By STEVEN HARPER

The Importance of Being Kevin

Published by DREAMSPINNER PRESS
www.dreamspinnerpress.com

THE IMPORTANCE OF BEING KEVIN

STEVEN HARPER

DREAMSPINNER PRESS

Published by
DREAMSPINNER PRESS

5032 Capital Circle SW, Suite 2, PMB# 279, Tallahassee, FL 32305-7886 USA
www.dreamspinnerpress.com

The Importance of Being Kevin
© 2019 Steven Harper

Cover Art
© 2019 Aaron Anderson
aaronbydesign55@gmail.com
Cover content is for illustrative purposes only and any person depicted on the cover is a model.

Trade Paperback ISBN: 978-1-64405-257-0
Digital ISBN: 978-1-64405-256-3
Library of Congress Control Number: 2018914541
Trade Paperback published July 2019
v. 1.0

Printed in the United States of America
∞
This paper meets the requirements of
ANSI/NISO Z39.48-1992 (Permanence of Paper).

To Michelle Singer, friend extraordinaire!

Acknowledgments

THANKS MUST go to the Untitled Writers Group of Ann Arbor (Mary Beth, Cindy, Erica, Christian, Jonathan, Diana, and Sarah) for their careful commentary on numerous drafts. Thanks also to my agent Travis Pennington for his patience and diligence.

Author's Note

THE CHARACTERS in this novel occasionally recite lines from Oscar Wilde's play *The Importance of Being Earnest*. Victorian prose, however, gets a little wordy for modern readers, and I condensed some lines for smoothness and to emphasize the parallel between Wilde's play and my book. I hope Mr. Wilde won't mind.

ACT I: SCENE I

KEVIN

A SINGLE piece of paper was supposed to keep me out of jail. My heart pushed against my spine like it was trying to drill out my back and run for it. A little voice that lived inside my head said, *You're an ass for even trying it. No one wants a loser. You're going to juvie, and you deserve it.*

The grimy tiled hallway was attic-room dim. Someone had turned off most of the lights, probably to save money. They had shut the AC off too, and it was close to ninety degrees in there. Sweat ran down my back as I scuffed down the corridor, eyes lowered. The laces on my shoes were knotted twice each because they'd been broken a couple of times. That made them a bitch to tie, so I usually just shoved my feet into them like old slippers and pretended I didn't want to play basketball with my friends anymore. Previous friends. I didn't seem to have many current friends.

At the end of the hallway was the bulletin board with the great and powerful paper on it. If my name was on it, I was in the clear. If not, *clang* went the bars. Fear dried my mouth and dampened my hands. You hear stories about what it's like in juvie, the stuff they do to new kids. I was sixteen but short and on the skinny side. I'd be someone's shower boy for sure.

I passed some doors and got to the end of the hall. The bulletin board had a bunch of flyers on it that shouted stuff like *Summer Stock Seminar* and *Youth Counselors Wanted* and *Have You Seen This Dog?* In the middle was a brand-new sheet, white as a grin, with the words *Teen Scenes Cast List: The Importance of Being Earnest* at the top. The fear jolted through me. The list. My probation officer said I either had to get a job or find a summer program, or she would recommend to the judge that my probation be revoked and I spend the next two years at Maximus Boys Training School, which was a fancy name for teen prison. There

1

were no jobs in Ringdale for teenagers, thanks to the toilet economy, and like a dick, I'd put off looking for a summer program. Yesterday I was in the library hoping they might be hiring for the summer—they weren't—and I saw a flyer for summer theater tryouts, which my watch said I had just enough time to make.

I knew zip-shit about theater, but by then I had nothing to lose, so I ran across the street to the Ringdale Community Art Center. In ten minutes I was on a stage pretending to be some weirdo from England while the director pushed her glasses up her nose and whispered to a guy scribbling on a clipboard.

Today was the absolute, last-ditch, no-shit deadline. Unless I called Ms. Blake this afternoon with good news, I was heading for shower-boy hell.

I was panting like an overheated dog. My eyes started to travel down the cast-list sheet, and suddenly I couldn't stand it. Not knowing was better than finding out. I didn't care what Ms. Blake said. I spun around to run away—

—and crashed straight into someone else. It was like hitting a suitcase filled with hammers. I said, "Oof!" and went down. The floor rocked. I shook my head like a cartoon character who'd been whacked with a Ping-Pong paddle.

"Geez, are you okay?" A hand stuck itself into my field of view. "Let me help you."

"Yeah, I'm—" I looked up and totally stalled out. The guy standing over me was about nineteen. His hair made me think of a blackbird, and his eyes were green, like the first day you mow the grass in May. His jaw was long, and his nose turned up at the end a little. My insides twisted around, feathery and fluttery at the same time, and all my words ran away. It felt weird, and I didn't know what to do.

The guy pulled me to my feet, and I could feel the strength in his arms. He wore a crisp T-shirt, and the cuffs around the lower sleeves were filled with muscle. Way more than my skinny-ass arms. I ran my hand through my hair. It's ordinary brown, always a little too long, and so thick it's hard to comb. At least my eyes are a decent blue.

"You're in a big hurry for someone who didn't even check the board," he said.

My brain kicked back into gear. His name was Peter. He had auditioned too. The director had called us up onstage to read together, in fact. My words came back, and they tumbled around like a bag of oranges spilling across a table. "I didn't—I mean, you were—wow!"

"I was wow?"

Shit. My face grew hot, and I wanted to fade into the wall behind me. "No, I mean you were good. Yesterday. Really good. You did… a good accent."

Aw shit. In my head I was putting a pistol to my temple.

"Thanks." He held out his hand again. "Kevin Devereaux, right? I'm Peter Finn."

"I know! I can't forget you… I mean, how good you were." *Bang.* "They put the cast list up."

Peter tried to lean around me to see it, though he had half a head on me. He smelled like sweat and sunlight. "So did you check it?"

"I didn't have to. I sucked. I'm gonna go to—" I stopped myself. "Go home, I guess. Uh, you probably got a lead, though. You really had me believing you were from England and stuff."

"What part were you hoping for?" Peter asked.

"What does it matter? I didn't get it." I leaned back against the bulletin board, refusing to look at it. "You probably got Jack. The lead. Or Algy, the other big role. I just… I figured I'd get the butler or something. But I didn't. I sucked."

Peter grinned at me, and all the stars came out. While I was recovering from that, he pushed me aside. In my head I said something witty, maybe even a joke with a pun in it. What came out was, "Hey!"

"Dude, I want to know." Peter examined the board with his hands behind his back. He wore brown cargo shorts and sandals, and that made me feel better because no one wore cargo shorts anymore, and it meant he was less than perfect. I chewed my thumbnail.

"Well, you were right," Peter said with a sigh. "You didn't get the butler."

My knees wobbled, and only the wall kept me from falling over. The voice in my head said, *What did you expect, dipshit?*

"T-told you…." My throat was thick. The air was close, and I needed to get out of there.

3

"You got Algy," Peter finished.

It took a second for that to sink in. The idea flowed across my mind like blueberry syrup. Peter was grinning his bring-the-stars grin and pointing at the bulletin board.

Teen Scenes Cast List: The Importance of Being Earnest
Jack Worthing (Earnest).... Peter Finn
Algernon Moncrieff (Algy).... Kevin Devereaux
Lady Bracknell.... Melissa Flackworthy
Cecily Cardew.... Meg Kimura

There were more, but my eye kept going to the second line on the list. I couldn't move. If I did, my name would disappear.

Peter clapped me on the back. "Congrats, dude."

That broke the spell. I jumped up a little and punched the air, so light with glee and relief I didn't think I'd come back down. "I'm saved!" I yelled, and then I flung both arms around Peter. "Omigod, omigod, I can't believe it!"

"Yeah." Peter's voice was a little muffled by my shoulder. "Great news."

I realized what I was doing and froze. Peter had really broad shoulders. I slowly released the land mine I was holding and backed away. "Uh... sorry," I mumbled. My face was hot enough to set ice cubes on fire. "Got carried away."

"It's okay, dude." Peter leaned against the wall. "We're gonna spend the next month together in close quarters anyway. You know how it goes in theater—the play becomes your life, and the cast becomes your family."

"Oh, um... actually, I *don't* know." I found myself scuffing the floor with one shoe. "I've never done a play before."

Peter raised dark eyebrows. "You haven't? Geez. Algy's a huge part too. That's—"

"The cast list is up!"

A herd of teenagers thundered down the hallway toward the bulletin board. I swear the tiles shook. Peter and I leaped out of the way only just in time.

"Did I get it?"

"You got it!"

"Les Madigan is stage manager? What a creep."

"Who got Jack?"

"Meg Kimura? Who the hell is that?"

"Omigod! I'm Lady Bracknell!"

Peter grabbed my arm and drew me away. "I thought cattle calls came *before* the audition. Let's get out of here."

"Aw man—I didn't even get the butler."

I trailed after Peter like a dumbstruck duckling. Okay, I wasn't going to jail, and that still made me rubber-legged relieved, but I didn't even know what the hell a cattle call was. What was I getting into?

Outside, the hard June sun made me flinch after the soft darkness in the backstage area. A few trees leaned over a tiny parking lot behind the Art Center—the lot with a sign that said Cast and Crew Parking Only. Most of the slots were taken. The metal door clanged shut behind us.

"Where's your car?" Peter asked.

I glanced away. It was really hard to look at him, especially out here in broad daylight. "I rode my bike. Over there."

Before I could get more embarrassed about it, I stalked over to the bike in question—I had chained it to the cast and crew parking sign—and fiddled with the lock. My bike was a Schwinn POS I got from a police auction for ten bucks, and I spent more time repairing it than riding it. I don't know why I bothered locking it up, especially since my hi-tech security system was just a hunk of chain and a rusty combination lock.

The sun was breathing down my neck, and I was sweating worse than inside. Summers in Michigan are brutal, and they start fast. One day you're fighting off polar bears to take the trash out, the next you're frying grilled cheese on the sidewalk. And it's so humid you can get a drink by inhaling hard. It's crazy.

"How about I give you a ride home?" Peter said behind me. "We could talk. About the play, I mean. Algy and Jack are best friends, and we need to figure out—"

"No!" I rounded on him, the lock and chain wrapped around my fingers. "No. I don't need a ride!"

He blinked. "Hey, it's no big deal. I didn't mean—"

"I'm fine! Just fine!" I was almost yelling but couldn't seem to stop myself. "I don't need a ride!"

The theater door slammed shut again. "There's my guys!" Iris Kaylo trotted toward us between the parked cars. Her dark hair was pulled into a loose bun with two pins the size of knitting needles stuck in it. She wore square dark-rimmed glasses over her nose and a pencil behind her ear. She also wore a purple polo shirt with Teen Scenes written in white where the pocket would be.

"You saw the cast list, right?" she continued.

"Iris," Peter said. "Yeah, we saw. Geez, thanks for giving me Jack."

"You deserved it. And you, Kevin." She gave me a sudden kiss on the cheek. My face went hot again, and I felt squirmy. "I couldn't believe your audition. Brilliant! Where have you been all my life? What did you think, Peter?"

Peter grinned. "I couldn't take my eyes off him. No one could. He walked right into the role."

"Uh…" was all I could manage.

Okay, here's the thing. I kind of got what they were talking about. When I walked into the cool darkness of the theater auditorium yesterday afternoon and looked at the scenes Iris handed out, something sort of took over. I read how Algy and his best friend Jack accidently-on-purpose put together this elaborate game of fake names and let's pretend, and I got it. I understood Algy, knew what he wanted, who he wanted to be, what flipped his switches. In a weird way, Algy became real, became *me*. My own self, my real self, retreated into a shell painted with "Algy" on the outside, so when Iris called my name and I climbed up the steps to the stage, it wasn't me, Kevin Devereaux, up there. It wasn't Kevin pretending to be Algy either. It was Algy himself, with a seed of Kevin inside him. If that makes sense.

Earnest is a buddy show about two best friends, Jack and Algy. They lived in England in the 1800s, when society was super strict. Jack has a bunch of embarrassing secrets, like that he has no money and that his parents left him in a handbag at the train station when he was a baby, so he grew up a poor orphan. He likes this girl named Gwendolen, but she won't date a poor guy, so he tells her he's a rich guy named Earnest. But then they fall in love, and the longer they stay together, the harder it gets for Jack to tell her the truth. Meanwhile, Algy—that's me—falls in love with Jack's cousin Cecily, but it turns out *Algy* says his name is Earnest too. Then all four of them end up at the same country house for the weekend, and stuff gets awkward. A guy named Oscar Wilde wrote it. Iris said *Earnest* was like a sitcom, and I guess she was right. Even though it's like a hundred years old, it's still funny.

Anyway, Iris called Peter up onstage too, but I didn't see him. I only saw my best friend Jack. I didn't see a bare stage with a few pieces of old furniture scattered across it. I saw a drawing room in an English manor in 1865. I totally swallowed myself and became someone else. And since Algy wasn't knocked flat by Peter's—Jack's—looks, neither was I.

"*My dear boy,*" I'd said to Jack, "*I love hearing my relations abused. It is the only thing that makes me put up with them at all. Relations are simply a tedious pack of people who haven't got the remotest knowledge of how to live nor the smallest instinct about when to die.*"

Everyone in the audience who was waiting to read died laughing, including Iris. Peter—Jack—made his own lips a hard line so he wouldn't laugh too. The part of me that was curled up inside the Algy shell spun like a Ferris wheel, discovering a new kind of glee. *Holy shit! They laughed! This is awesome!*

Peter, as Jack, said, "*Well, I won't argue about the matter. You always want to argue about things.*"

"*That is exactly what things are made for,*" I said and made a little face that cracked everyone up again, and my inner self did handstands. It was incredible fun.

But when I walked off the stage at the end of the scene, Algy disappeared, taking his brains and self-confidence with him, and my own self emerged like a worm crawling out of the ground after the rain. I realized everyone was laughing at how awful I was, how dumb I looked. I even checked to see if my fly was open. Peter might have called something out to me, but I didn't hear because I was already leaving.

I got what Peter was talking about when he said I walked into the role, but that didn't make me an actor. What did I know about acting? Still, I had loved it on that stage and wished I could stay up there forever.

Iris was saying, "You've never done theater before, Kevin? Most of the Teen Sceners have done three or four plays by your age."

"Nope." I was feeling self-conscious with Iris and Peter staring at me and really wished I could get out of there. Liquid heat poured down from the sun and flowed back up from the parking lot. The air shimmered with it. A trickle of sweat ran down Peter's forearm, pressing against the faint dark hairs and following contours of muscle.

"What made you try out, then?" Iris asked.

Their twin spotlights landed on me like headlights on a deer. *Say something,* my little voice said. *Your mom was a famous actress, and this was her dying wish. You read the play and had to get in on the action. You're a double agent masquerading as a teenager and need cover for the summer. Anything!*

I scuffed the tarmac again with my shoe. "I... just thought it might be a good idea."

Lame lame lame!

"Well, I'm glad you came in." Iris sketched a wave and headed back for the theater door. "See you tonight at seven sharp."

Peter turned to me. "You sure you don't want that ride? It's getting hotter by the minute."

I looked at his green eyes, cooler than autumn water, and nearly shouted *yes.* Algy would have. But that would have been stupid. I grabbed my handlebars. "No, thanks. I gotta go."

"Okay, sure. See you tonight." He chirped open a brand-new blue Mustang and peeled out of the lot without even looking back. That made me feel weird and hollow, and I didn't like it.

To get home I had to pedal past the Genevieve Morse Memorial Library and down what looked like a gentle country lane, even though it was in the middle of west-side Ringdale. Lush trees stood around perfect lawns like giants having tea. Houses straight out of *Killionaires Magazine* were sprinkled among them. See, Ringdale is home to Morse Plastic and the Morse family. No one outside of Ringdale had ever heard of either one, even though Morse made like a third of all plastic used in the country. Toss a spork in the trash, and chances were Morse created the raw material. All that plastic in your computer and your pop bottles and your car? Morse, Morse, Morse. And Morse Plastic put a lot of rich people in Ringdale. Hell, that Mustang Peter drove probably meant Peter's dad or mom—or maybe both—were Morse higher-ups.

I passed a wooded area and a big rustic-looking sign that said Morse Nature Center at the beginning of a wide trail with wood chips on it. Morse Plastic contaminates the water, pollutes the air, and poisons the ground, so the family bribes the city with stuff like nature trails, a huge library, big parks, school grants, and summer programs for teenagers.

But there's still the stink. Some days it's rotten-egg sulfur. Other days it's oil and diesel fumes that hang on the air in greasy droplets. Sometimes it's the sharp smell of burned plastic. There's always something. But no one complains about the smell because the wind carries it to the east-siders, and who gives a shit about them?

I crossed an old one-lane bridge over the Hellburger River and coasted onto a narrow road that wove between a golf course and yet another park. Guys in weird pants and half gloves whacked white balls and buzzed after them on electric carts. I climbed a little hill and emerged onto the sidewalk next to M-127, a busy road that tries to be a highway. I had crossed out of the west side into the east side.

The farther I rode, the smaller and shabbier the houses became. Out here, the roads crossing M-127 don't even have numbers. They have names—Two Mile, Three Mile, Four Mile. No one cared enough about the people even to give the streets nice names like Whisperwood Lane or No Bankruptcy Drive. Today's east-side stink featured toasted tin foil with a hint of lighter fluid.

Was Peter a west-sider? Had to be, with a car like that. He probably didn't even know where the east side was.

I pushed harder on the pedals. Cars rushed by, leaving exhaust behind. I could still feel the heat of his touch despite the hot sun above me. God help me, I wanted to jump in his car, and not because it probably had AC. Stupid. *Sure, take me home*, I'd say. *Or just take me!* Wonder how he'd react to that?

I turned down Six Mile, a badly-paved road with ruts in it. The houses down here flop in their yards like old dogs. Dirty, broken toys litter old grass, and a couple-three always have Realtors signs out front with Price Reduced printed hopefully across them. The one saving grace is that it's a lot of old woods and farmland between the houses, so if you look in the right direction, it's kind of pretty, especially when fall turns the trees into a fireworks show.

My bike found the driveway by itself—dirt and ruts, just like the road. A bunch of trees made a dark space over my house. Well, it wasn't really a house. Yeah, I lived in a single-wide, and if that made me trailer trash, then fuck you too. At least me and my dad kept the place up, and better than some of the real houses up the road. The lawn might have been patchy because of all the trees, but there was no junk anywhere, and we painted last year. We didn't do flowers and shit because, you know, that was girly, but the grass was raked and mowed, and Dad built a decent little wood porch for the front. Dad's truck was old and rusty like my bike, but there was nothing we could do about that.

Still, there was no way in nine kinds of hell I was going to let Peter see it. I'd rather ride naked through a poison ivy farm.

I always got a little mad when I came home, especially when I got home after riding my POS past all those huge houses. It was beyond unfair that me and my dad were struggling in a rattrap trailer while only a few miles away, rich people thought the world was unjust because the champagne on their last Bahama cruise wasn't chilled right. The anger leaped up like a tiger and grabbed me. It was worse now that I was living *After*.

I divided my life into *Before* and *After*. *Before* was before all the shit that landed me in front of the judge. *After* had only been the few weeks since then, but it felt like half my life. Sometimes I thought the anger had finally gone away, but then it roared out of the grass growing around my soul and ate me alive. The play was good news, and I had fun with it, and there was Peter, so yet again I thought it had gone, but when I got home and thought about Peter's car and the house he probably lived in, the anger rumbled again, and my hands went white around my handlebars.

It was cooler under the trees, at least. I parked my bike and climbed up the short flight of steps to go inside. The living room, like everything in the trailer, was tiny but clean. Dad was kind of a neat freak. We only had a couch and a beanbag chair—both used—and an old TV on a milk crate. Our AC was a box fan in the window.

But the thing that was truly weird about my place was the books. They were everywhere, in simple stacks and tidy piles, shelved two and three deep on bookcases made of bricks and boards. There was no system to them. *Harry Potter* nudged against Charles Dickens, nonfiction leaned against a mound of manga. Bestsellers, romances, science fiction, thrillers, poetry collections, even graphic novels—all of them used, scammed from library or garage sales, or even snatched from the dumpster behind the bookstore downtown. Usually I barely noticed the books, but that day, they made me mad. Why did we have to live in a fucking library instead of a normal house?

Dad was reading on the couch. He's kind of an older version of me, or maybe I'm a younger version of him. We have the same plain brown hair and blue eyes and the same long nose, though Dad keeps his hair short and his arms are thicker than mine. His bare feet were propped up on the old trunk we used as a coffee table, but he sat up when I came in.

"Hey, kiddo," he said. "How'd the interview at the library go? Good news?"

Pissed without knowing why, I went into the kitchen—like everything else, it was narrow but neat—and drew a glass of water. "Bad," I said slowly. "They wanted somebody older."

He got up and came to the kitchen doorway. "Did you show them the recommendation your teacher wrote?"

"Yeah. They didn't care."

"Your probation officer called," he said, also slowly. "She wanted to know what to tell the judge. Kev…."

"It'll be okay, Dad." I was suddenly reluctant to say anything. It was dumb, but the play felt like a cool secret, like I'd found a doorway into another world or something, and I didn't want to wreck it by telling someone else. And I was kind of mad he was asking.

"The terms of your probation said you have to get a summer job, Kev. You want to go to juvenile?" Dad folded his arms. He was still holding his book. "Besides, we could use the money."

I opened the refrigerator. "We got anything to eat? I missed lunch, and I'm starving."

"Sandwiches—your favorite."

"Yay," I said. "What about *your* job situation? Any drywall stuff come up?"

His face hardened. "Nothing. No one wants to hire an ex-con. That's why I'm so worried about your situation. If you turn out like me—"

"You were released from jail years ago." I plopped jelly on a slice of bread. "Who cares now?"

"In this economy? Too many people." He sighed, and I could see he was struggling not to get mad too. I sort of wanted to fight, but not really. "You're changing the subject. Kevin, Ms. Blake gave you two extensions to find something already. I don't know if she'll give us another one. What are you going to tell her?"

I sat down at the chipped table with my sandwich and a glass of Kool-Aid. No milk for the wicked. "I actually kind of... found something."

"You did? Holy god, why didn't you say so? What is it?" Dad's expression was still tense.

Here we go. "I tried out for the Teen Scenes program at the Art Center. I was cast in a play."

"A play?" Dad dropped into the other kitchen chair. "What do you mean, a play? What play? Why a play?"

"Because I wanted to, Dad. Because I thought it might be fun. It's called *The Importance of Being Earnest*, and it's about two guys who create a fake friend named Earnest to get girlfriends." I took a bite to cover my mixed-up feelings. The audition and Peter and the hot ride home were all pissing off the tiger that paced inside my rib cage. "The director said I was really good too. I got a big part. Not the lead role, but a big part."

"Kevin." Dad's voice was dangerous now. "Your PO said you have to get a job this summer to show that you're not—"

"The rehearsals are in the evening," I interrupted. The tiger was growling. Why couldn't he just be glad I'd found something I liked? "I can still look for work during the day. Besides, Ms. Blake told me that getting involved in a summer program is just as good as getting a job as far as she's concerned."

"But you aren't earning any *money*," Dad said.

"Neither are you!" I roared.

Silence slammed across the table. Dad looked down at the book in his hands. The tiger fled, leaving a trail of black guilt.

"You're right." Dad got up. "Fine, then. You're in the play. That's good. Glad things worked out, son."

"Dad, wait," I said.

But he was gone. His bedroom door clicked shut, leaving me with two bites out of a jelly sandwich.

ACT I: SCENE II

KEVIN

I DID call Ms. Blake to tell her what was going on. At least *she* was glad for me. No juvie.

That was a relief. I paced around the trailer after that, not sure what to do with myself. Dad stayed in his room. I went down the short hall and raised my hand to knock on his door. I felt guilty because I'd made him feel bad about not finding work. Then I got angry that he was making me feel guilty. Then I felt unhappy that I was angry at him. And finally I felt angry that I didn't know what the hell was going on. I stalked into my own room and flung myself on the bed. It sucked living *After*.

My room had nothing in it. I mean, there was *some* stuff—my bed and an old dresser and my clothes. My school backpack was shoved in the back of the closet, and a digital clock reported regimented time on a warped table next to my bed. But nothing real—no posters on the walls, no souvenirs of trips to Florida, no old toys from when I was little—just four walls and me. The only nongeneric thing in my room was a framed photo next to the clock. It was a school picture of a kid about fourteen years old. He had red-brown hair with a curl in it and a few zits, and he was smiling at the camera. His name was Robbie, and before I went to sleep at night, I tapped his picture three times, hoping he'd forgive me, hoping he'd take away the nightmares about what I'd done. It never worked, but I kept trying. I didn't know what else to do.

I lay back and thought about taking a nap, but that would risk a nightmare, and I didn't want to do that. Besides, Peter's face kept swimming around inside my head, and who could sleep through that?

Okay, look—this is the twenty-first century, and I'm not stupid. It's not like I've never heard about men who are attracted to other men. Shit, you can't turn on the TV anymore without seeing a couple guys smooching it up. But Ringdale is a really conservative town, run by

14

conservative people. I mean, a couple years ago, a teacher at the high school let one of her kids show an internet music video that said it was okay to be gay, and the school board fired her ass. People around here aren't good with that kind of stuff. I hadn't been... still wasn't... either. Ringdale kind of does that to you. The factory warps people along with the plastic. So I kept my damn mouth shut.

And there was other shit too. Now that I was living *After*, I didn't deserve someone like Peter. I didn't deserve *anyone*. So I needed to keep it all inside. Besides, I told myself, Peter was nice and freakin' amazing, but he wasn't interested in me. He was rich and good-looking and had a dozen girlfriends lining up to blow him and another dozen begging to marry him. Even if he swung in the same direction I did—huge, Jupiter-class, nova-size *if*—he wouldn't be attracted to me and my shitty shoes and my POS bike. So why even let him inside my head?

Which was why he spent the rest of the afternoon living there in all his starlight grinning glory. Why couldn't the tiger just eat him?

That evening I biked all the way back to the theater. It occurred to me I was going to have legs of steel by opening night. The back door was propped open, and I threaded my way through the maze of hallways and dressing rooms and storage areas to the stage. The other cast members were there, some of them talking among themselves, others standing around, looking uneasy because they didn't know anybody. I searched for Peter but didn't find him. Was he coming? Then I shrugged to myself. It didn't matter.

The theater was big and echoey, a space that might swallow you up. I hunched into myself at the edge of the stage and tried to call up confident, funny Algy, without luck.

A guy with longish blond hair and a lean swimmer's build came up to me. He looked about twenty or twenty-one. "Hey, buddy. You're Kevin Devereaux, yeah?"

"That's me," I said.

He handed me a script for *The Importance of Being Earnest* from a bag he was carrying. "I'm Les Madigan. Don't lose this—we don't have the money to give you another one—but you can highlight your lines and write blocking in it."

"Blocking?" It sounded like combat.

"You know—stage directions. Where you move and when."

"Oh. Got it."

"You were pretty good at the audition." Les held out a hand. "Welcome to the show."

"Thanks." I shook. He gripped hard for a long second and then let go, gave me a tight smile, and moved on to someone else.

Peter came in at that moment. He was talking with Iris and pointing to his own copy of the script. My heart gave another stupid flutter when I saw him, and I remembered how it felt when I grabbed him in a hug when we saw the cast list. I tried to shut it all down, but how does anyone shut down feelings?

"Let's get started, everyone," Iris called. "Circle up on the stage floor, please."

We all scooted into a circle and sat like kindergartners with our legs crossed and an air of anticipation. I don't know if I was trying for it or if he was trying for it, but Peter and I ended up next to each other, and I was excited and relieved and scared all at once. He gave me an ironic salute, and a smile crept across my face.

"You all have your scripts," Iris continued, "and we'll do a read-through in a minute. But first, a few rules."

I made myself look around the circle. There were nine of us in the cast—five boys and four girls—along with Iris and that guy Les, who I remembered seeing at the auditions sitting next to Iris with a clipboard.

"Rehearsals start onstage at seven sharp, so you need to be here ten minutes before then. Early is on time and on time is late. After two tardies, you'll be replaced." She gestured at Les. "Les Madigan is our stage manager. Once the performances start, my job ends and he becomes god. Good stage managers are hard to find, so don't piss him off."

Les tapped his clipboard with playful menace, and everyone made dutiful laughing sounds. I glanced sideways at Peter. He was flipping through his script, not really paying attention. I guessed he had heard this stuff a dozen times already.

"Last rule—remember that we're all volunteers. The only payment we get is experience and a whole lot of fun." Iris pushed her glasses up on her nose. "So let's start with an icebreaker."

I wasn't sure about this part. I'd done so-called icebreakers in school, stuff where someone wrote a label on your back and you had to guess what it was based on how people treated you. I hated shit like that because I always got something like East-Sider or Delinquent, and everyone treated me like dog crap in a bag even after the game ended. I looked around to see how the others were handling the idea. All the other members of the cast were strangers to me, though I thought the blonde girl with the round body might be named Melissa. They seemed relaxed with the whole icebreaker thing, but they probably all knew each other anyway.

"This is called Two Truths and a Lie," Iris said. "Everyone has to introduce themselves, then tell two truths and one lie. The rest of us have to guess which one is the lie. I'll go first." She cleared her throat. "I'm Iris Kaylo, the director. One—I'm studying to be a teacher."

Peter shifted, and his knee brushed mine, light as a dragonfly. It stayed there. I had another deer-in-the-headlights moment. The contact was casual, could be accidental. Maybe he hadn't noticed.

"Two—I listen to a lot of reggae music."

Or was it on purpose? I didn't move, and neither did he. My knee turned into a hot coal. Out of the corner of my eye, I could see Peter's face. He was looking at Iris, and he was smiling just a little, as though he was into the lie/truth thing.

"Three—I once worked as a roadie for the Grateful Dead," Iris finished. "Which one's the lie?"

"Three!"

"Two!"

"Two!"

"One!" people called out. Peter shifted his weight and put his palms on the floor behind him, but he didn't move his knee. I couldn't have moved if a *Tyrannosaurus rex* had burst through the door.

"Two was the lie." Iris grinned. "I definitely don't listen to reggae. Melissa, you're next."

The round blonde girl waved to us, and most waved back. "I'm Melissa Flackworthy, and I'm playing Lady Bracknell. I'll start with this. One—I'm the oldest of four sisters."

I decided it was time to take some action. What the hell did I have to lose, right? I mean, it might be an accident, and I could just apologize. Still, tell that to my adrenaline levels. They zoomed off the chart. I casually leaned back like Peter was and put my hands flat on the floor behind me, close to Peter's.

What the fuck are you doing? said my nasty inner voice, but for the first time in my life, I told it to shut the hell up.

"Two—I was born in Germany. Army brat."

Everyone was watching Melissa, and my body blocked the view anyway. My hand crept closer to Peter's like a shy inchworm. *Just be cool.*

"Three...."

My little finger touched his. I felt his skin on mine, and a little jolt shoved my heart into my throat. My shorts felt too small. I didn't dare look at Peter.

"Hmmm...," said Melissa. "I'm not sure."

What felt like a long moment passed. I was dead. Peter would freak out, pull his hand away, and shake it like I'd given him a disease. His arm muscles tensed, and I braced myself for it. Then he pressed the side of his hand more firmly against mine. My heart flew from my body like a released falcon and shot into the sky, screaming its joy.

"I know. I didn't learn to ride a bike until I was ten. Which one's the lie?"

A chorus of guesses followed, but Peter and I stayed silent, our hands pressed secretly together. I risked a glance at him, and this time he smiled fully at me, and I smiled back. A hundred suns flashed into existence and went nova.

"It's three. I never did learn to ride a bike."

Some laughter and a little conversation among the cast followed that one. By now my arms were cramping up from the way I was sitting, and I was forced to shift, which pulled my hand away from Peter's, but I made eye contact with him so he would know it was okay. He nodded. It felt amazing good that someone else might feel—

"Kevin! Yo, Kevin!" My head snapped around. Les was pointing at me with his pencil. "Your turn, man."

The suns and novas and falcons evaporated with a *fwoop*. "Oh! Sorry. I'm Kevin Devereaux, and I play Algy. Lemme see." I thought fast. "One—I have family in New Orleans."

One—I've figured since I was twelve that I'm gay.

"Two—I'm really good at chess."

Two—I'm sitting next to the greatest guy I've ever seen, I think he likes me back, and my heart is pounding so hard I can barely talk.

"Three—I ran away from home once and didn't come back for almost a month."

Three—I'm a loser who lives in a white-trash library with an ex-con, and I'm turning out just like him.

"Three!"

"One!"

"One!"

"Three!"

Oops. One of those was supposed to be a lie.

"It's two," I said. "I don't even know how to play chess."

I saw Les looking at me for a moment. He pushed his hair out of his eyes with a long-fingered hand, winked at me, and went back to scribbling on his clipboard. What was that all about? A pang hit me—had he seen me touching Peter's hand?

"Okay, Peter," Iris said, which snapped my head around again. "You're next."

Peter ticked his off on his fingers. "I'm Peter Finn—Jack Worthington. One—I'm a licensed pilot. Two—I've dated someone who was ten years older than me. Three—I'm going to be an architect. The lie is number one."

"Hey!" Iris shook an admonishing finger at him. "You're supposed to make us guess."

"Sorry. I don't like guessing games." Peter raked a hand through his hair and looked straight at me with eyes that stopped my breath. "And that's not a lie."

Les tapped his pencil hard on the clipboard.

After that Peter and I carefully pretended nothing was going on. The others went through their truths and lies, and then we read through the script. That was kind of fun, though with everyone just sitting in a circle, I didn't really feel like Algy. It was the first time I'd actually read *The Importance of Being Earnest* all the way through, and I decided I'd have to look up some stuff about Oscar Wilde, the guy who wrote it.

When we were done, Iris gave us all a copy of the schedule, a list with contact information, and a website where we could get updates. I shoved it into my pocket and didn't tell anyone I didn't have a computer. I met some of the other cast members, but I was a little shy around them. Melissa seemed nice, and two of the guys in the show—Joe and Thad Creeker—were brothers.

Once we were done, everyone scattered, and I lost track of Peter. A little disappointed, I headed out back to the tiny parking lot, which was nearly deserted. I didn't see Peter's Mustang. It was ten o'clock, and a gibbous moon coasted over silvery treetops. When I was little and Mom was still around and we lived in a real house, I thought it was *gibbon*s, and that a gibbon monkey lived up there, making the moon more and more full. The dark, warm night lay soft between streetlight puddles, and hidden crickets peeped as I unchained my bike.

Footsteps scuffed on the cement. I whirled. It was Peter. My heart kept on whirling.

"Hey," he said. "I didn't see you leave."

I shrugged. Suddenly the touching game seemed dumb and distant, probably a mistake. "Yeah. Are we the last ones?"

"Except for Les. He has to lock up."

"I missed your car," I said.

"It's in the front lot. You're riding your bike home in the dark? Kind of dangerous."

"Nah. I do it all the time." I wrapped my chain around the seat post. "I like riding at night. It's peaceful."

Peter stepped closer. "You were really good during the read-through. Everyone else was stumbling, but you were really smooth."

"Really? Uh… thanks. I thought you did pretty good too, Jack."

"Algy."

We both kind of grinned, and uncertainty hung in the air between us, unclear as cracked glass. Neither wanted to move closer, and neither of us could move away. Peter's breath smelled like chocolate. My hand

20

was on my bike seat. Silence stretched. I didn't know whether to run like hell or fall at his feet.

"Do you go through the park when you ride home?" Peter asked at last. "I can show you a cool shortcut."

I couldn't say anything for a second. Then I managed, "Sure. But… how come? It's kind of out of your way."

"You heard me at the icebreaker." And then he put his hand on top of mine on the bike seat. It was warm, and that touch made my crotch go tight. "I don't like guessing games."

The stupid little voice in my head said, *He's toying with you. Get the hell away. Be safe! Run!* A sick feeling tried to come up through my stomach like sewage.

I opened my mouth to ask him what the hell he was talking about, that he was making a huge mistake. But then it was as though funny, confident Algy pushed me aside and took over my body. From my mouth came the words "You don't have to guess," and I flipped my hand around to take his.

There was a tiny moment when nothing happened and I thought I had fucked it up. Then Peter gave a heavy sigh and grabbed my hand tighter. "Oh, thank god. I was terrified that you were screwing with me."

"Holy shit! So was I." We both laughed then. It felt really good to do that with someone.

Peter's head came around, and he dropped my hand. "What was that?"

I looked around too but didn't see anything. "What?"

"I thought I heard—never mind." He led me away with my bike. "Come on. It's a damn beautiful night."

"It damn sure is," I agreed, and we laughed again.

We wandered down the fake country lane past the huge houses with their tea-party trees to the park. The summer night was a cloak drawn soft around us, giving us a private world overseen by the moon, and she wouldn't say anything. I walked between Peter and my bike, and our shoulders touched as we moved. It sent happy little shudders through me. How could such a small thing as a touch make me so happy? It didn't seem real.

"So was that really true?" I asked. "You really dated someone ten years older than you?"

"Yeah." Peter ran his hand through his hair again, and I admired the gesture. "I was fifteen. It broke all kinds of laws. But man, it was great while it lasted."

"Er... just so we're on the same page... it was a guy, right?"

Peter halted on the sidewalk. I stopped too, suddenly afraid. What had I done wrong? Shit. Was he still...?

"Dude," he said, "the last girl I kissed was my cousin Shelly at her wedding, and I way wanted to kiss the groom instead."

More laughter. I felt the tiger retreat. Peter could do that.

We crossed the bridge and wandered into the park. Peter's arm came slowly around my shoulders. I had never felt the weight of another guy's arm there. It made me feel secure, like the world would never touch me again. It also made me excited. My shorts felt too tight again, and I swallowed hard.

"Did you always know that you were... that you liked guys?" I asked him.

"No way." Peter snorted. "It took me forever to figure it out. Well, forever until I was fifteen."

The river flowed like a silver snake under the gleaming stars. I could feel Peter's body heat like the summer night around me. I could jump over the trees. I could walk on the moon. I wanted... I needed....

And then Peter's arms went all the way around me. Before I completely understood what was going on, he was kissing me. I dropped my bike. His mouth was warm on mine, and every part of my body melted and froze at the same time. Even as it happened, other thoughts—

This is it! My first kiss!

You don't deserve this, asshat.

Is that his dick pressing against me?

—crowded through my head, trying to ruin it.

We parted, but our foreheads were still touching. His breath moved across my face.

"Jesus, you're gorgeous," he whispered. "From the second you walked on that stage, you were beautiful, you know that?"

A shadow moved at the corner of my eye. Was it a person? I backed up and turned away a little, feeling weird and heavy all of a sudden. My left hand stole around and clasped my right elbow. "Don't call me that. I'm a frigging loser."

Peter looked mystified. "You're not, Kevin. You're so talented and smart. Anyone can see that. Iris sure did."

"I'm a loser, okay?" The tiger was growling again. "Just like my…. I'm a stupid loser."

"Because I kissed you?" Peter put his hand on my shoulder. "Oh my god—I didn't mean to—"

"No!" The stupid anger flashed back. I had thought Peter could help me keep it away, but he couldn't. "It's not you, Peter. You don't want me. You *can't* want me."

I snatched my bike from the ground and started to leap on it so I could pedal away. Anger and fear drove me, and I couldn't stop moving.

A hand grabbed my arm. Peter's hand. Hot as a chemical fire. "Hey," he said. "What I *want* is to find out for myself."

Run, I thought. *Flee. Hide.*

But I stayed. For a little bit.

I barely remembered riding home after we left the park. Dad was still up and waiting for me in the stuffy living room, book in hand.

"I thought rehearsal got out at ten," he said narrowly. "It's quarter after eleven."

"My bike chain popped off." I held up my grease-stained fingers, which I had thought to wipe across said bike chain before I came in. "It was a bitch to fix in the dark."

"Language," he said. His eyes were hard, and I knew he was suspicious, but hey, my story was plausible. My bike broke down all the time. And it wasn't like I was out dealing drugs or getting drunk.

No, said my stupid inner voice. *You were kissing a guy.*

"I'm gonna wash up and go to bed," I said, and I fled before he could say anything else.

In the bathroom I scrubbed my hands with soap. My reflection above the tiny sink duplicated my movements. Did Dad really know something? Or was he just still mad at me from before?

I stared at the mirror. Blue eyes stared back. Did I look different? I brushed my hair away from my forehead with damp fingers. Wow. He had kissed me. And I had kissed him back. It was hard not to spread my hands and shout. I never thought it would feel like this, like I was touching everything in the whole wide world.

I slipped into my room to undress for bed, though I wanted to spread my wings and leap into the air. I wanted to shout and sing. I had a boyfriend! A significant other! A BF! Maybe! Probably! But who could I tell? If word got around that Kevin Devereaux was queer… shit. Some of my euphoria slipped away, and I tapped Robbie's picture three times. This was so bad.

But it felt so good.

It took a long time to fall asleep.

The boy huddles on the ground in a circle of male figures. The others shout and yell and pump their fists.

"Kick his ass!"

"Smash his face!"

"Bash his nuts!"

"Come on dude—fight!"

"What are you waiting for? Come on!"

A fist falls. A foot kicks. A chain swings. A rock crushes.

The boy shrieks, "Leave me alone!"

I shot awake. The sheet was bunched around my waist, and my hair was stuck to my scalp. More sweat ran down my stomach. My heart beat terrible rhythms inside my chest.

The dreams wouldn't go away. I didn't know what to do. I really wished that Peter—

No. The darkness pressed in around me. I was glad Peter wasn't there. He'd know I was a loser for sure.

I curled sideways in my bed and waited for the next dream to come.

ACT I: SCENE III

KEVIN

"OKAY, FOLKS, let's try it this way." Iris pushed her glasses up and waved her script at us from the audience, which I learned was called *the house.*

Onstage, a girl named Krista Benson sat on a couch. She was playing Gwendolen, and she was supposed to be crazy in love with Peter—Jack, I mean. Someone had dragged a bunch of furniture onto the stage and put down masking tape where the stage crew would build the walls and doors. I could have saved myself a lot of agony by just volunteering to work crew—they took anyone—but I hadn't known that. Course, then I wouldn't have run into Peter.

I was offstage with Les, the tall, blond stage manager guy. He carried a big loose-leaf notebook with Master Script written on the cover in Sharpie. On the other side of the stage was the round blonde girl, Melissa, who was playing my character's snotty aunt, Lady Bracknell.

Peter was also onstage. He was sitting beside Krista/Gwen with her hand in his. Their scripts lay on the couch. Next to me, Les was scribbling stage directions—blocking—in the master script.

"Peter—I mean, Jack—let's have you kneel in front of Gwen and take both her hands," Iris called from her seat in the house. "But stay in profile—don't turn your back to us."

Peter obeyed. I shifted next to Les, who continued to scribble.

"Now lean in close. Closer. You're in love."

Krista/Gwen ducked her head a little and smiled as Peter moved in. She was pretty, and I suddenly didn't like her very much.

"Don't do that," Iris admonished. "I know it's uncomfortable, but this is the man you love. Lock eyes with him. A marriage proposal is the biggest moment of a Victorian woman's life."

Gwen did so. Peter stared back, and I saw a spark between them. Weird. I knew it was just a play, that they were only acting, but it made me nervous to see Peter look at Krista that way.

Les tapped his pencil against the notebook. I glanced at him, and his eye caught mine. I gave a little half smile. He shrugged nonchalantly and went back to writing again. The margins of the script were filled with *L*s and *R*s and *X*s in circles with arrows going all over the page. It was gibberish to me.

"Enter Lady Bracknell," Iris said.

Across the stage, soft, blonde Melissa puffed stiffly into Lady Bracknell and stalked between the masking tape marks, script in hand. *"Mr. Worthing! Rise, sir, from this semi-recumbent posture. It is most indecorous."*

"Mamma! I must beg you to retire," Gwen said. *"This is no place for you. Besides, Mr. Worthing has not quite finished yet."*

Les stopped writing and dropped his hand as though it had cramped up, but I was too caught up in what was happening onstage to pay much attention. Some curtains were half hiding me and Les from the stage, so it was hard to see. Peter was still holding Krista's hands and leaning close.

Lady Bracknell looked shocked. *"Finished what, may I ask?"*

How dumb was it to be jealous of—

A hand caressed my left buttcheek. Cold water crashed over me. I jerked my head around. Les pulled his hand back with a weird smile.

"I am engaged to Mr. Worthing, Mamma."

For a second I couldn't move. Nausea squirted through my stomach. I all but jumped sideways a few steps and turned away. I didn't know what to do.

"Pardon me, you are not engaged to anyone. When you do become engaged to someone, I will inform you of the fact."

Les went back to scribbling in the notebook again, though he looked a little pissed off. No one seemed to have noticed anything. They were all watching the stage, and we were mostly behind the curtains. What the hell had that been about? Did I give off some kind of gay radiation? Did everyone know?

"For goodness sake, don't play that ghastly tune, Algy. How idiotic you are!"

My stomach turned again, and I stared down at the stage floor. When Les touched me... it felt... gross, like he was squeezing a roll of toilet paper at the store. Was it always gross? I liked it when Peter touched me, but he didn't grope me like that. Did I just attract weirdos?

Loser!

Maybe I was just overreacting. Maybe I had just imagined it, or he had brushed up against me accidently. Maybe—

"Algernon! Algernon! Yo, Kevin!"

I snapped back to the real world. Everyone was looking at me, including Iris, the one who had spoken to me.

"That's your cue, Algernon," she said. "Pay attention. And Les— it's *your* job to cue him if he forgets."

Les saluted with the pencil. "Sorry, Iris. My fault. I didn't prompt him."

"Go back to your entrance, Algernon," Iris said.

I entered and tried to call up the Algernon shell from the audition, but Les's handprint burned my skin, and I couldn't concentrate. Peter looked down at his script, and his hair fell across his forehead. I wanted to touch it.

"Gwendolen is as right as a trivet," he said in a crusty English accent. *"As far as she is concerned, we are engaged."*

"For your next line, Jack, clap your friend Algy on the shoulder in a stiff, British sort of way," Iris called.

"Her mother is perfectly unbearable," he said as he clapped me on the shoulder with an air of sorrow. *"Never met such a gorgon. I don't really know what a gorgon is like, but I am quite sure that Lady Bracknell is one."*

For a moment I was back in the park with his hand on my shoulder. Then I was back in the theater. I let Algy smile a little at what his friend was saying. Out of the corner of my eye, Les looked annoyed. I decided to ignore him.

"I beg your pardon, Algy." Peter moved his arm around to my other shoulder so he was half hugging me. I liked that a lot. *"I suppose I shouldn't talk about your own aunt in that way before you."*

"She said clap, not hug, Peter," Les interrupted. "Save the love for later, dudes."

I pulled away from Peter like he'd turned into a snake. "Hey—what?"

"He's right, Jack," Iris put in. "Save the love hug for when you find out Algy is your long-lost brother. A clap on the shoulder will do for now."

"Got it," Peter said in a neutral voice.

Shit, I thought.

"Your line, Algy," Iris said.

At ten Iris called it quits. "See you all tomorrow onstage at seven sharp," she said. "Work on memorizing those lines. I want everyone off book in two weeks. Kevin and Peter—"

Both of us jumped a little as everyone else drifted away.

"I'm seeing great chemistry between you two. Keep it up."

I didn't know how to respond, so I said nothing. Peter whacked me on the back, hard, and said, "Thanks" to Iris. In a lower voice to me, he said, "See you outside in a bit."

A while later I was outside, unchaining my bike from the silver street lamp. My heart pounded. My hands shook. I couldn't wait to see him.

The steel door creaked open, and I turned. "Hey—" I began.

"Hey," said Les.

I straightened, startled. "Oh! Uh… hi, Les." What the hell?

He strolled toward me, hands in his back pockets. I backed up a wary step, bike lock still in my hand. The memory of the way he'd touched me oozed around my head. I didn't like him, didn't like *this*.

"Long ride home?" he asked.

"Kinda," I said.

And then he was directly in front of me. He put his hand on my shoulder the way Peter had done. I felt cold and unhappy, but I couldn't move either. The thought of running was… frightening. Like I'd make him mad if I did. And Iris had said not to piss him off because he was the stage manager. What if he got me kicked out of the play? My probation could get revoked.

"I thought I'd walk through the park with you," he said with a half smile. "I could show you a cool shortcut."

28

It took a second for it to sink in. When it did, another chill ran over me. Those were the exact words Peter had said to me. How had he known?

Les grabbed my crotch. I froze. Thought fled my brain like a flock of frightened birds. I had no way to think, no way to react. His hand groped around, tugging and feeling through the fabric of my shorts.

"I like shortcuts," Les was saying. "And you're pretty short."

The tiger in me roared to life. I shoved Les with both hands hard. He fell back on his ass, face twisted by surprise and then anger of his own.

"Don't touch me!" I snarled. "Leave me alone!"

Les sat on the warm tarmac. He didn't look sly or slender or half-wry. He looked furious as boiling poison. "I know what you are, you little shit!" he shouted. "You *want* me to—"

"What's going on?" Peter was suddenly there, tall and strong. I swear for a second he was wearing a suit of armor. "Is something wrong here?"

"Nothing." Les scrambled to his feet and stormed toward the door. "Nothing at all." He slammed his way inside.

I rubbed my face. My crotch felt bruised and violated. Peter turned to me. "Are you okay? What happened?"

"I'm fine," I said quickly. "It's nothing. Nothing happened."

Peter looked at me, then at the door, then at me. "You sure?"

"Yeah. It was just... stupid." No way was I going to talk about this with Peter. He'd think I attracted weirdos. I'd deal with it later. "Come on. The shortcut, right?"

We walked through the park, my bike ticking along beside me. The nearly full moon floated serenely above us, and the road stretched ahead like a silver river beneath soft air. Peter brushed my shoulder as we walked, and I let the entire shitstorm with Les fade away. I was walking with a guy who had kissed me and who might kiss me again.

"Can I say something stupid?" Peter asked.

"Uh... sure."

"I couldn't stop thinking about you all day today. And I couldn't wait for rehearsal tonight."

I was going to float away, but I said, "That's pretty stupid."

"Hey!" Peter glared at me. "You're supposed to say I'm *not* stupid."

29

"Oh. Sorry. I'm not very good at being a… you know."

"Boyfriend?"

"Is that what I am?" The road crunched beneath my shoes. "I mean, we've gone on exactly two walks and had exactly one kiss."

In answer Peter turned and kissed me. It wasn't as powerful as the first time, but it was close. When we finished, I was surprised to find we were still standing on the ground instead of up in the clouds. I had to remember how to breathe.

"Two," Peter said.

"You don't even know me," I murmured. "I could be a jewel thief or an ax murderer for all you know."

"Okay." Peter took a deep breath, and I wondered if he was remembering how to breathe too. "Have you ever murdered an ax?"

"Smartass." I slugged him on the shoulder.

"Ow!" Peter staggered with mock pain. "You'll pay for that!"

He flung himself at me, and we rolled across the soft grass, grunting and laughing like puppies. My muscles pushed against his; his body was hard against mine. I felt free and safe at the same time.

Abruptly I was sitting on Peter's stomach, pinning both his wrists above his head with my hands. Panting a little, I looked down at him. He grinned. There was no way I had gotten him in this position without his permission, and he knew I knew. The bastard. I grinned back, then leaned down and kissed him. This time we were slower, more careful. I let myself explore his mouth and got a little rush at the way his hands were pinned. The grass rustled beneath us, and the entire world narrowed to just us.

I pulled back. "Three."

Peter grinned again and turned his head. "What was…?"

"What?" I looked too but didn't see anything.

"I thought I saw a light over there. I guess not."

He pushed me aside and sat up with his arm around me. I would have preserved that moment in glass forever. We were next to the river, and the current made small rushing sounds in the darkness.

"You were right. I don't know anything about you. Where do you live?"

Normally those kinds of questions would have thrown me or made me uneasy, but at that moment, I would have told him anything. "With my dad. Outside of town."

"What about your mom?" He picked up a pebble with his free hand and tossed it into the river. It vanished with a tiny splash.

"She left a long time ago, when I was about nine. I don't even know where she is."

"Oh. Sorry."

"I'm okay with it," I said, not quite lying. I avoided thinking about Mom as much as possible. "What about you? You're in college, right? Studying drama?"

"Nah." He tossed another pebble. "I'm not good enough to go pro, and I don't want to teach. I'm studying architecture. I love drawing buildings, and I want to see them made real."

"That's right—it was one of your truths." I inhaled his scent, one I was learning to recognize as completely his own. "You'll do it. I can see you."

We sat that way for a moment longer, me happy in Peter's arms. Then he said, "I hate to do this, but I have to get up early. Summer class."

I sighed. "'Kay."

We retrieved my bike, and Peter gave me another long kiss. "Four," he said and walked down the path the way we had come, hands in his pockets. I watched him go until the darkness swallowed him.

I have a boyfriend! It was the strangest idea, and one I never thought I'd hear inside my own head. For once the nasty little voice was silent about it. *A boyfriend! Who likes me for me!*

"Hey."

I whipped around. Les was standing there, a lazy smile on his face. A smartphone glowed faintly through his front pocket. A jolt went through me.

"Jesus!" I yelped. "What the hell are you—"

Les grabbed my shirt, yanked me toward him, and kissed me hard. I froze a moment, just like I had done when he groped me, but this time I recovered faster and broke away from him.

"One," he said, and the word sent a chill down my back. He knew about me and Peter. He had seen us, listened in with his cell phone on.

I felt like someone had run a dirty hand over my soul. The tiger snarled inside me.

"Who do you think you are, asshole?" I yelled. "Leave me—"

He shoved me hard. I went sprawling backward on the grass. Les was on top of me in a flash, his hands pinning my wrists just like mine had done to Peter's moments earlier. Les looked down at me and grinned. Saliva glistened at the corner of his mouth.

"You'll kiss him, but you won't kiss me? You give some to him and won't give any to me? Little pervert."

Les's head came down in a snake strike, and he kissed me again. It stole my breath. I tried to squirm away, but he was heavy, and I couldn't get any leverage. Terror tore through me.

"Two," he said.

My heart pounded. My hands shook. I couldn't wait for him to leave.

"Leave me alone, asshole," I tried to growl, but I couldn't get much air, and it came out as more of pitiful gasp. "I'll call—"

"The cops?" Les sneered. "And tell them what? That you're a little faggot? Gonna tell everyone in the police report that you're a little faggot? A little pervert?" He leaned closer, his iron grip around my wrists. "I'll tell the cops what you did with Peter. He's nineteen. You're sixteen. They'll tell the news. They'll tell your dad, little pervert."

The terror was crushing my chest. They'd tell my probation officer. She'd send me to juvie if I got in trouble with the cops. Everyone in school would know. And Dad—what would Dad say?

In a fast move, Les flipped me over on my stomach with my hands behind my back. He was so strong. My face pressed into the grass, my nose mashed dirt. What came next hurt worse than anything I thought could ever hurt. I went away for a while. At last Les's weight left me. I lay on the ground.

"I can tell you liked that, little pervert," Les said. "It'll be even better next time."

Next time? The words were red snakes.

Les knelt next to me and put his hand on my shoulder. "We'll be seeing a lot of each other over the summer. I'll definitely be seeing a *lot* of you." He kissed me on the temple. I flinched—I couldn't help it. "Three," he said. And then he was gone.

For a long time, I lay there. I didn't want to move. Everything hurt. I wanted to sink into the ground and let that spot become my grave. But finally I had to get up. Moving like a zombie, I pulled up my shorts and put one foot in front of the other until I reached my bike. I couldn't ride. Slowly, I wheeled it out of the park.

I barely remember the walk home. It must have taken hours, but time passed in a haze. When I got to the trailer, I had the presence of mind to get a screwdriver and open the air valve on my front tire. It hissed flat. Then I went in.

Dad was on the couch, staring at the book in his hands, but I didn't think he was reading. The box fan stirred the hot air. He shot to his feet.

"What happened to you?" he snapped. "It's almost two in the morning. I've been worried sick."

I looked at him. For half a second I wanted to grab him in a hug and bawl like a little kid until he stroked my hair and said it would be all right. Then I remembered what Les had said in the park. The cops. The news. Peter. Dad.

Little pervert.

"I got a flat tire and had to walk my bike home six miles," I said in a tired voice. "Check my bike if you don't believe me."

Dad wasn't ready to give in. "Why the hell didn't you call?"

"No pay phones between here and there." I had to get out of there before I started to cry. "I'm wiped. Need a shower, then bed. Night."

I turned the shower as hot as I could stand it, then made it a little hotter than that. I washed every inch of me, but the memories hovered around me in the steam.

It'll be even better next time.

It still hurt. I scrubbed myself dry and swallowed some ibuprofen from the medicine cabinet. When I lowered the towel in my room, Les yanked my shorts down again. I clutched the towel tighter around my waist.

I'll definitely be seeing a lot of you.

Somehow I got another pair of shorts on and curled up on my bed. Robbie looked at me from his picture frame. I stared back without knocking on it.

ACT I: SCENE IV

KEVIN

ROBBIE STILL looked up at me from his frame, though now it was morning, and I was outside under one of the trees in the front yard. I hadn't really slept. The morning air was cool, especially in the shade of the yard. A cute little birdie twittered on a branch over my head. Any second it would shit on me.

I heard Dad's footsteps coming, and he squatted next to me in thick work boots and a blue denim shirt with the sleeves rolled up. "You shouldn't do this, Kevin. It ain't healthy."

He reached for the picture, but I whipped it out of his reach. Dad sighed and ran a hand through his hair. I set the photo facedown on the grass where Dad couldn't reach it. I didn't want to talk.

"Listen, Kev," he said, "I don't know how to help you. I wish we could afford for you to talk to someone, but—"

Anger burst out of me. I rounded on him. "Why? You think I'm crazy? I need a shrink?"

Dad looked tired. It wasn't the first time we'd had this conversation, and it always went the same way. "I'm saying I don't know what's going on with you. This started long before all that stuff with... with those other guys."

I picked up the photo again and looked down at Robbie.

"Look, I know you think I won't understand. I thought the same thing when I was a teenager. But I haven't forgotten what it's like to be sixteen. Talking about it can help."

Dad, I'm gay, I have a boyfriend, and last night I got...

Robbie looked up at me like he always did. Dad squatted next to me, silent.

... raped.

My hand shook, and the photograph trembled a tiny bit. *It was my fault. I should have fought back more, should have made sure Les hadn't seen me and Peter together.*

I looked at Dad. He tried to be a good dad. I knew that… mostly. Even if he'd missed most of my childhood because of prison. He could help. I wanted to talk. I opened my mouth to say the words. But what came out was, "You're wearing work clothes. You get a job?"

Dad looked disappointed, and I felt even guiltier. "Yeah. Temp thing putting up drywall for a few days."

"Under the table?"

"No taxes that way." Dad gave a small smile. "Every cent for us. What are you doing today?"

I managed a small fake smile of my own. "Probably memorizing my lines. The play opens in four weeks, so I have to get to work."

"Okay. Don't forget to eat lunch. See you this evening." He rose to go, then hesitated. "Kevin…."

"I'm fine, Dad." I looked down at the photo again. "Go to work. You'll be late."

He hovered there a moment longer, then clumped away. The truck drove off in a cloud of dust.

Just then the phone rang inside the trailer. "Shit," I muttered and ran inside, the photo still in my hand. I had to be the only teenager in America who didn't have a cell. We couldn't afford one. Even our landline had a cord, and it always twisted. I snatched it off the wall.

"Hey, Kevin," said Peter.

All the strength went out of my legs, and I slid down the wall to the floor. I couldn't decide if it was because his voice made me happy or scared. "Hey," I said. "Uh… how did you get my number?"

"It's on the contact list Iris handed out, doofus."

I wrapped the cord around my hand. "Oh. Right. So… what's up?"

"My class is out for the day. You want to get together? We could work on our lines or just hang."

For a second I was back in the park. Peter was kissing me. Then it was Les. Then it was worse. I pulled my knees up to my chin.

That'd be great! Where? "I can't. I'm supposed to do stuff around home today."

"Oh. Okay." I could hear the hurt in his voice, but I couldn't face him. Not now. "Well, see you tonight."

"Yeah." The phone cord was cutting off the circulation in my fingers. "Gotta rehearse, right? See you."

We hung up. My hand stayed on the phone for a second, then convulsed there. Rehearsal. Les would be at rehearsal.

Nausea rushed over me in a black wave, and I barely made it to the bathroom in time. I clutched the cold toilet and threw up. Acid burned me up and down.

This was all because I'd kissed Peter. If I hadn't done that, Les would never have seen me and gotten those ideas. He wouldn't have come after me like that. It was my fault.

I threw up again and again until there was nothing to throw. I sat on the thin bathroom carpet. Just sat. And sat. I didn't have the energy to move. Time passed. The bathroom grew darker as the sun shifted. I didn't move. The bathroom grew darker still. I didn't move. Finally I dragged myself to my feet. Almost time for rehearsal. My legs cramped up, and I bore the pain as my due.

Outside I inflated my bike tire with the hand pump. I couldn't let everyone else down. It wouldn't be fair. I pedaled the long way into town so I could avoid the park, and I tried not to think about rehearsal, but when I arrived at the Art Center, my mouth dried up, and iron bands of fear tightened around my chest. Les was waiting beyond that iron door, and I had to go through it. I was so scared. He—

The rear door banged open, and I jumped. My bowels went loose. I cried out and hated myself for being such a coward. Iris poked her head outside.

"There you are," she said. "You're late, kiddo. Remember, you lose the role if you get more than two tardies. I don't make exceptions."

I locked my bike with shaking hands. "S-sorry, Iris. Coming."

She followed me inside, and we walked side by side down the hallway toward the theater. I remembered how scared I'd been about the idea that this hallway might lead me to jail. Now that idea seemed a much better option. Maybe I should just drop out and go to juvie. Get it over with.

"Are you okay, Kevin?" Iris asked. "Your face is white as milk."

"I'm fine," I said. "Really. Just a little tired. I'm… I'm…."

The room tilted. I fell dizzily against the cinder-block wall. Iris made a startled sound and caught me by one arm. "Kevin!"

Then I was sitting on the floor with my head between my knees. The hallway was dark around the edges. Iris knelt beside me with her arm around my shoulders. Words built up and spilled out. I couldn't stop them.

"I'm so scared, I'm so scared, I'm so scared," I chanted.

"Kevin, what's wrong?" Iris's voice was filled with concern. "Tell me."

I had to tell someone. I couldn't keep it in. "I was attacked. Last night. On the way home from rehearsal."

I waited for disgust, but Iris sounded worried instead. "Attacked? Kevin, what happened? It's all right—you can say."

"I… I was…." Fear drained some of the words away. I couldn't quite say everything. "This guy jumped me."

"Do you know who it was? Did you call the cops?"

"I don't know who it was. I didn't call anyone." My eyes were hot, and my nose felt swollen.

She helped get me to my feet. "Let's go into the green room and we'll talk, all right?"

A few minutes later, I was sitting on a lumpy couch in the green room, which is what theater people call the place where actors wait until they're needed onstage, even if the walls aren't actually green. Iris handed me a can of Coke and sat down.

"I've got the others running lines," she said. "Tell me what happened."

I held the cool can against my wrists. It calmed me a little. "There isn't much to tell. A guy jumped me in the park. He wanted money, but I didn't have any. So he hit me a couple times and ran away."

"Would you recognize him if you saw him again?"

Les's grinning face floated in front of me for a second. "Maybe," I muttered.

"We should call the police. Even if you can't tell them who did it, you should file a report in case he's caught later."

I tensed. "No."

"Kevin, I know it's hard." She touched my wrist. "A lot of assault victims react this way. And it's how people like your attacker get away with it."

"It's not that." I hated lying to her. It made me feel like a worm under dog turds. "I'm sort of… on probation."

Iris straightened her glasses. "Probation?"

"My PO told me I had to get a job or do a summer program like the play. So I did. If I call the cops… I'm already on their bad side. They won't believe me—or I'll just get in trouble again."

"Look, kiddo." Her voice was gentle and made me want to cry again. I took a hard breath so I wouldn't. Crying in public is embarrassing. "The cops won't care that you're on probation. You're the victim here. What did your parents say?"

I almost dropped the pop can. "Don't tell my dad! He'll pull me out of the play."

"All right, all right. I won't." She got up. "Look, I really have to get back to rehearsal. Do you want to go home, get some rest? We won't count it as an absence."

"No! The play…. It helps me deal." That hadn't been what I meant to say, but it was true. I could be someone else for a while. Algy didn't give a shit about Les.

"Sure. I'll have Les read for Algy until you're ready." She paused. "I saw Peter at the pop machine. He's worried about you, but I told him we needed to talk in private."

I sat there for several minutes after she left, drinking the Coke. It was the only thing I'd had all day, and the sugar rush flooded my veins. Finally I got up and slipped into the backstage area. Ropes and pulleys with weights at the bottom lined the back wall, and black curtains hung in a velvet maze. Everything was painted black back there. On the stage, Meg Kimura, an Asian girl I didn't know very well yet, was sitting on a couch. Meg was playing Cousin Cecily, my character's eventual girlfriend. Jack, Peter's character, was looking after her because her parents had died. We were all supposed to ignore Meg being an Asian girl in a white family. I guess lots of plays did that kind of thing now.

Beside her on the couch sat Les. He was playing Algy, my character. I didn't want him to do that, but I didn't want to go out there either. I felt hot and cold, angry and scared, all at once.

Meg said as Cecily, "*I have never met any really wicked person before. I feel rather frightened. I am so afraid he will look just like everyone else.*"

Les said as Algy in a really bad English accent, "*Oh! I am not really wicked at all, Cousin Cecily. You mustn't think that I am wicked.*"

I watched with a sick fascination and didn't notice a hand reach out of the darkness behind me.

"*If you are not, then you have certainly been deceiving us all in a very inexcusable manner.*"

The hand landed on my shoulder. I jumped and twisted like a fucked-up cat.

"*I hope you have not been leading a double life, pretending to be wicked and being really good all the time. That would be hypocrisy.*"

Peter pressed me against the stage wall, a hand over my mouth. He was grinning his starlight grin. I felt like I'd been slammed into a cage.

"Sh," he whispered. "It's just me."

"*Oh! Of course I* have *been rather reckless,*" Algy said.

I grabbed Peter and clung to him there in the dark. He looked surprised.

"*In fact, now you mention the subject, I have been very bad in my own small way,*" Algy said.

Peter held me at arm's length. "Are you all right?"

"*I don't think you should be so proud of that, though I am sure it must have been very pleasant,*" said Cecily.

I had to feel something, anything, nice. I kissed Peter. Hard. He kissed back.

Algy said, "*It is much pleasanter being here with you.*"

The kiss ended, and Peter smiled at me. It did feel nice. "Five," he said.

Les whispered his own numbers in my head. Suddenly Peter's face merged with Les's. I felt sick. The air grew close and still. I spun and had just enough time to see shock cross Peter's face before I fled.

"That is a great disappointment," Algy said behind me. *"I have a business appointment that I am anxious to miss."*

I grabbed my bike and pedaled furiously toward home. It was mostly dark out. Low black clouds hung in the sky, and lightning lanced across them ahead of me. The temperature dropped. I pushed harder as rain fell in fat drops. It turned into heavy sheets that rushed over the street and wet me through. I didn't care. Nothing mattered. I was nothing.

The downpour continued all the way home. When I turned into the driveway, my front tire hit a rut or a rock or something, and I wiped out. My bike went one way, I went another, and I stomach-surfed across the wet grass with an *"oof."* Once I slid to a stop, I just lay there, arms cradled around my head, hoping the rain would melt me into the ground. I wasn't sure if I was crying or not. Thunder rolled and crashed above me, but I ignored it.

I lay there a long time in the heavy rain and gathering gloom. Eventually I heard a soft "Hey."

Peter. I didn't know how to feel, though I was rock tired. My arms jacked me half-upright of their own accord. "What do you want?"

"I was frightened, man. Iris told me you got into a bad fight. Are you… I mean…."

"I'm fine. I'm…." Air rushed out of me. "I'm scared shitless."

"If you wanna talk about it, I'll listen." He sounded like Iris. "It's what boyfriends are for."

"I dunno if I *can* talk about it." Rain bucketed over us both. My feet were soaked inside my shoes, and my fingers had wrinkled up. Stupid thing to think about. "I'm scared all the time, Peter. I'm scared he's gonna come back and… and do it again."

"Do what?"

I didn't answer.

"Look." Peter was sitting next to me now, not caring that he was getting just as wet. That made me feel a little better. A lot better. He cared enough to sit with me in the rain. "You got into a fight. It's shitty, but it happens, you know? You don't have to—"

"He raped me."

A long moment passed. I drew my knees up under my chin without looking at Peter. Why wasn't he responding? Jesus, why had I said anything? *Now he thinks I'm some kind of fag slut.* I tensed myself to get up and run.

Peter grabbed me in a heavy hug. "Oh my god. Kevin, I'm so sorry. Jesus, I'm so sorry. This is all my fault."

That gave me pause. "What? How is this your fault?"

"I only realized it after you ran out at rehearsal—the attack happened just after I took off, didn't it? If I hadn't left you alone, it wouldn't have happened." He let me go and ran a hand over his wet face. "I'm a shit. I'm sorry, Kev."

"It's not your fault." I took his hand. "You couldn't have known."

Peter wiped at his eyes. Was he crying? "Yeah, well… if it's all the same to you, I'm going to feel guilty for a while yet."

I managed a small smile and noticed Peter's Mustang parked in the mouth of the driveway. My driveway. Shit. Peter was seeing where I lived. But in comparison with everything that had happened, that didn't seem so important.

"How did you know where to find me?" I asked.

"Iris had your address on the audition form." Water dripped off his nose. "She thought someone should check on you. I took off before anyone else could volunteer. My car's pretty fast."

"Yeah. Sweet ride," I said with envy. "Geez, are you rich?"

"Kinda." With a sheepish grin, Peter pushed back his soaking hair. "My grandfather left me a fund."

I pointed at the trailer. "Yeah, well, mine didn't."

"I can see that. And you know what?" He towed me to my feet and hauled me toward it. "Who gives a shit? If it's dry, let's go in."

Seconds later we stood dripping inside the front door. Peter let out a low whistle. "Hell of a book collection. Yours?"

"Nah. I like to read okay, but my dad's the book fiend." I covered my discomfort at having him there in my crappy home by grabbing a pair of towels and tossing one so it landed on his head. "You can use this."

He rubbed it over his hair. "Look, I don't want to sound like a bad porn movie, but we should get out of these wet clothes. You got anything I can borrow?"

41

And then we were in my bare bedroom. Peter leaned against the doorway while I rooted through my dresser, throwing clothes around with wild abandon because I didn't know what else to do. He was in my room, in my freakin' *room*, and he was going to take his clothes off. Were we going to do it? Did I want him to? I wasn't sure. Not after Les. Even before Les, I wasn't sure. Everything was so mixed up. If he wanted to and I didn't, would he not want to be boyfriends anymore?

"T-try these." I handed him some stuff, and our hands touched. My eyes met his, and all the air went out of the room.

"Thanks." His voice was soft. "I'll hang the towel in the bathroom while I change. Be right back." And he left.

I dropped onto the bed with my head in my hands. Robbie watched me from his picture frame on the nightstand. I was kind of mad that Peter didn't want to and also totally relieved. How could I be both at the same time? It was so fucked-up. *I* was so fucked-up.

Noises came from the bathroom. I yanked off my wet clothes and pulled on dry ones. My shoes were a sloppy wreck, so I went barefoot. Peter appeared in the doorway wearing a pair of baggy basketball shorts and the biggest T-shirt I owned. It was still too small for him, and it clung to every muscle of his chest and torso. I couldn't stop staring.

"Way better." He stretched out an arm that threatened to burst from the sleeve. "I think."

"You look great," I said, glad I was able to say it out loud. "You should dress that way all the time."

Peter dropped onto the bed like I had earlier, and I noticed his face was a little red. Had I embarrassed him? Hmmm…. He picked up Robbie's photo. "So who's this?"

"Don't." I snatched it from him angrily. "Don't ever touch it."

"Oh. Sure, okay." Peter got up, but I was looking down at the photo and didn't see the expression on his face. "Look, maybe I should go. See you."

He headed for the door. A lump gathered in my throat, and I kept staring down at the photo. It was ending before it even began. The nasty inner voice said, *See? You don't deserve him or anything else.* I just couldn't keep it together. I never could.

The empty doorway stared at me. *Idiot!*

I ran into the living room with the photo still in my hand. Peter's hand was on the knob to the front door. "Wait!" I ran up and put my free arm around him. He was warm. "I'm a shit. I don't want you to leave."

We sat down on the sagging couch with Robbie's photo amid the books on the coffee table, our arms around each other as if we might float away if we let go.

"I'm glad you ran out when you did," Peter whispered in my ear.

"Why?"

He grinned at me. "Because I was getting pretty bored standing there with my hand on the doorknob."

I leaped at him. "You jerk!"

We wrestled on the couch, both laughing. Somehow I got him pinned to the cushions by the wrists. Peter smiled up at me. And then it was me and Les in the park. I leaped away and huddled on the far side of the couch.

"Sorry...," I muttered.

Peter turned sideways on the couch to face me. The smile left his face, and he looked both serious and sympathetic. "This is about what happened in the park, isn't it?"

I didn't answer.

"And about that kid in the picture."

Now I looked at him. "How did—"

"Dude, it's written all over you."

An insane image popped into my head. I was covered with tattoos of my life story, and everyone could read them.

"Was he... you know... your first boyfriend?" Peter said.

I stared at him, wide-eyed. Peter looked sorry he asked, but he resolutely met my gaze. And then I burst out laughing. I clutched my stomach and laughed and laughed. "Oh my god. First boyfriend. That's great!"

"Glad you liked it." Peter looked a little put out.

The laughter passed, and I wiped my eyes. "Oh man. No, he wasn't my boyfriend. Kinda the opposite."

"So what about him, then?"

I got up and went to the window. Outside, the rain came down like the clouds were trying to wash away every tragedy in the world. "I tried to kill him."

ACT I: SCENE V

KEVIN

I WAS angry, I said to Peter. *Like, all the time. I had no real friends. My mom was gone. She left the second Dad got out of jail. I think she was counting time out here just like he was in there. He got home, and she took off. Couldn't wait to get rid of a shitty kid like me. That was when I was nine.*

Anyway, I only had Dad, and I still didn't know him very well. He wouldn't understand anything. Besides, I was pissed at him. Pissed at him for going to jail, pissed at him for not being around, pissed at him for making Mom go away.

What? No, I have no idea if he really made her go or not. I was just pissed. Some other shit was bugging me too, but I didn't want to think about any of it, so I went out and made friends with some extreme east-siders, guys I knew Dad would hate. They were a little older than me—I was fifteen—and they did some wild shit. Broken bottles and crystal meth lightbulbs in abandoned single-wides was just the start of it. I drank and stole, yeah, but at least I wasn't stupid enough to try the meth. Oh hell, that's not true. I was too scared to go through with it, though I pretended I was hitting it.

Then, over spring break, Hank—he was kind of the leader—said it was time for a real bash. I... I liked Hank. A lot. I also hated that I liked him so much. It was another reason to be pissed off so much. It wasn't just Hank who gave me those kind of feelings. It was... well, you know how it goes.

Hank's bashes turned out to be a lot of fun. We picked a west-side neighborhood, grabbed up baseball bats or rocks or chains or whatever else we could find, and bashed stuff after dark. It felt good, like I was part of a strong and powerful group.

First it was mailboxes. We smashed 'em. Then it was cars. We bashed a bunch of those. The next step was easy. Hell, it was even logical. I mean, you go out after dark when there's been a lot of gang activity, and what do you expect, right?

So yeah—this kid was outside on the street. Only we decided it was our street, at least until the cops showed up and we scattered. Hank saw him first, but we all caught on fast. The kid was maybe a year younger than me. He had brown hair, like me, and these really big eyes. He looked like a baby bird.

I don't really remember everything that came next. It seemed like the kid didn't even try to run when we surrounded him. I do remember thinking my baseball bat was really heavy, and tiny bits of glass stuck in the wood glittered like diamond dust. The kid was so scared, he was panting.

We were all waiting for someone else to start. It was weird, but no one really wanted to go first.

Then Hank said, "Hit him, Kev! Cream the little faggot!"

I was holding my bat high, ready to hit a home run. This kid was rich and had everything I didn't. And Hank, tall and handsome and strong, was telling me to do it. And I was pissed.

Hank shouted, "What are you waiting for? Do it!"

The kid put his hands up to his head. I won't lie. I wanted to do it. But I couldn't quite make myself.

Hank said, "He wants to suck your cock."

Something in that sent me over the edge. I swung my bat and hit the kid in the arm. He screamed. The gang laughed, and they swung too. Chains and rocks and hands and feet. I couldn't stop. I was hitting everything that made me angry, everything I hated.

Everything that was me.

That was when the cop cars showed up, with lights that slashed the dark like blue knives. Everyone scattered, but one cop took me down in a football tackle and got me in handcuffs so fast I didn't even have time to understand what was happening. I'll never forget the awful, sad look on my dad's face when he came down to the station to get me. I wanted to flush myself down the toilet.

The kid almost died. He was in the hospital for three weeks. He was released the day I got sentenced. Because I had a clean record, the judge gave me two years' probation instead of jail. She said I couldn't see or talk to any of the people I used to hang out with. If I see them or get into any other kind of trouble, I go straight to juvie.

She also gave me a picture of the kid I beat up. It's this one here.

"His name is Robbie Hunter," the judge said. "He's fourteen. He has an older sister and a younger brother. He likes reading and playing video games. He loves woodworking and built his little brother a treehouse last summer."

Every word beat me black and blue. I couldn't speak or think. All I could do was stand there with my head hanging down. If she had swung an axe to chop it off, I wouldn't have stopped her.

"You beat up a person, Kevin. A person with hopes and feelings and a family who was terrified he would die. You aren't allowed to forget that." And she hit her desk with that hammer thing.

What? No, I've never talked to Robbie. But I keep him on my nightstand and knock the frame three times before I go to sleep so he knows I haven't forgotten him.

So no... he's not my first boyfriend. Or maybe, in a weird way, he is.

MY HANDS were twisting in my lap like a nest of spiders. It was the first time I'd ever said any of this stuff out loud, and it was both easier and harder than I thought. I was sweating a little and was glad for the box fan churning damp air in from outside. The rain had slowed to a trickle.

Peter was still sitting next to me on the couch. I faced forward; he faced sideways. "I don't know what to say," he told me.

I shrugged. More words swarmed inside me. I didn't want to let them out, but I was already leaking. "You don't have to say anything."

"No, I feel like I should have something profound to say, but I can't think of—"

"I deserved it," I said.

There. The last of the words were out. All of a sudden, I wanted to take them back. My chin trembled, and I worked my jaw.

"What?" Peter asked.

47

My mouth moved by itself. "That thing in the park. I deserved it."

Peter put his arms around me then, though I didn't move. "That's not true, Kevin. Absolutely not."

"Yes, it is." The words rushed around, faster and faster, trapped in the circle of Peter's arms. "I beat up Robbie Hunter, and then that guy… attacked me. I'm being punished, and I deserve it."

"The universe doesn't work that way, Kev." Peter's voice was soft. "No one's trying to punish you."

"Yeah, whatever." It was nice to hear, but I didn't believe it. Why else would it have happened? Shit, because of what I'd done to Robbie, I'd gotten involved in the theater program, and that put me in the park that night so Les could attack me. It was all so obvious.

Peter leaned in closer and pecked me on the cheek. I was too wrapped up in inner blackness to respond. He pulled back a little. "Six?" he said hopefully.

Okay. That made me smile. A little.

The front door banged open. Peter jerked away from me. I nearly smacked the ceiling as Dad stomped into the trailer. His hair was tousled, his work shirt and jeans filthy, his boots muddy. And he was wet.

"I'm home!" he shouted. "Whose car is that in the driveway?"

"Dad!" I bolted to my feet. "Hi! How was work? Are you hungry? Boy, you must be tired! I could make you a sandwich!" I almost ran the five steps to the kitchen. "Put up lots of drywall? You look like you've been slaving pretty hard! Are you working tomorrow too?"

Dad set down his lunch bucket. His eyes were narrowed. "What are you up to, Kevin?"

"Me?" I answered too loudly. I couldn't seem to help myself. "I'm not up to anything. Why would I be up to anything?"

"The only time you babble is when I've caught you at something." He jerked a thumb at Peter. "Who's your friend? Is he involved? That his car out front?"

I had out bread and a knife and no idea what to do with either one. "Uh…."

"Hi, Mr. Devereaux." Peter got to his feet, elegant and smooth, and held out his hand. "I'm Peter Finn. Kevin and I are in the play together. We got out of rehearsal early today, so I gave him a ride home."

They shook hands. A too-wide grin had plastered itself across my face, and I reined it in. If Dad suspected anything....

"I see. Nice to meet you, Peter." Dad dropped his hand and looked at him. "Is that Kevin's shirt you're wearing?"

My heart collapsed like a dead balloon.

"Yeah." Peter slid his hands into his back pockets and smiled that perfectly charming smile, the one that could stop a charging jaguar. "I fell and got soaked through when we ran in from the car, so Kevin loaned me some stuff. We hung my clothes in the bathroom. I hope that's okay."

"Sure, that's fine. Glad Kevin has a friend." The last bits of suspicion fell away from Dad's face, and I thought I might faint with relief. "I'm ordering pizza for supper. You can stay if you want."

"No, thanks. I should get home. Is it still raining?"

"Not as hard." Dad was rummaging around one of the end tables where we kept takeout menus. I shoved the sandwich bread aside—pizza!—and snagged the umbrella from the little closet near the front door.

"I'll walk you to your car so you don't get wet this time," I said.

"Thanks," said polite, charming Peter.

"Nice meeting you, Peter," Dad called as we walked out. "You're always welcome."

We huddled under the too-small umbrella and avoided puddles out to Peter's blue Mustang. Rain drummed on the cloth above our heads. His hand and mine held the handle together, and I suddenly wanted to keep on walking down the driveway, onto the road, and into forever with him.

"Thanks for coming over, Peter," I said as he opened the door. "I... I feel kinda better." And it was true.

"I'm glad." An odd look came over his face. "Look, Kev, I wanted to tell you...."

"Tell me?" Our hands were still on the umbrella handle. "Tell me what?"

He broke away and dropped into the driver's seat. "Never mind. I gotta go. *Earnest* forever!"

I waved as he drove away, wondering what he had wanted to say but not wanting to think too hard about it.

Dad was on the couch, pulling off his work boots, when I came inside. "Pizza's on the way, kiddo. They paid me pretty good, even for a short day."

"Cool. I'm suddenly starving." I put the umbrella away and headed toward my room.

"So what is Peter to you *really*?" Dad asked.

The whole world stopped. For a moment I couldn't move. *Oh shit.* Had he seen something? What did he know?

"What do you mean?" I forced a casual note into my voice. Algy would have been proud.

"You haven't had a friend over since… since before court." He unlaced his other boot. "He a good friend?"

Oh. Jesus. It was okay. Probably. The ice was still thin, though. Dad wasn't looking directly at me, and that meant he was keeping things too casual. "Sort of. I mean, we have a lot of scenes together in the play, and he's pretty cool."

"He has a car. And he's a couple-three years older than you."

"Sure, but we get along." I needed to change the subject, and fast. "You gonna take a shower before the pizza gets here? Drywall dust doesn't mix with mozzarella."

Dad stretched and headed for the bathroom. "Yeah, I better."

I let out a relieved sigh when he got out of sight and then almost hit the ceiling yet again when he shouted, "Kevin!"

A shirt and a pair of shorts flew through the air and *fwapped* on my head. "Your friend left these in here."

I restarted my heart, then took Robbie's picture and Peter's clothes into my room while the shower hissed in the bathroom. Robbie's picture went onto the nightstand, and Peter's clothes went onto my bed—old boyfriend, new boyfriend. I sat cross-legged and crumpled Peter's damp T-shirt to my face. It still smelled like him. I lay back on my bed, and for a moment I forgot about Robbie and Les and was back on the couch with Peter's arms around me.

ACT I: SCENE VI

PETER

IN HIS own room, Peter peeled off Kevin's shirt and crumpled it to his face. It still smelled like Kevin. He lay back on his bed for a moment. What the hell was he doing? Kevin was sixteen, for god's sake, barely a junior in high school. Peter was nineteen and starting his sophomore year in college this fall. Sure, when they were old, like in their thirties, three years wouldn't be any big deal, but right now those few years yawned like an abyss.

But when they were together, that abyss melted away. Kevin had been through a lot, and he didn't act like other high schoolers Peter knew. At the audition he had barely glanced Kevin's way. And then Kevin walked on the stage and become Algernon. The transformation was so quick, so complete, it left Peter staring, and he almost dropped his lines. And shit, the guy was good-looking. That tousled brown hair and those merry blue eyes yanked Peter straight in. Peter rarely shied away from risks, but it took all his courage to touch Kevin's knee during that first rehearsal and take his hand later in the parking lot. Now everything was moving so quickly. Peter had been in love before, but never this hard or fast. And then he learned some whack job had raped Kevin.

Fury bunched the shirt in his hands. It had taken all his self-control not to... what? Yell? Shout? Scream? Go hunt the guy down? He didn't even know who the asshole was. But if he ever found out....

Peter stuffed Kevin's shirt under one of his pillows and followed them with the borrowed shorts. Then he got out shorts and a shirt of his own from the walk-in closet. The french doors to the deck outside his room showed the rain was ending at last. Most of the trailer where Kevin lived with his father would have fit into Peter's room, where hardwood floors scattered with heavy throw rugs stretched to walls of molded plaster. One section was more like a living room, complete with a plasma TV set into the wall, a fireplace, and comfortable furniture scattered with an array of video games. Peter's desk and computer took up surprisingly little space, and the shelves sported a respectable book collection, though nothing close to what Kevin's dad had amassed. A door led to his bathroom. Peter wondered what Kevin would think of the place and exhaled hard at the thought. East-sider and west-sider. Romeo and... Romeo.

Someone rapped sharply at the door. Peter recognized the knock. "Come in, Mom."

Helen Morse entered the room. She wore her business clothes— conservative gray dress suit and flat shoes. Her silvering hair was pulled back into a bun. An unhappy expression creased her face, and Peter tensed. Now what?

"I thought rehearsal ran until ten," she said.

"Schedule change. No biggie." He pulled on his shoes. Kevin's had duct tape on them. Peter hadn't even thought twice about dropping a thousand dollars on his. "What's up?"

Mom brandished a piece of paper. "You got a letter from the chair of the architecture department. It says they've approved your request for a change in major."

"You opened my mail?" Peter got to his feet in both surprise and outrage.

"Your father and I are paying for that education." Mom pointed an accusing finger under his chin. "If it comes from the school, I'll damn well open it. I checked your schedule too. All the classes you've signed up for are in either architecture or theater. You're supposed to be studying business."

Peter stubbornly folded his arms. He'd known this argument was coming, but he didn't want to have it right then, not with what had just happened to Kevin looming behind him. "I hate business. It's frustrating and boring, and I'm no good at it."

"Your grandfather didn't found Morse Plastic so you could—"

"—fritter my life away drawing pictures of buildings and parading around on a stage. I've heard it before, Mom." Peter dropped back to the bed. "I'd ruin Morse Plastic if I took it over. We both know it."

"You'd do no such thing, Peter Finn. You're a *Morse*, and being a Morse means you get respect."

"Whether it's earned or not," Peter said wryly.

"Don't talk that way. You're an intelligent, talented young man who's a natural leader. All you need is a push in the right direction."

"How do you know what the right direction is, Mom?" Peter countered. "Look, I don't want to talk about this. I was in a good mood until now."

"Peter Finn—" Mom reined in her temper with obvious effort, though her foot tapped the rug with firm little thumps. "I'm not going to be around forever. Your grandfather wanted Morse Plastic to stay in the family, so the next CEO has to be you or your sister, and you know it can't be Emily."

"She'd do a better job than I would." Peter's hand crept under his pillow to touch Kevin's shirt for reassurance. Kevin was strong. Peter could be strong too. "Maybe it's time to take the company public, Mom. You know what an IPO would do. It'd be the biggest thing to hit the market since Google."

"There, see?" She came over to stand near Peter's bed, and he smelled her perfume. "You *do* have a head for business."

"Two classes don't make me a CEO," Peter sighed.

Mom strode for the door. "I have a business thing over dinner. We're not done discussing this, Peter Finn."

"Sure, sure," Peter said to her retreating back. "Would you tell Dennis that my car needs to go in the garage?"

Mom paused at the door. Without turning around, she said, "Emily's been asking for you. You should go see her before bedtime."

She shut the door. Peter sat on the bed for a long moment, then dropped his head into his hands for a moment longer. Shit. He hated arguing with Mom. He hated it even more when she was right. Better to get it over with.

He left his room and followed a long, wide corridor through the mansion. A number of the help stood aside to let him pass, and Peter nodded absently to them. Eventually he came to a heavy oak door. He steeled himself and knocked exactly twice.

"Enter," called a musical voice from within.

Peter opened the door. "Hi, Em."

"Peter Finn!" she called. "Peter Finn, come in! I want to see you so much, Peter Finn!"

He shut the door behind him.

KEVIN

A NEW guy was at rehearsal, huge and bulky, with bowling-ball arms and a shovel beard. He made me nervous, but not nearly as nervous as Les did. It took all my nerve to stand on the stage with him there, even though I took care to stay far away from him. Les took up his usual place near the curtains at stage left with his notebook. My stomach grew cold and tight at the sight of him, though he ignored me. I thought about dropping out of the play, but then I'd be in trouble with my probation officer, and I wouldn't see Peter anymore. So I made myself go. Peter stood next to me, of course, and I was glad about that. Thad and Joe hovered around Meg, and Melissa stood some distance away from Les with her back pointedly toward him. I wondered if there was something going on there.

Even more furniture was on the stage now, along with a partially built staircase at the back. Iris was downstage—the part closest to the audience. She gestured at the big guy.

"This is my brother Wayne, everyone," she said. "He's designing the set and will be helping out as assistant director."

Wayne gave a curt wave. "Hey."

"Your brother?" Joe said. "Geez."

"We're twins," Wayne grunted, and I couldn't tell if he was kidding or not.

"Tonight I thought we'd start with an acting exercise," Iris said, "and then start blocking act two."

At this Wayne said, "Take a moment and get into character. When I say *go*, I want you to turn to whoever is closest to you and mime a conversation, using gestures and expressions your character would use."

Les glanced at me. I kept my eyes on Wayne but sensed Les looking at me with eyes of hardened glass. I started to edge closer to Peter, then stopped myself. I couldn't drape myself over him all the time, much as I wanted to. People would wonder. Besides, I needed to get to know the other cast members. And it would be nice to have some other friends. I made myself sort of stroll over to Melissa. Lady Bracknell. She was still keeping her back to Les.

"Remember, your character isn't you," Wayne rumbled. "No one here acts or moves like an English aristocrat or servant from a hundred and fifty years ago. So you'll have to think every moment how your character moves and avoid moving like an American teenager instead."

Peter seemed to realize I wasn't standing near him anymore. He looked a little surprised, then shrugged and turned to Joe. I wasn't sure how to feel about that. I mean, he should have been a *little* disappointed, right?

Wayne said, "Get into character and… go."

Melissa caught my eye and drew herself up, becoming stiff and stern. She huffed at me, her slacker nephew, and mouthed several things. I realized I had no idea what to do. A big part of Algy was his words, but Wayne had said we couldn't speak. It felt like something had been stolen from me. I made myself slouch a little, and I called up the Algy shell, but it was thin and pasty. I turned away from "Aunt Augusta" and rolled my eyes. No, that wasn't right. Algy was too afraid of his aunt to show disrespect, but he wouldn't show any fear either. On impulse I took her hand, kissed the back, and pretended to say something charming. Charmed but refusing to fall for it, Aunt Augusta took her hand back and waved it distractedly.

"Algy and Lady Bracknell—good!" Wayne called. "Lane—Thad—remember you're a decorous butler, not a street sweeper. Look at your partner, not at Les."

I was getting into it now. I fished a bit of paper out of my pocket and showed it to Aunt Augusta while I made puppy-dog eyes. I had no idea what was on it, but Aunt Augusta accepted it and made a questioning gesture. I clasped my hands under my chin. With a sigh of exasperation, she mimed signing it and handed it back to me. Of course—it was a check. I kissed her hand again with an outrageous flourish, then turned my back on her with a look of glee.

Everyone was staring at us. They burst into applause, Peter the loudest. I was caught completely off guard, and the Algy shell shattered. Melissa grinned and curtseyed. I flushed.

"There, you see?" Iris said. "You can tell a lovely character story without a word. Great opening, folks. Let's get to work. Les, who do we need?"

Les shot a glance at me. My insides turned black and rotten. I wanted to shrivel up. I wanted to hide among the curtains. I wanted to shoot him with a spear gun.

He's not going to do anything with everyone here. Maybe I could just avoid him. Then he wouldn't have the chance to touch me.

"Miss Prism and Cecily are onstage," he said. "Dr. Chasuble, Merriman, Jack, and Algy need to be ready to enter. Everyone else take five."

"No fives. Work on lines," Wayne rumbled.

Melissa headed offstage, away from Les. In the interest of staying with people, I came with her. Only the two of us were on that side of the stage. Impulsively, I said in a low voice, "You don't like Les very much."

She gave me a hard look, a lot like Aunt Augusta might give Algy. "What makes you say that?"

"I can see it. I don't… I don't think I like him either. What'd he do?"

"He's a fuck," she said, also low. "He sold some shit to my younger sister, and when she was on it, he tried to…. Anyway, he's a fuck."

My eyes widened. "No shit?"

"No shit. Stay away from him. Seriously."

"Did he…?" I found I couldn't bring myself to finish the question. Instead I asked, "Did you call the cops?"

"And get my sister in trouble?" She shook her head. "Course, that's how he gets away with it."

"How come he's working here, if he's doing… you know."

Melissa blew out a puff of air. "You heard Iris—adult volunteers are hard to find. And anyway, there's no proof unless my sister wants to report him. And she won't." She pointedly changed the subject. "I'm getting a pop from the machine before I get called up. You want one?"

"No, thanks."

She trotted away, leaving me alone in the wings and feeling tense. Now what should I do? The judge had said associating with known criminals was a violation of my probation, so being in the play with Les as a stage manager could get me into trouble. On the other hand, dropping out would leave me without a summer program, and that would get me into trouble too. Plus I didn't want to screw over the rest of the cast. Les was fucking with me no matter what I did.

Peter slipped around the rear of the stage and sidled up next to me. I elaborately pretended he wasn't there but couldn't help a little smile. His presence made me feel better, lighter. It was the fact that he made a special effort to sneak over to see *me*.

"Miss Prism, you're sitting at the table, ready to teach German grammar," Iris called from the darkness. "Cecily, you're upstage, watering plants. Les, can you get a watering can from the prop room?"

"Know what?" Peter said out of the side of his mouth.

"What?"

"I really want number seven."

I looked down to keep from smiling, but it didn't work. No one had ever made me feel this way before. I still didn't completely trust it. Peter kept his eyes straight ahead and pretended to be absorbed in the action on the stage, but then he flicked his green eyes my way. He was also keeping something from me, something he had started to tell me, then stopped. Was it something bad?

Onstage, Meg as Cecily said, *"He has many troubles in his life. Idle merriment and triviality would be out of place in his conversation. You must remember his constant anxiety about that unfortunate young man."*

The rehearsal continued. Sometime later, Joe was onstage as Dr. Chasuble, with Charlene Feverfew as Miss Prism. The two of them played older people who had been half in love with each for years but were too shy to say anything about it. The watering can was supposed to symbolize the fountain of their love or something. I had already gone through a scene and was watching from the sidelines again with my knees under my chin.

Iris, who was still out in the house with Wayne, called out, "Jack, you enter upstage at Dr. Chasuble's line, '*Perhaps she followed us to the schools.'* You're pretending to be sad that your fake brother Earnest is dead, so you have two layers of acting going on."

"Got it," Peter said from underneath the half-built staircase. Eventually we'd have a door underneath it, but for now we had to ootch around the boards and pretend.

Out of nowhere, Les plunked down beside me. "Hey."

My entire body turned to ice. For half a second, I was back in the park—

"We'll be seeing a lot of each other over the summer."

—and I couldn't think what to do.

"This is indeed a surprise," said Miss Prism onstage.

"What do you want?" I whispered.

Peter as Jack replied, *"I have returned sooner than I expected."*

"To see you," Les whispered back. "I missed you, little pervert."

"Leave me alone," I managed.

"Nah. I have a deal for you."

"Deal? What do you mean?"

Les pulled his smartphone from his pocket, the one I had seen glowing that night. "I got a cell phone video of you and Peter making out. An adult man kissing a male minor. Peter would get in big trouble. You would too, probation boy."

Little black spots swam in front of my eyes. A flash flood was thundering down the canyon straight at me. "What… what do you want?"

"Let's go where we can talk about it some more." Les got up. "Now."

I didn't know what else to do. My insides filled with acid, but I followed him out a side door into one of the hallways that ran around outside the theater. Les looked casual, as though we were two friends about to share music lists. The door clicked shut like a safe.

"Here's the deal," he said. "You're gonna come over to my apartment after rehearsal tonight and every night and make me happy like the little pervert you are. My address is on the cast list. Once I get tired of you, I'll delete the video. Don't show up even once, and the cops find out about those stolen moments in the park. Your dad will too. A minor kissing a legal adult. They'll love that."

Oh god. My legs weakened, and I leaned against the cold cinder-block wall. He would tell my probation officer. I would to go juvie. Peter would go to jail. Dad would find out about everything.

"Why are you doing this?" I burst out. "What's it to you?"

"*Psh.* I already told you." He put his hands on the wall on either side of my head and trapped me there so he could lean in and kiss me on the mouth. My stomach roiled, and I wanted to throw up. "You're going to give me the same thing you gave Peter. It's only fair. And that's four. I'm looking forward to five." He backed away a little bit. "Speaking of five, you're on in that many minutes. Break a leg."

When he opened the door back into the stage area, Miss Prism said, "*And now, I will not intrude any longer into a house of sorrow. I would merely beg you not to be too much bowed down by grief.*"

I hid inside Algy for the rest of rehearsal. He made a safe place for me. I didn't notice Les or Peter or Melissa. Iris and Wayne were ghost voices telling me where to walk and when to pause. And when it all ended, Algy evaporated, and I found myself in the parking lot, staring at a POS bike chained to a streetlight. I was supposed to ride it over to Les's apartment so he could… do more stuff. I felt worthless as a broken bone. My whole body dragged at me. What would I be doing half an hour from now? How much pain would I be in?

A pair of hands grabbed me from behind. I yelped and spun and fought them. They let go, though I was clutching one of the arms in as cruel a grip as I could muster. The arm belonged to Peter.

"Oh geez—I didn't think," Peter said. "You're nervous because of what happened. I'm sorry."

"Yeah." I was panting. "Yeah. Sorry."

"You're not sorry. I am."

"Okay, we're both pretty sorry." I was aiming for flip but got flat.

"Sure. Uh, want to go for a walk through our favorite shortcut? I don't have class tomorrow."

I still held Peter's arm. Of course he wanted to go through the park. He wanted number seven. Just like Les wanted number five. I couldn't stay, but what was I supposed to say to Peter? "I… can't," I said lamely. "I have to…. I can't."

And then it was just too much. I flung myself forward, intending to push past Peter and run away, forget my bike, let the dark swallow me whole. But somehow I ended up tangled in his arms with my face pressed against his shoulder. Peter stroked my hair, and it felt so good. I wasn't even aware I was crying at first.

"What's wrong, Kev?" he asked softly. "Jesus, I hate seeing you like this. It cuts me to pieces."

I tried to stop crying. It felt stupid, bawling in a guy's arms, but once I got started, I couldn't seem to stop. An image of Miss Prism's dumbass watering can popped into my head.

Peter guided me to the curb at the edge of the parking lot, and we sat down together, his arm around my shoulders. I leaned on him, shameless as a rag doll. A streetlight threw silver light to the sidewalk several feet away, but where we sat, the darkness made us invisible.

"Just tell me," he soothed. "You'll feel better if you tell someone. Is it the attack?"

I nodded into his shirt. "Sort of."

"What, then?"

The words were building up again. "I… I lied before."

"About what?"

"I told Iris I didn't know the guy who attacked m-me. But that's not t-true." I swallowed. "I know who it was."

"Who?"

I still couldn't quite say it. "It didn't stop there. He saw you and me in the park beforehand. He got a phone video of us k-kissing. He said he'll use it or tell my dad unless I go to his apartment and… and let him do it to me all over again."

Peter's expression remained neutral. Lamplight pooled around us, and the summer crickets peeped everywhere, caught up in dramas of their own. A car drove quietly up the street, pulled by its headlights.

"Who?" he asked again.

I didn't want to say it, but I did. "It was Les."

Peter's body stiffened, and every muscle went tight against mine. He didn't move. Shadows hung over his face.

Fear slid down my spine. "Peter?"

He got slowly to his feet, and his face twisted under the shadows into an angry mask. I didn't even recognize him and pushed myself backward.

"Oh my god," I said. "Please don't be mad at me, Peter. Please don't."

His fists clenched white as ice, and his voice was soft as death. "I'm going to kill him."

He took six measured steps across the lot to his car, climbed in, and screeched away, leaving me alone on the pavement.

LES

LES MADIGAN sat on the crappy-ass, lopsided couch he had scammed from the Fuck You Too section of the Goodwill store. A board laid across two milk crates made a rough coffee table, piled with dirty dishes. In the kitchen corner of his apartment, the microwave door stood open, and the smell of burned popcorn hung in the air. In the opposite corner sat his rumpled bed. The summer night pressed against his window screens, open to let in any semblance of a breeze.

A smartphone occupied a tiny corner of the milk-crate coffee table, and Les tapped at it. An old text message—*M. Flackworthy, UR dead asshole*—flicked across the screen for a moment, and then a video ballooned open. A shaky version of Peter reached for an equally shaky Kevin, and their lips met. Les remembered catching every detail in the park. He had seen the two of them in the parking lot behind the theater and suspected the little fuck might put out. The memory of Kevin shoving him away still pissed him off. Les tapped a cigarette on the wood and lit it. *Little pervert.*

At least it hadn't taken long for Les to get what he wanted. What he needed. Hell, *deserved.* All the work he put in around that theater, and for free. The shit he sold to snooty-ass west-siders and their bored MILFs barely kept the lights on. Volunteering at the theater program kept him in touch with the local teenagers, but that was business. He deserved some fun too.

"Ooh, Kevvie, you kiss like an angel," Les said in a high-pitched voice as the video continued to play. "Aw, just keep your tongue in your mouth, Pete. I'm way too butch for that. Besides, I have a date with Les in—" Les checked his watch. "—two minutes."

Three sharp knocks rattled his door. A little wave of anticipation thrilled through Les, and he shut off the video. The little fuck was early. This was going to be fun. He could take his time, not worry about being seen or heard. His crotch grew tight, and he opened the door.

"You're early," he said. "Good. I like it when—"

What felt like a steam shovel smashed Les flat. He stared upward, dazed. His ribs and back ached, and the room swam. Standing over him like an angry freight train was Peter Finn. Les's balls shriveled up. Peter kicked the door shut.

"You son of a bitch!" Peter roared and smashed him in the face with his fist. Pain flashed white-hot through Les's skull. Peter hauled up on the front of Les's shirt with one hand and pulled back the other to punch him again. Fear flooded Les's veins.

"No," he gasped. "What are you doing?"

"You know what I'm doing!" Peter smashed him in the face again. Les heard and felt his nose break. Blood gushed. "And you know why!"

"Please!" Les begged. "Stop!"

Peter yanked Les half-upright. His eyes were hard emeralds. "Did you listen to Kevin when he said stop? *Did you?*"

Les tried to scramble backward, escape, but his legs wouldn't obey. His mind couldn't keep up with what was happening. It wasn't supposed to go this way. It wasn't supposed to—

"You're *dead*, asshole!" Peter pulled back his fist again.

ACT I: SCENE VII

KEVIN

THE IRON gate closed off the way ahead of me with an angry frown. Stone walls stretched away on either side. A long, long driveway wound into the distance past the gate. I double-checked the address. This was it. Huh.

An intercom was set into one of the pillars that flanked the gate. A little nervous, I pushed the call button. Almost immediately a man's voice said, "May I help you, sir?"

Sir? How had he known I was a guy? I glanced around. Ah— cameras above the gate. That made me more nervous.

"Uh… I wanted to see Peter Finn? My name is Kevin Devereaux. Is Peter here?"

A long pause followed, and then the gate slid open with an oiled hum. "Please continue up the drive," said the intercom.

Okay, then. Me and Peter hadn't spoken since last night. After Peter drove off, I went home instead of to Les's apartment. Dad was working again today—yay—and I got more and more restless as the day went on. And I figured if Peter could look up my address on the cast list, I could look up his, right? And if he could drop in on me, I could drop in on him, right? Besides, I had reasons to come see him—two of them.

My bike clattered up the curved driveway, and I wondered how many cameras were on me. A rich green lawn scattered with shady trees, bright flower gardens, and occasional fountains spread out in all directions. A herd of hedges carved into animal shapes—giraffe, lion, zebra, antelope—froze in a green stampede. Geez, the place practically dripped money. I had to remember not to let my mouth hang open. Peter had said he was kind of rich, but I didn't know he meant Scrooge McDuck rich.

The sun shone hot, and I was sweating both from the long ride and from nerves. The driveway curved past a four-story white mansion with massive steps and tall pillars out front. It seemed to stare down at me like an elephant deigning to notice a mosquito. I swallowed and automatically looked around for something to chain my bike to. Then I smacked my head. East-sider paranoia meets west-sider luxury. Though this place was so far past west side, it warped gravity.

I left my pitiful little bike at the bottom of the steps and climbed toward the pillars, feeling very small and shabby. Maybe I should go around to the back door or something. Then I snorted. Back door? There were probably a hundred back doors, and which one led to Peter? I made myself climb the marble Mount Everest and approach the big door set back in the shade of those pillars. My heart sped up. I didn't want to make a mistake and be fingered for a stupid east-sider, but was I supposed to ring or something? I had already talked to the intercom guy, so ringing seemed like overdoing it. And what if a butler opened the door? I didn't have a name card or anything to give him like I'd seen rich people do on TV. On the other hand—

The door whipped open when I approached. To my relief, it was Peter. His grass-green eyes were as wide as that starshine grin of his. He wore a yellow polo shirt and dark shorts and sandals I now realized probably cost more than my dad's truck.

"Kevin," he said, a little too loud, and thrust out his hand. "Dennis told me you were at the gate. Come in."

"Uh… hi." I shook his hand, and Peter hauled me inside. Cool air wafted around us, and the sunlight cut back as though someone had turned down a faucet. The entry foyer was huge and echoey. Shiny hardwood floors and high, airy ceilings, white walls and alcoves and staircases, tall windows and stained glass—a church married to a skyscraper. I didn't see any other people.

"It's great to see you," Peter enthused. "Really great."

I cocked my head, still at the door. Why was he acting so funny? "Yeah. I thought I'd drop by. You know, because of last night and stuff. I thought we could—"

"Let's go up to my room." Peter said, again a little too brightly. "We can talk up there."

64

He led me upstairs through part of the house. I got more impressions—expensive silk rugs, museum statues, a room filled with more books than even Dad had read—before we arrived in a room that could have eaten mine ten times over. I blinked at the fireplace, the dinosaur-sized TV, the racks of video games, the living room furniture, the bed that could sleep five, and the glass doors that led onto a private deck with a hot tub on it.

"My abode." Peter gestured with false extravaganza-ness. "Have a seat wherever. Promise not to tell my parents I brought a boy up to my room. Ha-ha."

All I could say was "Wow" in a real small voice.

"How about a snack or something to drink?" Peter got out his phone. "I can text the kitchen, and they'll send something up. It's no problem."

"I'm still recovering from the shock. This is your *room*?"

"Look," Peter said uncomfortably, "it's just a house. No big deal."

"Just a house? Just a *house*? That's like saying the *Titanic* was just a boat." I laughed a little. "You related to the Morse family or something?"

Peter looked away sheepishly. He rumpled his hair with one hand. I finally realized the clue fairy had been whacking me with a board for the last twenty minutes. "No fuck," I gasped. "You're a *Morse*? As in a Morse Plastic Morse?"

"Caught."

"But… your last name is Finn." I staggered, not altogether untheatrically, to the bed and sat down. Only later did I think the couch might have been a better choice, but who the hell has a couch in their bedroom?

"Finn is my middle name. I'm named after my grandfather Peter, and when I was little, everyone called me Peter Finn to keep us separate. My family still calls me that, even though Grandpa died several years ago." He shrugged. "I use Finn as my last name when I don't want to spread around who I am."

I stared at him from the edge of the bed and tried to make sense of it all. It was like learning your favorite stuffed animal was a one-of-a-kind collector's item or that the bike you bought at a police auction and usually left in the rain was a custom race job built in

Holland. Peter continued to look away as though something on the deck fascinated him.

"Why didn't you tell me?" I said at last.

Long pause. At last he replied, "Scared to."

Out of all the answers on the "List of Reasons My Boyfriend Wouldn't Tell Me He's a Bruce-Wayne Billionaire," that particular response ranked somewhere after "I'm spending my entire fortune on a sex-change operation, so I didn't think it was worth mentioning."

"Scared?" I asked.

He sighed. "Look, when you're a Morse, you never know if people like you because of you or because you're a Morse. With money."

"Money," I echoed. Peter made the word *money* sound like *dryer lint*.

"I wanted to keep quiet until I knew you better." Sunlight slanting through the window got caught in Peter's dark hair. "I didn't want to scare you off or change the way you... the way I *hoped* you felt about me."

"Oh." That made a weird kind of sense... I guessed. But it wasn't easy to understand. What it cost to buy just the stuff in Peter's room could support me and Dad for months and months. If I had that kind of money, I wouldn't give a box full of cat crap what anyone thought of me. Bring it on.

"So," Peter said in a soft voice, "now you know my dirty little secret. Are we... okay?"

I had never seen anyone with such broad shoulders look more like a scared puppy. He really was freaked about the idea I might be interested more in his money than in him. And I'd been worried he'd hate me because I lived in a single-wide. Suddenly it all seemed so ridiculous.

A bubble of laughter burst out of me. "You gotta be kidding. Are we okay? I knew you were hiding something, but I was afraid it was... I don't know... an alcoholic grandmother or a strange attraction to feet." I flung myself backward on the bed. "This is a relief."

Peter sat next to me, still a little wary. "Really?"

"Totally. I fell for Peter Finn, not Peter Moneyballs." I sat back up and kicked off my crappy-ass shoes so I could wiggle my toes at him. "Unless you want some of these bad boys. In that case, I'm outta here."

"You're a shit," he said, laughing. "All right. You win. I was stupid."

"Yeah. But I was stupid because I thought you'd run away when you saw *my* house. We're evenly stupid."

He let that pass. "So what brings you by? I mean, I'm glad you're here, Kev, but—"

"Two reasons. First…." I leaned in and kissed him for a long moment. The room vanished, and my world pulled in to just him. It was incredible, being able to do that without worrying someone might come along. When the kiss ended, I pressed my forehead against his and touched his hair. "You said you were looking forward to number seven." My voice had dropped into a husky register even I didn't recognize. My hands were a little shaky, and yeah—my crotch was tight and hard. "So seven."

Before I knew it, we were lying down on the bed, and our arms were around each other. I never thought I could feel so safe and excited at the same time. My hands wandered over Peter's back and sides, across the solid muscle under his shirt. He explored my chest with his hands and touched my face. I could eat and drink this for the rest of my life.

Peter's hands started to move lower—down my stomach and lower still. I froze then like the green gazelle on the front lawn. I ached for him to keep going, but I was also scared. Should I touch him the same way? God, I wanted to. I tentatively touched his hard stomach, but the memory of pain pushed its way into my head, and my heart sped up. I didn't know if it was from fear or excitement, and I felt a little sick. My dick ached. I wanted Peter's hands on me, and I wanted to run away and hide from them. My face was hot and my stomach was cold. Then Peter stopped and pulled his hand back. Relief and disappointment made a strange mix inside me. He lay back on the bed, and I faced him, my head propped on one hand. My heart slowed down.

"Was that eight?" I asked.

"Oh yeah," he said.

A silence stretched out between us, and more words built up inside me. It was like the sex situation a second ago—I wanted and

67

didn't want at the same time. But this was why I had come over, and I had to speak.

"Peter," I said at last, "what happened last night? After you left the theater? You were pretty mad."

He sat up and put his hands in his lap. Apprehension rumpled his face. That made *me* apprehensive.

"I don't know if I should tell you," he said.

Whenever people say that, it means they're going to tell you, and you aren't going to like it. I steeled myself. "Why not? I told you what happened to *me*. That was the second reason I came over here—to make sure you were okay."

"I'm okay." He twisted his hands in his lap. "Really, I'm—"

"Holy shit!" I pulled his hands out of his lap. It was the first time I'd gotten a close look at them. They were way bigger than mine, and the knuckles were bruised and blue. A half-healed cut scored the back of his left middle finger. "Look at your hands. Did you… did Les…?"

"Yeah." Peter took his hands back. We sat side by side on the bed, our elbows resting on our knees in identical poses. "I pounded the shit out of him."

"Wow." It was the second time I'd said that in this room. "You did that because of… what he did to me?"

Peter's jaw trembled, and he looked away. "I couldn't let the son of a bitch get away with it. He won't bother you anymore."

"What about the video?"

"Grabbed his phone and deleted it. Les wasn't in any condition to stop me."

"Huh."

We sat there in silence for a while longer. Peter wouldn't meet my eyes. He looked like he was trying not to explode or melt or break into pieces. I wanted to touch him, but I felt… weird. The hands that a second ago were touching my face and skimming over my skin had, last night, smashed and broken Les Madigan. Les had planned to rip me up again, but Peter had gone to see the demon in my place.

"I… thanks…," I said in a small voice.

A sigh came from the bottoms of his feet. He looked unnerved, like he'd just missed getting hit by a bus. "Okay."

"Peter?" I said. "Peter Finn? What is it?"

"I was nervous. Shit, I was terrified."

"Of what?"

He let out another long breath and seemed to get control of himself. "I thought you'd hate me when you found out. After what happened to that kid Robbie... I thought you'd hate someone who could get that angry."

"Oh."

I thought about that. I thought about Peter smashing Les's smirking face, about Les begging for mercy and Peter hitting him again and again. Then I thought about Robbie. They weren't the same. Maybe I deserved what Les had done to me, but I was still angry at him for doing it, and the image of Peter taking him apart only made me feel satisfied.

"I'm not mad," I said. "Maybe I should be, but I'm not. If you hurt Les... good. Maybe that's wrong, but that's the way I feel." I gently took his bruised hand. "So *we're* good. Hell, we're awesome. Thank you, Peter Finn. Thank you for kicking the shit out of the guy who—" I'd said the *R* word aloud once and found I didn't want to say it again. "—who hurt me."

"Okay. Okay." He gave me a rough one-armed hug. "Look at us. Couple of emo boys. Come on. I'll show you around, and we can grab some supper before rehearsal."

It turned out Peter's parents weren't home, so we had the place pretty much to ourselves. Except for "the help," as Peter put it.

"You have, like, servants?" I asked as we wandered down a massive staircase to the first floor. "Do they live here?"

"A couple do," Peter said. "Most of them live in town, though."

"Do they help you get dressed and stuff?" I asked.

"No," he scoffed. "Unless I have to get ready for something really complicated."

"I'll help you get dressed," I said with a wide grin. "Or undressed. Could be fun."

He stopped halfway down the stairs. "Don't," he said quietly.

I stopped too. "Don't what?"

"Look, my family is really conservative. They donate mil—lots of money to political candidates on the right, and they don't know I'm into guys. Okay? And if the media got hold of it, the whole Morse clan would go batshit nutso. They might cut me off or, worse, try to invalidate my trust fund. Anything you say in front of the help will get back to my parents too, so be careful around them. Publicly we have to be just friends, and that's it."

That kind of hurt, though I got it. I mean, Dad didn't know about me either. Who was I to judge?

"Understood, sir." I saluted.

He rolled his eyes. "This way. You might like the art gallery."

"Art gallery?"

Yep. They had an art gallery. Peter showed me paintings and sculptures by masters no one else got to see, though I didn't recognize any of the names. Then we went swimming in their indoor/outdoor Olympic-sized swimming pool, complete with water slide, though I paid more attention to Peter in his bathing suit than I did to the water. We went riding on honest-to-fuck horses (though Peter actually rode while I just clung to my horse's saddle and tried not to let my teeth mash together). And then we played video games in his room (though Peter kept cheating by rubbing the back of my neck and distracting me so I lost every game... and I didn't care one bit). And then we rehearsed *The Importance of Being Earnest* (though Peter just wanted to watch me do some of Algy's longer speeches). And then we had supper in the formal dining room (though it was only two of us at a table that seated twenty, and it was awesome homemade sausage-and-pepperoni pizza and deep-fried chicken fingers served by "the help" on white china with crystal, and afterward Peter admitted he'd texted the kitchen to do that in order to impress me, and whoa—he wanted to impress *me*).

Later, that Dennis guy texted to say he'd brought Peter's Mustang around, so we headed down to leave for rehearsal. I wondered what it would be like to grow up with invisible people who did stuff for you and never worry if the lights would stay on or if there would be heat in winter or if you had holes in your shoes. Going back to the single-wide library would be a major comedown after this place. The anger tiger made ugly noises inside me. I couldn't even tell people Peter and I were seeing each other. Hell, even if I could, everyone would probably figure I was just digging for gold. Or plastic.

"What's in there?" I asked, more to distract myself than out of real curiosity as we passed a door. Peter stiffened and then sped up and took me past the room and faster down the hallway. It caught me off guard, and I had to hurry to catch up. "Did I say something wrong?"

"No," he said shortly. "It's just…. That's my sister's room. Her name is Emily."

"You have a sister?" That caught me off guard again. "You never said you had a sister. Is she here?"

He was almost running now. "Nah. Come on. I think Dennis put your bike in the trunk."

There was a shut-the-fuck-up note in his voice that made me nervous, but I shut the fuck up. We didn't say a whole lot on the drive to rehearsal either. What was going on? I wanted to ask, but the hard look on Peter's face was a little scary, so I said nothing. Maybe he and his sister didn't get along. It wasn't really my business, I guessed.

We arrived at the theater in plenty of time for Iris's 6:50 rehearsal rule. When we came inside, everyone who was on the schedule was already onstage—Thad, Joe, Meg, and Melissa. And Iris and Wayne, of course. I looked around apprehensively for Les and then remembered he probably wasn't coming. Or was he? Maybe he would resign as stage manager. That would be a huge relief.

Everyone turned to look at us when we entered through the side door, and I got nervous all of a sudden. Something felt off. Did everyone know what had happened? I could tell Peter felt it too, and he brushed my arm.

A woman I didn't recognize was talking to Iris. She had brown hair twisted into a braid around her head, and she had a lean, athletic build. In contrast to all of us in our shorts and sweats and T-shirts, she wore a white blouse and snappy blue blazer. The woman noticed everyone looking at me and Peter, and she turned as well. I caught it then—the woman was a cop. After a while, you can just tell these things. Acid churned in my stomach, and fear turned my hands icy. I had violated probation somehow, and she was here to arrest me.

"What's going on?" Peter said.

"This is Valerie Malloy," Iris told us. "She's a police detective."

My breath was coming fast now, and my insides cramped up. I should run away, find a place to hide.

"I'm afraid I have some bad news," Iris continued. "Last night—"

"Thank you, Ms. Kaylo, I'll take it from here," Detective Malloy interrupted. She was standing in front of both of us now. Everyone else was staring with unabashed curiosity. My feet felt nailed to the floor. "Peter Finn Morse and Kevin Devereaux?"

"Yeah," Peter said. I nodded.

"Mr. Devereaux, you're a minor, which means I can't question you without a parent or guardian present. I'll have to talk to you later when I can arrange for your dad to be here. Mr. Morse, you're nineteen and a legal adult, so I can talk to you now."

"But what's *happened*?" I blurted out.

"Last night at 10:45 p.m., the police received an anonymous tip. Officers arrived at the scene and found Les Madigan. He'd been severely beaten. His face was a mass of bruises and broken teeth."

Oh shit. The focus of my fear shifted sideways. Les was pressing charges. *Peter* would go to jail now. Guilt mingled with the fear and threatened to overwhelm it. Peter had done that for me. It was my fault.

"I see," Peter said.

"Mr. Madigan was dead," Detective Malloy finished.

The three words plowed through me like a charging bull. My knees weakened, and the floor wobbled. Dead? Les was *dead*? But Peter had only—

"How did you bruise your hands, Mr. Morse?" asked Detective Malloy.

Peter slipped his hands into his back pockets. "I don't think I should talk about it."

"A witness who lives in the building saw a car leave the scene at about the time Les was probably murdered," Detective Malloy continued relentlessly. "The witness didn't get a license plate, but the description of the driver matches you, and the description of the car matches your blue Mustang, Mr. Morse. Can you explain that?"

Peter's face was a rock. "No."

"Then you leave me no choice." She spun Peter around and whipped out a pair of handcuffs. "Peter Morse, you are under arrest for the murder of Les Madigan."

ACT II: SCENE I

KEVIN

PETER WOULDN'T look at me while Detective Malloy hauled him away, and a black feeling oozed through my stomach. Everyone freaked out at hearing that Les was dead and seeing Peter arrested, so Iris canceled rehearsal. I wasn't in very good shape either. An image of Robbie huddled all broken on the ground came into my head and mixed with thoughts of Peter beating Les to death with those hands that had touched me. I ran out of the theater and made it all the way to the golf course on my bike before I threw up at the side of the road. This was my second barf-o-rama in two days. Shit.

It was a long, scary ride home under lengthening evening shadows. Acid burned at the back of my throat, and I really wanted some cold water. Peter had killed Les. Over me. The guy who had attacked me was dead. It didn't seem real. He had attacked me, and now he was gone, wrenched out of the world by a guy who had kissed me eight times. I couldn't figure out what to do about that. Les scared the shit out of me, but I hated him too. Could I feel good about him being dead? I'd been okay with it when I thought Peter just beat him up. Shit, I'd felt great. But dead? I didn't know.

And what was going to happen to Peter? He *killed* a guy. Fear put a black lump in my chest. Peter was strong and powerful, but I remembered the awful sound my bat had made when it hit Robbie—that wet snap of wood breaking bone, the scream of pain that followed. And I remembered how angry I'd felt because Hank said Robbie thought I was gay. I was ready to kill Robbie, and I didn't understand why. Not then, anyway. It was why I felt like a bug at the bottom of a skunk's burrow when I stood in front of the judge and why I was ready to go to juvie, where they'd beat *me* and smash *me* like I had done to Robbie—because I deserved it.

74

All this mixed up inside me, and it scared me, and it pissed me off. How could Peter do this to me? To us? What was happening to Peter right now? Fingerprinting and photographing? Interrogation in that little room in the police station? I'd been there with steel handcuffs around my wrists. So had Dad.

I turned down Six Mile Road and coasted past the tired old houses. Dad. This wasn't the first time someone... important to me had been arrested for murder. The same thing had happened to Dad, back when I was just little and Mom was still here and we lived in a real house because Dad had a good job as a construction worker for Morse Plastic. I was maybe four years old, but I remembered that day. I was drawing a picture with crayons at the kitchen table, and the walls were painted yellow. It was sunny outside, and I was thinking about going outside to wait for Dad to come home. He was late. Really late. And I was hungry.

Then some other stuff happened—I don't remember all of it—and Mom was talking to me. She looked really mad.

"Your daddy's in jail," she said in a flat voice. "He killed a man."

I didn't know how to handle that, so I started to cry. Mom wasn't much help. She spent all her time on the phone. I was scared and didn't know what was going to happen. It seemed like I was scared a lot after that. How could my dad have killed someone? I knew Dad could get mad, and sometimes he would yell. Once he punched the wall and put a hole in it, and that was really scary, but he fixed it the next day and you couldn't see the hole anymore.

Later I found out that Dad had gotten into a fight at work. Both of them were up high in the building they were working on. The other guy punched Dad, Dad punched back, and the other guy stumbled backward. He fell off the building and died. Some of the other workers said that Dad definitely didn't throw the other guy off the building and that the other guy had started the fight, but the court said that Dad was still at least partly to blame. The judge sentenced him to eight years in prison for manslaughter.

Dad lost his job when he was arrested, right? Mom's job as a file clerk at Morse didn't pay very much, so we lost the house and had to move into a tiny apartment. I slept on the couch and never brought friends over because I didn't want them to know I didn't have a bed and my dad was in jail. By then I stopped being scared. I was tired of that, and I spent a lot of time being mad instead. I was mad Dad had gotten himself sent to prison, and I was mad we had lost our house, and I was mad Mom didn't take me to see him more often, and I was mad I had to go visit him. Being mad was easier than being scared. I guess raising a kid who was mad all the time was hard on Mom, because she didn't talk to me very much, and I ran around on my own a lot and did what I wanted and got into trouble. Three or four times I got suspended from school, but Mom never yelled at me. She didn't seem to care.

Michigan's prisons are way crowded, and Dad was a model prisoner who spent most of his time reading—a new habit—so they let him out after five years instead of eight. I was nine years old. By then I'd grown up going to visit Dad once a month. He got out of prison a week after my ninth birthday, and I thought we'd have a celebration, maybe even go for hamburgers. But Mom opened a couple cans of beef stew like she always did on Thursday. It felt weird with Dad sitting at the little table when I was used to seeing him in the visiting room with guards and other prisoners and their families. Mom and Dad didn't talk very much. Dad tried to talk to me, but I didn't know what to say, so I kept my eyes on my bowl and ate.

Two days later Mom was gone. Just left. I still don't know where she is or what happened. It was probably because I was a crappy kid. Who would want to hang around with me?

Dad couldn't find work. If you want to work construction, you have to be bonded and licensed, and convicted felons can't get bonded. Michigan doesn't give you welfare either, unless there's something wrong with you, like you're blind or in a wheelchair or something. Dad got some money because of me—that made me feel real good—but it wasn't enough to stay in the apartment. One of the guys he met in prison owned a trailer on some east-side land outside of town, and he said me and Dad could stay there if we paid the property taxes and kept the place up. So that's what we did. Dad got some under-the-table jobs here and there, enough to pay utilities and buy an occasional pizza. I didn't know what would happen when Dad's friend got out of prison. I tried not to think about that.

So now both my dad and my boyfriend were up for murder. Was there something about me that attracted this shit? There had to be something wrong with me.

A strange car was sitting in the driveway by Dad's truck. I dropped my bike on the ground nearby. Now what?

When I went inside, I found Dad standing in the living room with Detective Malloy. My skin went cold. They both turned.

"There you are." Dad's voice was tight, and I remembered he hated the police, though mostly he was scared of them. "This is—"

"We've met," Malloy said. "Kevin, I need to talk to you, and your dad said it was okay."

I felt like I was going to throw up. "About what?"

"Come on, Kev." Dad sighed. "About that boy Peter. He was over here the other day."

Malloy flipped open a notebook just like they did on television, just like the detective who had arrested me the first time. "What's your relationship with Peter Morse?"

"What? What?" Dad interrupted before I could answer. "He's a fucking *Morse*?"

"He is." Malloy's face was bland.

"Holy shit." Dad sank to the couch. "What the hell is he doing at the Art Center?"

I had never heard Dad swear so much all at one shot. It almost made me forget what was going on. The trailer was growing warm despite the box fan in the window, and I wanted to hide in the forest of books.

"Your relationship with Peter Morse?" Malloy asked me again.

"Do I have to talk to you?" A shaky note entered my voice. "I don't want to."

"You don't have to," Malloy replied. "I can go down and talk to your probation officer and see what she thinks about you not cooperating, though."

A pang went through me. "You know I'm on probation."

"Kid, I know everything about you. I saw the photos of what you and your friends did to that boy. Now you're connected to another beating, one that ended in a death this time, and you won't answer questions. That's really suspicious in my book."

My insides turned to water, and my knees went rubbery. The walls closed in from all directions. I had no way out. She would find out everything.

Malloy continued, "Maybe we should continue this down at the station—"

"Hey, hey, hey." Dad held up his hands. "That's not necessary. Kevin will tell you anything you want to know. Won't you?"

And then I thought of Peter in a jail cell. Peter, who had taken my place at Les's. Peter, who had defended me.

Killed for me.

I couldn't figure out how to feel about all this, but I did know I owed Peter. I could at least be strong for him, like he had been for me. I made myself stand up straight.

"Peter and I are friends," I said. "We're in the play together. So what?"

"Mouth," Dad said.

Malloy scribbled in her notebook. "He came over here a couple days ago, and you went over to his house today."

"You did?" Dad said.

I started to answer, then shut my mouth. The first time I had been in court, my public defender attorney had warned me it was dumb to say the first thing that popped into my head. He told me always to count five *Mississippis* before I answered any questions. So I counted—*one Mississippi, two Mississippi....*

When I reached five, I realized something. "You didn't ask a question."

"Why did you go to Peter's house?"

One Mississippi, two Mississippi.... She was looking for proof that Peter had killed Les, and she was looking to see if I was involved. But there was no connection between me and Les, or none anyone knew of. No one had seen what he had done to me, and Peter had deleted the video from Les's cell phone.

Hadn't he? I hadn't actually seen him do it. And what if the police found Les's phone at Peter's house and they used some kind of computer program to recover the video? They were always doing shit like that on TV. I was getting scared again.

...five Mississippi.

But the police wouldn't even know to look for Les's cell phone, let alone look for it at Peter's house.

"I went over there to rehearse," I said. "He has the lead, and I have a big part. It's a lot of lines."

"All you did was rehearse?"

One Mississippi, two Mississippi.... In my head, Peter kissed me and ran his hands over my body on his bed. "That wasn't really a question."

"Did you do anything besides rehearse?"

One Mississippi, two Mississippi.... "We played some video games and went swimming," I said. "This might go faster if I you just asked me what you wanted to know."

"Did he talk to you about Les Madigan?"

One Mississippi, two Mississippi.... I couldn't see any good way to answer this. I would have to lie or get Peter into serious trouble. The lie won. "No."

"What was your relationship with Les Madigan?"

All the *Mississippis* went flying out the window. My heart beat hard, and I felt the blood leave my face. "My... relationship?"

Malloy's face was a stone. "Yes. How did you know him?"

"He is... was... the stage manager. We did some theater games. I didn't know him very well."

"We'll be seeing a lot of each other over the summer. I'll definitely be seeing a lot of you."

Les's last words after the attack burned in my brain. I was pale and shaking, and I knew it, and what's more, Malloy knew it. All the *Mississippis* in the world weren't going to save me. Peter was going to jail because I couldn't keep my fucking act together. Then inspiration struck. I staggered to the couch next to Dad and slumped onto it. "He's really dead, isn't he? Oh my god—he's really dead."

"Are you all right, Kev?" Dad turned toward me.

I put my head in my hands. "He's *dead*. I just saw him yesterday, and now he's *dead*."

"You're freaking him out, Detective," Dad said, but without much conviction. He was as afraid of Malloy as I was. In that moment, I hated him. I wanted him to stand up for me, yell at Malloy, throw her out of the house. But he just sat there and acted like she had a bigger dick than him. Red anger made my fingers white but also made it easier not to be scared of lying to Malloy.

"Just a couple more questions," Malloy said. "Where were you last night between ten and midnight?"

One Mississippi, two Mississippi.... "That was just after rehearsal, right?"

"You tell me."

"After rehearsal I rode my bike home and went to bed."

"Can anyone verify that?"

"He got home at ten forty-five," Dad put in. "It usually takes him forty-five minutes to ride here from the Art Center."

"Why don't you pick him up?"

Dad looked down at his hands. "We can't afford the gas money."

"Did you go anywhere after that?" Malloy pressed.

I shook my head. No *Mississippis* this time.

"Can anyone besides your dad verify that?"

The anger tiger roared to full power in me and devoured every *Mississippi*. "You think *I* did this? After everything I went through with Robbie? You think after all the fucking nightmares and the throwing up and shitting my pants, scared I'm going to jail, that I'd do it *again*? You're a fucking moron!"

"I think it's time for you to go now." Dad got to his feet and stood between me and Malloy. "We're done."

Unfazed, Malloy handed him a card. "If either of you thinks of anything to add, call me, night or day." And she left.

Dad didn't move until the sound of her car faded in the distance. Then he let out a long, deep breath. "Shit."

I didn't say anything. Suddenly I was exhausted—but still scared and pissed off.

We sat on the couch in silence for a long moment. Then Dad went into the kitchen and came back with a bottle of whiskey I didn't know we had, and two glasses.

Two?

Without a word he poured a lot into the first glass and a thin drizzle into the second. He thought a moment, poured in a little more, and handed it to me. "Here."

I stared down at it. The fumes from the alcohol smelled like they might catch fire. "But—"

"Have a drink with your old man. You can handle it. But only that much." He knocked back half his glass and shut his eyes.

Okay, sure. I wasn't going to turn that down. Hank and the others in the gang had gotten drunk more than once, and a couple of times I had too, but that was cheap beer with sort-of friends. This was whiskey with my father. Feeling strange and grown-up, I knocked back the glass like I'd seen Dad do. It tasted awful, and it felt like swallowing molten lava. I coughed hard, and Dad pounded my back with a broad hand.

"Good. When you're old enough, you'll learn not to do that, but for now, you're okay."

Warmth like Peter's swimming pool spread all through me, and I felt my muscles loosen. The anger faded. "Thanks, Dad."

He sipped. "So. You have nightmares, huh? You never told me that."

"Oh." Caught out, I nodded. "Yeah."

"About Robbie?"

One Mississippi, two—wait. "Every night, just about."

"That's why you keep his picture by your bed," Dad said. "To try and keep the nightmares away."

"Kinda."

There was a long pause. We both stared straight ahead at nothing. For a second, time seemed to flicker. We were sitting on the same couch, but way older. I looked like Dad, and he looked more like someone's grandpa, and we both had the same glasses with whiskey in the bottom. Then time flickered again, and everything was back to normal.

"I get them too," Dad said quietly.

"Get what?"

"Nightmares. Used to be every night, but now it's maybe two, three times a week."

I blinked at him and wondered if I could handle another drink. The room looked soft around the edges. "About... that guy?"

"His name was Mark. Mark Brown." Dad picked up his glass and stared at it. I didn't move. Dad never, ever talked about this, and I was afraid I'd scare him off like a shy deer. "We were on the fourth floor of the building we were putting up, and we got into a stupid argument at lunch. He shoved me, and then I shoved him back, and then he tried to punch me, so I ducked and punched him hard without even thinking about it. My stupid temper. Half a second after I hit him, I knew I'd done something wrong. He stumbled backward like he was drunk, and he tripped on a riveter. I tried to grab him, I swear to god, and my fingers brushed the front of his shirt, but he was already going over. The last thing I saw was the terror in his eyes. I heard him scream all the way down."

Dad poured more whiskey for himself. "The nightmares change. Sometimes Mark is falling and I can't get to him. Sometimes I'm falling and Mark is laughing at me. Sometimes it's you falling. But the scream is always the same. I woke up almost every night in prison with his echo in my ears. I know what it's like. You go to bed with acid and wake up with sweat."

"Yeah," I said.

"Look, Kev," Dad said. "What I did to Mark was… bad. But I'm a different man now than I was then. Slower to anger. I read. I'm trying to figure out something better to do with my life. You're a different person than the boy who hurt Robbie too. You don't sneak out at night, you were more focused on your schoolwork at the end of the year, and you're doing this play. You made yourself better. You don't deserve torture."

"Will talking about it make the dreams stop?" I waved my glass. "Or should I just drink more of this?"

Dad stayed silent for a moment, then took the whiskey bottle into the kitchen and put it back in the cupboard. "That's a bad path to follow, son."

The room was a little spinny, now, and my tongue was loose in my head. I heard myself say, "Peter has a whole bar in his house."

"Yeah. About that." Dad sat down again. "What's going on with you two?"

"What do you mean?"

"You weren't freaked about that guy being dead. You were freaked about Peter. Or something close to him. Is it just because he killed a guy? Or because you two are closer than what you told that detective?"

My mouth was dry and slack at the same time. Words piled up in the back of my throat, but no way in hell was I going to say any of them. Not to Dad. Instead I said, "Me and Peter just hung out. His house is unbelievable."

"Kevin—"

"And Peter is my boyfriend, Dad. I'm gay."

The words fell out of my mouth like lead weights and landed on the couch between us. I stared straight ahead, totally not able to believe I'd said that. It just popped out. Dad froze. His mouth was partly open, and his face got red. Silence made the air hot and stuffy. My heart was pounding again, and I couldn't look at him. My hands shook. He was going to blow a piston. The awful silence went on and on. A weird thought crossed my mind—when Dad threw me out, would he at least let me keep my bike?

"Jesus fuck." Without another word, Dad drained the last bit of whiskey and slammed the glass back down. I cringed. Then he grabbed me around the shoulders and held me so tight I could smell the alcohol and sweat. "Jesus fuck. It's okay, Kevin. It's okay. Jesus, I love you, and it's okay."

It was the last thing I expected to hear from him. A big lump burst in my throat, and I was crying again. Shit. How many times was I going to do that? I felt light and airy and safe all at the same time, tight in my dad's arms like a little kid. He knew and he didn't care. Or he did care, but it wasn't bad. Or—I don't know what the hell I was thinking. It was just… good. For once. And it made me bawl like a first grader.

But I felt guilty too. Peter was in jail, and I was getting feel-good hugs from my dad. Still, I wanted it to keep going. Dad didn't care that I was gay. An anvil I'd been carrying on my back for years had disappeared. I wanted to cheer and leap into the sky and punch the sun. Why hadn't I told him earlier?

"Okay," Dad whispered into my hair. "Okay. We're all right. We're going to be all right. You're my son, okay?"

I pulled back a little, into the adult world, and scrubbed at my eyes with the back of my hand. "Okay."

We both inhaled and let out the same heavy sigh at the same time. That made us crack up. Both of us laughed hard on that saggy old couch. It was stupid and not that funny, but the more we tried to stop laughing, the more impossible it became. I laughed until my stomach hurt and I was gasping. Dad did too. That felt nice.

At last Dad said, "So Peter's your boyfriend."

"Uh-huh." I sat up straighter and had a strange urge to reach for my whiskey glass. Hm. "We kind of started seeing each other when rehearsals started."

"Son of a billionaire. You could do worse."

That made me laugh again.

Dad said, "You know I've got a lot of questions, right?"

I was grinning. "Right."

"But since this might take a while," he continued as he got up, "I want to see if there's any pizza left to go with this whiskey."

ACT II: SCENE II

KEVIN

IRIS CALLED to say rehearsal was still on tomorrow evening and she was calling for an extra one in the afternoon. Could I be there? I said I could. She asked how I was doing, and I said I was fine. That wasn't much of a lie. I was in-the-freezer scared for Peter, but I was on-the-beach happy about Dad, so it kind of averaged out. Iris sounded like she wanted to say more. I quickly said goodbye and hung up.

Night pressed against the windows, and the muggy summer air felt heavy on my skin. The box fan barely made a difference. I paced the trailer like a lion because I had no idea what was going on with Peter. Worry pushed me back and forth, back and forth. Peter was going to prison for life. I would never see him again. The police would find out about me and Peter.

Other stuff pushed at me too, stuff I couldn't put my finger on. It was awful. A thing with jagged teeth was going to jump out of the bushes at me any second, but I couldn't say what the thing was. For a minute I seriously considered calling Peter's house, but what could I say? "Hi, I'm your son's boyfriend and the reason he beat up that guy Les. Maybe he killed him because of me. Anyway, is he still in jail or what?" Sure.

Dad finally looked up from the book he was reading. "I'd offer you more whiskey, but I think you've had more than enough this year."

"Sorry," I muttered and leaned against the front door. "I can't sit still."

He set the book facedown. We'd already done some talking. I'd told him that, yeah, I'd known for a long time I was gay, and no, I'd never been interested in girls, and yeah, I'd fallen pretty hard for Peter, and no, we hadn't had sex, geez, why do you have to get so nosy, even if you're my dad?

"You can't sit still about the gay thing, or the police thing, or that guy dying?" Dad asked. "Or is it all one big junkyard?"

"I don't know what's happening to Peter," I burst out.

Dad checked his watch. "If you want the truth, he's probably getting out about now."

That stopped me. "Out?"

"Look, buddy." Dad leaned forward with his elbows on his knees. "I met a lot of guys in prison, and they were all dirt poor, like us. Didn't matter if they were innocent or guilty. They were all in jail because they were poor schlubs who couldn't afford anything but a public defender. The rich guys, they were born with Get Out of Jail Free cards in their mouths. And you can bet the Morse family has a high-powered lawyer with a whole deck of them. Your Peter won't spend more than a few hours in there."

I considered that. It didn't seem fair. Dad had gone to jail, and quick, because he'd had a public defender, while Peter—

No. Dad had gone to jail because he'd pushed Mark Brown off a building, and I was on probation because I beat Robbie Hunter almost to death. And Peter....

"What if he did it?" My mouth formed the words before I could stop them. "What if he killed... that guy?"

A moment passed. Dad sighed in the way that always meant he was going to say something I wouldn't like, and my jaw went tight.

"You would know better than I would, buddy," Dad said. "I only met him once. But I gotta tell you... he's a Morse, and in my experience, rich people do what they want, and the hell with everyone else. *Would* he want to kill that guy Les?"

Peter's voice echoed in my head. *I'm going to kill him.*

"I can't think," I said abruptly. "Going outside."

The door slammed behind me, and darkness closed its warm breath around me. I grabbed my bike and pedaled down the starlit road. The pavement stretched in front of me, long and pale. My chain rattled softly, and my tires hummed on the asphalt. So much was going on, and I couldn't sort it all out. I tried to empty my head and let it slide away, like the silver road sliding under my tires.

What did they do with Les's body? I tried to imagine it lying in one of those steel drawers in a morgue somewhere with a sheet draped over it. Or was it naked? They always put a sheet over bodies for TV shows and stuff, but I read somewhere that real morgues kept them naked so the examiner or coroner or whatever could look. A cold chill clenched my stomach. What if they took swabs of Les's skin and found my DNA on it? I stopped pedaling, and my bike whooshed silently for several yards while I got myself under control. They wouldn't. They couldn't get my DNA off Les because his own DNA would contaminate the sample, right? And that was even if they thought to look and if Les hadn't showered after he attacked me. Jesus, I hoped he had.

Houses stared at me with dark eyes as I glided past, and my thoughts wandered back to Peter. His hair was black as the night, and his arms were strong as the asphalt, and he slipped his big-guy hands over my face… and pretty soon I would be writing poetry or some other dumb-fuckery about him.

I wanted to. I ached to write long love letters to him and sneak them into his room so he'd find them on his pillow. And I thought how sweet it would be to send him flowers—did guys do that for other guys?—and I longed to stand on the stage and shout to everyone in the show that we were a thing.

I also felt scared. What if his black hair was like the black hair of a bad guy in a movie? What if his strong arms had punched Les into that steel drawer? What if his big guy hands had crushed Les's skull? I could be in love with a killer.

Soft summer wind skimmed through my hair. So what if Peter *had* killed Les? Les had… he had raped me. If anyone deserved to die, it was Les Madigan. But people who killed were *bad* people. Deep inside there was something wrong with them. I knew because I had almost been one of them. I remembered the complete rage that filled me when I hit Robbie Hunter with a baseball bat, and I remembered how awful and satisfying it was to hear the wood crack his bones. The sound still woke me up at night with ice running down my chest and Robbie's picture staring at me from the nightstand. How could I have been so horrible? If the cops hadn't shown up, I would have been a murderer. I hated the police, but they'd stopped me from becoming the worst monster there was.

My dad was a monster. I was a monster. I came from a family of monsters. No way I would ever let someone get close enough to find out how bad I was.

But Peter did. And Peter had turned out to be a monster just like me. Except.

I had hurt an innocent person. Peter, on the other hand, had killed Les after Les had hurt me. He'd done it because he loved me. I was a monster. Peter was a monster hunter.

Was that love, being willing to kill? Love and murder pulled me in two directions until my tendons popped. I didn't know if I wanted anyone to kill someone for me, even if the someone was Les Madigan. I didn't want him alive, but I didn't want him to be killed by Peter either.

I needed to talk to Peter, but he scared me too. If Peter had killed Les, would he do the same thing to… someone else who got him mad? To my dad? To me? Peter was a billionaire. He could do whatever he wanted. He could buy my home, my stuff, my dad—even me—a hundred times over and never notice. Did people matter to someone like that? Was that why he killed Les? Because Les didn't matter?

My jaw tensed as I pedaled. Les was spit on a wad of gum on my shoe. I *hated* Les. His murder made my heart sing rock songs. But I didn't want Peter to be the one who killed him, and I didn't want him to go jail for it. Everything mixed up inside me like acid soup. I needed to talk to someone—yell, shout, scream—but I didn't have anyone. Dad had just found out I was gay, and my boyfriend had been arrested for murder. How could I tell him that I'd been…? That the guy Peter killed had…?

My stomach clenched, and nausea forced me to stop by the side of the road and take deep, damp breaths. *I won't throw up, I won't throw up, I won't throw up.*

I didn't throw up. But only barely.

It was weird. Sometimes I could think the word… the *R* word… and sometimes I couldn't.

The long grass rustled by the ditch. I dropped my bike and jumped back with a yelp. For a moment I was back in the park, and Les was running his hard, sweaty hands over me. His weight was pressing down on me, and his breath was in my ear. My insides shriveled, and my lungs dried up. My heart pounded hard in my ears. I was alone in the dark.

Then the feeling was gone. The grass moved, and a raccoon ambled onto the road. It caught sight of me and froze. I stared at it, and it stared at me.

"Get!" I yelled at it.

The raccoon bolted back into the grass. I stood on the road for a long moment with my dead lungs and my hyper heart until I finally got back on my bike to head home.

I SLEPT way in. Dad was gone when I woke up. He'd left a note on the kitchen table saying he still had drywall work—yay!—and didn't know what time he'd be home, but he loved me and hoped I would be okay alone, and he left a smiley face at the bottom. He hadn't left a smiley face at the bottom of a kitchen-table note in a long time. *Huh.*

The phone rang. I jumped up and stubbed my toe on a pile of books. They scattered like they were trying to escape. Forcing my heart back under control, I reached for the receiver, then jerked my hand back. The caller ID screen read Peter Finn Morse and a phone number. *Shit.*

The phone rang again, and I turned to stone. What the hell was I supposed to do? *Shit. Okay, okay, okay.* I took a deep breath and reached for it. But I couldn't pick up. Instead I ran outside and dropped onto the front stoop with my fingers in my ears for a count of fifty. When I unstopped my ears, the phone was silent. The morning pine-tree shade was already warm. I went back inside. No message light on the answering machine. We were the last family in the world to be stuck with an answering machine instead of voicemail. I guess we were lucky just to have a landline. People on welfare get those free government phones so they can look for jobs, but Dad was a convicted felon, and felons don't get a lot of government help.

I was still mixed up. I was glad Peter had called me. He must have a zillion things to do, and he called me rather than do them. I was important to him. *Wow.* I'd never felt important to a… to a guy like that before. Except he was a killer. Maybe. I still didn't know what to think.

To keep my mind off it, I poured myself a bowl of cereal and sat down at the kitchen table with my *Earnest* script. My lines were all highlighted in neon orange. I stared at them, willing them to go into my memory. I'd heard somewhere that the best way to memorize something was to start at the back and work your way to the beginning. That way when you ran through stuff, it got easier instead of harder. A lot of my lines were scenes with Peter—Jack—but I tried to ignore that.

ALGERNON: Where have you been since last Thursday?
JACK: In the country.
ALGERNON: What on earth do you do there?
JACK: When one is in town one amuses oneself. When one is in the country one amuses other people. It is excessively boring.
ALGERNON: And who are the people you amuse?

Gravel popped outside. I shot to my feet and flicked up the bent metal slats that covered the windows. A blue Camaro was pulling into the driveway. My heart jerked hard, and a metallic taste came to my mouth. It had to be Peter. He wasn't supposed to come here. Not right now. But he did. What should I do?

Peter got out of the car. His Mustang must have been impounded by the cops, but that wouldn't stop a Morse, right? His face looked pinched and unhappy, like his shoes hurt and his belt was too tight. I wanted to run out and hug him and tell him it would be okay. I wanted to feel his arms around *me*. And I wanted him to leave so I could sort out what the hell I was doing. Carefully, silently, I twisted the deadbolt on the door to lock it.

He took a deep breath, like he was sucking up courage, and stepped toward the front stoop.

I fled. I ran to the bathroom, jumped in the tub, and yanked the shower curtain closed. My heart was pounding yet again, so hard it made my eyesight jump. My hands shook with tension, and I cupped them over my ears. That didn't stop me from hearing him knock.

"Hello?" came his voice from outside, and I could hear how nervous he was. He knocked harder. "Kevin? Hello?"

I crouched in the tub, wondering if Peter could hear my breathing. If he would just go away. But at the same time, I also wanted him to come in. Why did I have to try out for that stupid play? Then none of this would have happened.

The front doorknob rattled. Peter was trying to open it. I almost swallowed my tongue. My toes were clenched tight enough to rip my socks. Through the thin trailer walls, I heard him sigh.

"Kev? I know you're there. You have to be. I need to talk to you. To someone. Please?"

The ache in his voice hurt my stomach. How did he know I was there? My bike. Was it parked at the front stoop? I couldn't remember. But the truck was gone. For all he knew, I was somewhere with Dad. *Shit.* Peter didn't even know I'd told Dad about us. Was there even an *us* left?

"Kev?" Another long silence. My legs ached from crouching so long, but I didn't dare move in case he heard me. "Okay. I guess I'll see you at rehearsal."

Rehearsal. He would be at rehearsal. I had been concentrating so hard on just memorizing lines and trying not to think about Peter himself that I'd forgotten. Of course he'd be at rehearsal. Or maybe not. Maybe Iris would get someone else to play the part. The thought turned my arteries to cement. I didn't want to play Algy if some other guy played Jack.

The car crunched away. I waited for a count of one hundred before I got out of the tub and checked the window slats. Empty driveway. Why did I feel so empty too?

AFTERNOON REHEARSAL was at one. I rode my bike down, glad the day had turned cloudy, though it was definitely still summer. The closer I got to the theater, the tenser my stomach got. Iris liked to say that "on time" was late and "early" was on time, which meant we weren't supposed to arrive when rehearsal began. We were supposed to arrive early so we could be onstage when rehearsal began. But the closer I got to the Art Center, the slower I rode. I didn't actually get there until 1:01, which meant I was late—one of those tardies Iris talked about on the first day. *Shit.*

I ran through the cool dimness of backstage and found everyone in a clump onstage. Iris and her (twin?) brother Wayne were there too.

So was Peter. He was standing to one side with his hands in his back pockets. He saw me come in, but he didn't move, and he didn't say anything. I wondered why, and then I remembered—no one knew we were seeing each other. If we still were.

Standing a little away from Peter was an old guy—white hair, glasses—in a blue suit with a crisp white shirt. I had no idea who he was.

Everyone turned to look when I joined them. I swallowed and gave Iris a little wave.

"Sorry," I mumbled.

"I was just saying," Iris said as she pushed her glasses onto the top of her head, "that Les's death was a major shock to everyone. It's difficult and nothing anyone ever expects to deal with, even adults. A lot of you have questions, but before we go on, Peter wanted to speak."

"I know everyone is freaked out about what happened yesterday," Peter said, and the sound of his voice made my knees shake. "I mean, you saw me get arrested and stuff, and I want everyone to know that I didn't do it. I did not kill Les. My attorney, Mr. Dean"—he pointed to the old guy—"says I shouldn't say more than that, but I don't want everyone to think I'm some kind of killer. The police have a bunch of circumstantial evidence, and that's why they arrested me, but I didn't murder anyone."

"You brought your lawyer to rehearsal?" said Krista Benson—Gwendolen in the play.

The lawyer cleared his throat. "I'm Jeffery Dean, part of Mr. Morse's defense team. We've decided it would be best if Mr. Morse had an attorney on hand at all times. Just in case something comes up."

None of us knew how to respond to that—who the heck has a lawyer following them around?—so we ignored it.

"So you're really a Morse?" Meg asked.

Peter took his hands out of his back pockets. "Yeah. Can we pretend I'm not? When I'm here I just want to be Peter the actor, not Peter the Morse."

"You said your last name was Finn," accused Melissa.

"That's my middle name," he said in an echo of the conversation we'd had earlier. "I use it when I don't want it to look like I'm cashing in on family connections."

"You think your family can get you off?" said Thad. He was two years younger than me, the youngest guy in the show. Thad was staring at Peter pretty hard, and I couldn't tell why. "You have a lot of lawyers because you're rich, right?"

"Thad," Iris said in a warning tone.

"No, it's okay." Peter ran a hand through his hair in a way I liked a lot. "Yeah, my family is rich, and we've got a whole team of lawyers on the case. They bailed me out of jail this morning."

I staggered a little. "You spent the night in jail?" I blurted. That was the opposite of what Dad said.

"Yeah." Peter glanced at Mr. Dean, who nodded. "They couldn't hold a bail hearing until this morning, no matter how much pressure my family put on the court." He sighed and avoided looking at me. "I really didn't kill Les."

"All the evidence the police have gathered is purely circumstantial," Mr. Dean said.

"Peter said that," Meg pointed out.

"How did he die?" Melissa asked.

Peter shrugged uncomfortably, and Mr. Dean spoke. "According to the police report, there were bruises around Mr. Madigan's throat. He was probably choked to death. There is no hard evidence that Mr. Morse was responsible."

A murmur went through the cast. I thought about Les's face growing red and then blue as he choked under someone's strong hands.

"What's this mean for the show?" Joe asked. His face was unreadable.

Iris held up a hand. "I talked this over with Wayne and with Pete—with Mr. Dean. Peter is under suspicion, but nothing's been proven. Our system of justice says innocent until proven guilty, so we're assuming Peter is innocent. I've decided not to recast the role."

A murmur went through the rest of the cast. I played statue. Okay, this was great. It meant Iris thought he hadn't done it either. And it meant Peter and I would still be in the play together.

Yeah. It meant that Peter and I would still be in the play together.

"Let's rehearse!" Iris boomed. "Peter, Charlene, and Joe, onstage, please. The rest of you, Wayne needs your help painting scenery backstage."

Wayne took us to the scene shop behind the rear curtains and set us to work on flats, which are made of canvas stretched over huge wood frames, like giant paintings. When they're painted, they can look like wood paneling or stone walls or whatever you want—from a distance. Up close they're fakey-fake. Wayne lumbered around the flats and paint buckets like a shovel-bearded forklift, giving us directions and correcting us when we did something wrong. I lost myself in painting a wall—let my brain go off the hook while my body moved without me. Eventually I realized the others were talking.

"Kinda weird, Peter being in the play still." That was Meg. She was squatting over another flat, running a roller of gray paint over it. "I mean, he's super rich, right? Does that mean he bought the judge?"

"Who cares?" Raymond Nestorovich filled a paint pan. He played Merriman, another butler, and had about five lines. "Les Madigan was an asshole. If someone I know had to die, I'd choose him."

"How come?" Meg asked.

For a second it looked like Thad was going to say something, but then he hardened his mouth, and Raymond said, "Ask Melissa."

"No, seriously—tell me," Meg said.

By then I was barely pretending to paint. I was listening with everything I had. Even my hair was listening.

"He deals," Raymond said with a glance at Melissa. "Way I heard it, he gave some shit to Melissa's sister, and when he got her high, he was gonna rape her or something. Melissa stopped him."

"Kicked him in the nuts," Melissa said with a nod.

"*I have returned sooner than I expected. Dr. Chasuble, I hope you are well?*" Peter said as Jack from the stage.

Now I saw that Thad was looking at Meg really close, like a puppy looking at an open gate, and I got it. Thad had a thing for Meg. Jesus. He was two years younger than her. No way he had a chance. I knew how he felt, though. Peter was three years older than me. I just lucked out.

Joe as Dr. Chasuble said, "*Your brother Earnest is dead?*"

"*Quite dead*," Jack replied.

"*What a lesson for him*!" said Charlene as Miss Prism. "*I trust he will profit by it.*"

My breath came up short again—that stuff Les had said. Peter was way over eighteen, and I was a minor. The cops couldn't even question me without Dad being there. How much trouble would I get in if they found out? Dad hadn't said anything, but I'd just told him I was gay, and he probably wasn't thinking about that. Shit, *I* hadn't been thinking about it. Even with Les dead, I could still get in trouble.

I realized I was painting with a dry roller, and I dipped it again. I'd heard all this from Melissa before, but I didn't know Thad and Raymond knew it. What else was going on?

"Les is—was—a creep," Thad said. "Even if Peter killed him—big *if*—he shouldn't go to jail for it."

"*Poor Earnest*!" Jack said. "*He had many faults, but it is a sad, sad blow.*"

"*Very sad indeed. Were you with him at the end*?" Dr. Chasuble asked.

"*No*," Jack replied.

I had a lot to figure out. If more people hated Les than just me, did that make it okay that Peter had killed him? I worked my roller furiously back and forth. I had already decided Peter had done it, but Peter said he hadn't. Well, he *had* to say that, didn't he? I mean, I only pleaded guilty because the cops had caught me red-handed and I didn't have any choice.

Miss Prism said, "*As a man sows, so shall he reap.*"

"I heard the cops can't find his cell phone," Meg said. "They need it because they're hoping it has clues or something."

"His cell phone?" Thad said in a voice so quiet I could barely hear, and I was listening *hard*. "Where'd you hear that?"

"My uncle is a cop, and I heard him talking about it," Meg told him. "They're gonna get his phone records too."

"Will that tell them anything?" Raymond said. "Like, if he texted his killer or something?"

She shook her head. "The phone company doesn't keep text messages or voicemail. But they can tell who he called and who called him. Or texted."

"Then half of us are in trouble," Thad said. "He texted all of us when the play started to tell us about rehearsals."

Except me, because I didn't have a cell phone. I should have been relieved, but for some reason, the news only made me more nervous.

After a while, Iris called me onstage for a scene with Peter as Jack, the same scene Peter and I had done together at the audition. Mr. Dean was watching from the audience. When I entered with my script, Peter was standing at the other end of the ragged couch we were using until we got the real furniture, and Jesus, it seemed as though all the lights were shining on only him. His eyes were greener than all the leaves in a forest. I remembered how just yesterday afternoon we'd been lying on his bed and I'd kissed him hard with my hands sliding up his shirt. He caught my eye and then looked away and rumpled up his black hair, looking sexy as a rock star. My shoes were melting into the floor, and I thought my script might burst into flames.

"We've done this scene before, but I'm not happy with it, so I want to change it around," Iris said. "Algy, when you enter, you notice Jack is upset, so cross straight to him while you deliver the line."

Hoo boy. I edged toward Peter—Jack. *"Didn't it go off all right, old boy? You don't—"*

"No," Iris interrupted. "You need to get there faster. Go straight downstage and clap him on the shoulder when you get there. Start again."

Peter shot me a look that had the whole world in it, and my heart about split in half. I reentered and crossed downstage toward the audience. *"Didn't it go off all right, old boy? You don't mean to say Gwendolen refused you?"*

I reached Jack, who was looking out a window, or where a window would eventually be, and hesitantly touched his shoulder. He was wearing only a thin T-shirt, and his muscles were hot and tense on my palm. A little jolt went through me. That weird coppery taste came back, and for a moment, I was lying on Peter's bed with him again. For a second I couldn't speak. Peter flicked a glance at me with those green eyes, and I swallowed. To distract myself, I looked down at my script, even though I had these lines memorized.

"I know it is a way she has," I said. *"She is always refusing people. I think it is most ill-natured of her."*

"Oh," Peter-as-Jack said, and the vibration of his voice thrilled like thunder down my arm and into my chest—and lower. "*Gwendolen is as right as a trivet. As far as she is concerned, we are engaged.*"

"Hold it," Iris interrupted again. "This is the problem we had before. *Earnest* is probably the earliest bromance in English literature, but the Brits from this time are more standoffish with each other. Algy, you love your best friend here, but take your hand off his shoulder. And save the husky register for your love scenes with Cecily."

Fuck. I flushed and backed up. "Sorry."

"Rehearsal is for experimentation," Iris said. "Try something else. And, go."

I set my jaw. Algy wasn't in love with Jack. Algy wasn't me. Algy came from a rich family where his biggest problem was whether or not to have salmon for supper. That actually sounded supernova awesome right now. I could forget about Peter, forget about the shitty trailer, forget about Les. I summoned up the Algy shell, spun it around myself. My posture straightened, my head went up, and an ironic half smile crossed my face—not quite a sneer, but it could become a deadly one if I wanted. Algy had been through a lot of shit, and sometimes he used sarcasm to cover up how he really felt. I went for that.

"*Didn't it go off all right, old boy?*" I said with snarky sympathy and thwapped Jack on the shoulder. "*You don't mean to say Gwendolen refused you? I know it is a way she has. She is always refusing people. I think it is most ill-natured of her.*"

"Perfect!" Iris shouted. "Keep going."

A look of surprise crossed Peter/Jack's face, but he recovered. "*Oh, Gwendolen is as right as a trivet. As far as she is concerned, we are engaged. Her mother is perfectly unbearable. Never met such a gorgon.*" He paused, and I raised my eyebrows. Gwen's mother—Lady Bracknell—was my aunt. "*I beg your pardon, Algy, I suppose I shouldn't talk about your own aunt in that way before you.*"

I snorted. "*My dear boy, I love hearing my relations abused. Relations are simply a tedious pack of people, who haven't got the remotest knowledge of how to live, nor the smallest instinct about when to die.*" I crushed the last word.

This time Jack didn't hesitate. "*Oh, that is nonsense!*"

"*It isn't!*" The anger tiger was pacing inside me—the real me.

Jack turned back to the nonexistent window, though it wasn't in the script. "*Well, I won't argue about the matter. You always want to argue about things.*"

"*That is exactly what things were originally made for.*" I was still trying to get an argument out of him.

"*Upon my word, if I thought that, I'd shoot myself,*" Jack muttered and then paused. I wanted to keep arguing, but the script didn't have any lines for me, so I had to keep quiet. It bugged the hell out of me, and then for a moment, I couldn't tell if *I* wanted to argue, or if Algy did. "*You don't think there is any chance of Gwendolen becoming like her mother in about a hundred and fifty years, do you, Algy?*"

I hid inside Algy for the rest of rehearsal, and Iris said I was doing the best Algy she'd ever seen, even better than some actor she'd seen in New York. That made me feel good.

"Get something to eat and be back onstage by seven for second rehearsal," she said as everyone was getting ready to go. "Remember, early is on time—"

"—and on time is late!" we shouted back at her, and she waved us out. I let go of Algy, and suddenly it was just me, with my ordinary brown hair and crappy tennis shoes.

Peter caught up with me backstage as I was leaving, but to be honest, I wasn't leaving very fast. Mr. Dean was coming up behind us, but Peter held up a hand as everyone else boiled out the back door, leaving us in the cool, dim hallway.

"Give me some damn space," Peter ordered. "Kevin isn't a cop or a reporter."

Mr. Dean stayed back, out of earshot but within sight of us.

"Can we talk a sec?" Peter pleaded in a low voice. "Please?"

I ran my tongue around the inside of my cheek. "What?" The word came out flatter than I wanted it to.

Peter reached out to touch my shoulder but then dropped his hand. "Are you mad at me?"

I shrugged. For some reason it was hard to talk. Peter's eyes were filled with emerald pain, but this close, he smelled so good, and I wanted him to hold me. But not in front of Mr. Dean. I just shrugged.

"Kevin, I didn't do it." He glanced around like a nervous tiger. "I didn't kill Les. Yeah, I beat him up, but when I left his apartment, he was totally alive. He wasn't even unconscious."

"You said—" I began.

"I know what I said," Peter interrupted. "That was me being angry. I wouldn't kill someone."

"Yeah?"

Peter wet his lips. "I don't want to talk about this here. Can you come over to my house? Please?"

"I don't—"

Now he touched my arm, not caring what Mr. Dean might see. "Kev, please. I need you."

I couldn't say yes, but I couldn't say no either. Not with his warm hand on my arm. Instead I nodded. Peter sighed with relief and led me out to his car. Mr. Dean trailed behind.

ACT II: SCENE III

KEVIN

MR. DEAN followed us in a separate car. Peter and I didn't talk much on the drive to Peter's huge house. At the gate, a bunch of cars and vans marked with TV logos marched in a line down the road. People holding microphones and big cameras stood around looking bored until they saw Peter's car. Then they stampeded toward us. Peter swore and slapped a button. The gate slid open, and Peter made for it without slowing down.

"Are you going to hit them?"

"They'll move," Peter said. "Duck down and cover your face unless you want it on TV."

I dove to the floor. There were a few desperate knocks on the tinted windows, and then we must have cleared the crowd. I came up like a prairie dog scanning for danger.

"What the hell?" I said.

"I forgot to take the back way," Peter said. "They've been there since the arrest. Leeches. Never talk to a reporter, Kev. They'll twist what you say to make you look bad, and they never, ever take it back."

"Why?"

"Bad news gets more viewers than good news and apologies."

Mr. Dean's car came behind us, and we wandered down the long green drive to the Morse mongo house. Peter parked the Camaro at an angle near the front steps, and a guy in black sprinted out a side door to take it away. Peter hunched into himself and slouched up the stairs. I followed, feeling uncertain.

Another guy in black snatched open the front door for us before we could touch it. Peter didn't even look. I threw the guy a nod, but he stayed stiff as a coatrack, and I flushed a little. The anger tiger growled. Wasn't I worth noticing?

Mr. Dean followed us into the house. "You should have taken—"

"The back way, I know," Peter finished. "I don't need you in here. You can go write a brief or something."

Mr. Dean nodded and whipped out his cell phone. "Larry? Yeah, I need an update." And he walked away.

The house had a different feel to it. Before, I hadn't seen much of "the help," but now men and women in black and white zipped around with serious looks on their faces. A tight feeling hung in the air. Peter ignored all of them until a woman in a white apron hurried up.

"Do you need anything, Mr. Peter?" she said.

"No, Vicky. I don't—wait." Peter turned to me. "Are you hungry? I'm hungry."

He was going to order food from that kitchen. You're supposed to say *No, I'm fine*, when people offer you food, but Peter had said he was hungry, and I was always hungry, and anyway, screw it if I was going to turn down free food from a billionaire's kitchen staff.

"Starving," I said.

"Send some sandwiches and pop and stuff up to my room, please," he said. "And bring me a house cell phone—a blank one."

Vicky bustled away.

"You didn't want to text the kitchen?" I said as we climbed the stairs.

"She asked, I told."

Peter and I went straight into his room. It was as humongous as I remembered. The minute I shut the door behind us, Peter flopped onto the bed.

"Shit," he said.

I sat next to him, careful as a cat and trying not to be pissed off about the guy at the door. "Everyone looks freaked out down there. Is that because of you?"

"Yeah. They're all trying to look busy because Mom is on a rampage." He rolled over onto his back. "The whole family is going torpedo ballistic. I guess I can't blame them."

"Guess you can't," I said.

A long moment stretched between us like a rotting rubber band. I had no idea what to say next.

"Kev," Peter said finally, "I absolutely didn't do it. You have to believe me."

I couldn't stand it anymore, not with him sitting next to me looking so scared and handsome and... so Peter. I touched his hand, then grabbed it. "Tell me what happened."

"I told you once."

"Tell me again," I countered. "With more detail."

He paused and then nodded. "But you can't repeat any of this," he said in a dad kind of voice. "I'm not supposed to talk about this stuff to anyone but my lawyer. I could get in big legal trouble."

"Even though you already told me."

"That was... before." Peter's green eyes were dark and serious. "But I'll tell you everything anyway, if you promise not to tell."

For some reason that made me feel a little better. He was putting himself in danger by talking to me, and who would lie in circumstances like that? I crossed my heart and held up my right hand.

"Be serious, Kev."

"I *am* serious."

He told me. He talked about driving up to Les's craphole apartment, about pounding on the door, about knocking Les down, about the look of surprise and fear on Les's face. When Peter got to the part where he was pounding the shit out of Les, my heart was racing around my rib cage.

"Les was lying there on the floor, groaning," he finished. "I think his nose must've been broken, because it was bleeding pretty bad, but he was definitely alive, Kev. I said I wanted to kill him, but after I hit him a few times, I realized I didn't. Not really."

Peter swallowed, and I grabbed his hand again. His big, bruised hand that was so much larger than mine. "Okay," I said. "Then what?"

"I grabbed his phone and took off. It was unlocked, so I could disable the security. I needed to delete the video he said he had, but I didn't want to hang around to do it. When I got home, I found the video and wiped it. That's all." Peter swiped at his eyes. "But I guess someone saw me and my car, because the next day, Detective Malloy arrested me. I don't want to go through that shit ever again."

"What did you do with the phone?" I asked. It wasn't what I'd meant to say. The words just popped out.

Peter pointed. "It's in my desk drawer."

"Did you tell the cops about it?"

"Fuck no. Not even Mr. Dean or my other lawyers know about it. I put it in airplane mode and shut it off in case there's a GPS on it or something. I'll throw it in the river later."

"Why didn't you do it already?"

"I haven't had the chance," Peter complained. "After I got home, I spent like an hour finding that video. I didn't want that to get out, you know?"

Because Peter was over eighteen and I was only sixteen. Jesus, we had to be so *careful*. That didn't seem fair. It was only a difference of three years. But the thought of the police coming for me like Les said they would clenched my stomach up like a nest of snakes.

"I was going to give Les his phone back at rehearsal," Peter went on. "But I forgot to bring it. Thank god I did! I would've been fucked if Malloy had found it when she arrested me. Since then I haven't had the chance to sneak it out of the house without someone noticing."

"Let me see it," I commanded.

Peter gave me a look, then went to his desk and slipped it out. The phone was an ordinary smartphone, though a bunch of cracks spiderwebbed the screen.

"Don't turn it on," Peter warned. "If the GPS activates, the cops might be able to find it. It's still in airplane mode, but no reason to take a risk."

"Okay." I turned it over. The dark spiderwebs shattered the reflection of my face into a thousand pieces. "You're sure the video is gone?"

"Completely," Peter said.

I sighed and let myself feel a little relief. "It's bad enough you're up for murder. I don't want you to get in trouble for kissing a minor."

Peter blinked at me like a confused cat. "What?"

"The video showed you and me kissing in the park," I said, confused that he seemed confused. "I'm only sixteen, and you're nineteen, so it's statutory rape or something."

Now Peter faced me on the bed. "*That's* what you've been worried about? Our ages?"

"Well, yeah," I said. "Aren't you? I mean, we have to keep everything so quiet between us, and—"

"Kev"—Peter grabbed my shoulders—"age of consent in Michigan is sixteen. Once you're old enough, you can do whatever you want with anyone you want. It doesn't matter if the other person is male or female, sixteen or sixty. I asked one of my lawyers, and she told me."

"What?" My mind was a little mouse running in circles inside a cage, and the phone slipped out of my grip. "How can that be right? Les said... he said...."

"Les lied, Kev." Peter took both my hands. "He wanted to control you, so he lied."

Les lied. Even when Les was dead, he lied. That lie had chained me up, kept me quiet. I couldn't get my head around it. It seemed like I should feel relief, a sudden *wrench* as a bunch of tension disappeared. Instead I felt black-hole dread. I couldn't let go of the idea that Peter and I had done something illegal. Wrong. Les had dumped a burden on my back that had bent my body until I forgot how to straighten out.

"If it's not illegal," I said around the nonexistent weight, "why did *you* want the video so bad?"

"Are you kidding? Kev, we've been over this. My family doesn't know about me—about us. Marriage is legal, but that doesn't mean my family approves. My dad uses the word *fag* all the time, and Mom lets him. It's top-down policy at Morse that gay people get fired."

"Now *that's* illegal!"

"Not in this state. Marriage is equal, but you can still toss someone out of their job for being gay. The saying around Morse is 'Married on Sunday, fired on Monday.' The law is stupid that way. So are my parents." Peter looked away. "That video could wreck me."

"How... how can we be... you know—" I was hesitant all over again. "—together? If your family hates people like us?"

"When I turn twenty-one, the trust fund my grandpa left me comes under my control," he said. "It's enough to live on in decent style even if my parents throw me out. We have to look like just friends until then."

"Twenty-one?" I squawked. "That's two whole years!"

"I know," he said. "I've been waiting to turn twenty-one my whole life."

He leaned in and kissed me. The kiss was warm and nervous at the same time. Hesitantly, his arm went around me. Peter's kiss seemed to rush over my entire skin. It teased at my hair. He slid his tongue over my lips in a sensitive trail.

"Nine," he said in a husky, sexy voice.

I didn't say anything. I couldn't say anything.

"Are… are we okay?" Peter asked finally.

I thought for a long moment. The scared look on Peter's face made me want to run and hide. "I… want to be."

"But you don't know." Peter pulled away. "Sure. Fine."

"Peter Finn!" I said. "Don't even!"

He blinked at me. "Don't what?"

"This is a shitload of… shit for you to dump on me," I said. "It's scary, okay? I don't know what's going on with me or what's happening next or who I can talk to about anything. You can't make me sort this out all at once."

"I guess." I could tell he wasn't happy about it, but what else could I do? "Tell me something," he said abruptly.

My breath tightened a little. "Sure."

"Why do you call me Peter Finn?"

"Do I call you that?" Little pause as I thought about it. "I don't know. You said your family calls you that. I guess it's who you really are. Not Peter Morse or Peter the actor. Peter Finn. I guess I kind of fell into it." Another pause. "Do you want me to stop?"

Peter touched my hand. "I like it."

"Okay." I was little embarrassed for some reason, so I tried to lighten the mood. "Maybe we need to come up with your nickname for me."

"Hmm." Peter frowned. "Kevkev?"

"No."

Peter stroked the back of my hand in a way I liked very much. "Sugar buns?"

"Definitely not."

He raised my fingers to his lips. "Mr. Big?"

"Dude!"

We were saved from more conversation by a knock at the door. Peter jumped a little and dropped my hand, then pulled away from me and straightened his clothes. It was quick and automatic. I didn't like being pushed aside like a potato-chip bag. The anger tiger glowered, and my jaw clenched. But what was the other choice? Let the help come in while I sat on Peter's lap and stroked his hair? Hell, I was barely willing to think about Peter in my own head, let alone have other people think about it. I would have pushed him aside at my house. Dad knew about us, but I didn't think he'd be good with me and Peter kissing in front of him. It'd be too weird. So how could I be mad about Peter pushing me back?

Everything was so mixed-up and messy. I thought when you grew up, you know what to do when shit happened, but the older I got, the less I could figure out.

Peter called out, and I stuffed Les's cracked phone into my pocket. They wouldn't see it. Fuck Les. Fuck them.

Vicky and two other women entered with heavy food trays. I smelled ham and roast beef and mustard and cheese, and my mouth watered. Okay, not so mad anymore. The second woman's tray had bowls of sweet pickles and salty olives and home-made pita chips and onion dip. The third woman's tray had a sweating pitcher of pop, which must have been difficult to balance. I wondered why she even used the tray, then remembered how, in rehearsal, Iris always made Lane—Jack's butler—put everything on a tray. Huh. The women set everything up on a table in Peter's sitting area while I waited uncomfortably. Should I say something to them? Make conversation? Peter seemed to act like they weren't there, but he didn't talk to me either, kind of like the way you stop talking at a restaurant table while the waitress refills the glasses. I followed his lead.

When they were done, Vicky set a glossy black smartphone on Peter's nightstand. Les's phone felt heavy in my pocket. "There you are, sir. Will there be anything else?"

"Thanks, Vicky. That's all."

They left, and Peter picked up the phone. It was brand-new and still had the factory's plastic coating over the glass.

"What's a house cell phone?" I asked, though my full attention was on the food across the room.

"Dad set it up. The family and the people who work in the house use these phones. We even have our own app. I can use it to create a food order and send it to the kitchen or have my car brought around or tell the stable to saddle up the horses, but half the time it's faster just to text someone directly." He grinned. "Still, Dad likes tech, so he made the app. Anyways… here."

He handed the phone to me. I looked down at it, bewildered. "I don't understand."

"I'm giving it to you, dork," Peter said. "It's yours."

"Mine? Peter Finn, I can't take this."

I tried to give it back, but he folded his arms.

"You're insulting me, dude," he said. "I want you to have it."

I was a little out of breath. The sandwiches were far away and forgotten. "It's too expensive. This is the newest one."

"Kev, look." Peter's hands closed over mine with the phone in them. "Think of it as me being selfish. I'm tired of not being able to reach my boyfriend. Now I can."

"But it's too expensive."

"That's relative," Peter said. "If you gave me a present that cost a dime, would it be too expensive?"

"No," I said, though I honestly didn't have a dime.

"Okay, then. To me this cost a dime. Seriously, Kev—have you *seen* me? Just take the damn phone and say thanks."

"Uh… sure." I took it. "Thanks. But just because I have it doesn't mean I'll answer it every time you call."

"No." Peter gave me a small smile that set off tiny fireworks in my head. "But I can leave you a message. And protect you."

"Protect me?"

"If Les had seen you with a cell phone, maybe he wouldn't have attacked you."

"Hmm." I gestured at the trays. "How about we eat?"

We leaned against each other on his couch while we tested my new phone and ate the thickest, tangiest sandwiches I ever had in my life. His warm skin against mine felt so fine, so perfect. I found myself half lying in his lap, and I never wanted to be anywhere else. As a joke, Peter fed me an olive. His fingertips brushed my lips and generated an electric wave that tingled down to my soles by way of my crotch.

Peter said in a low, urgent voice, "Want me to adjust that for you?"

I glanced down and flushed. It was really embarrassing that Peter had noticed, but at the same time, it was… freeing. He had seen and thought it was great.

Then my heart beat quick and my mouth went dry. For half a microsecond, I was lying in Les's lap with Les's arms around me instead of the guy who had killed him.

Who *hadn't* killed him.

I sat up and shoved my new phone into my pocket like nothing was wrong. My fingertips touched where I was hard and made me shiver. "Uh… maybe later. There any pop left?"

I could tell Peter was hiding his disappointment. "Sure. How about—"

A scream came from somewhere outside the room. It was a long, high wail that scraped fingernails across my eyeballs. Peter shot to his feet, his eyes wide as semi tires.

"What's the matter?" I asked. "Who was that?"

Another scream. "Shit," Peter said and rushed out of the room.

He left the door open. I only waited half a second before following. Peter was already running down the wide hall. He rounded a corner with me right behind him. A pair of house workers, a man and a woman, were grappling with a girl about my age. The girl had black hair like Peter, but her body was softer, almost overweight, and she was throwing a world-class tantrum. She snarled and struggled with the two people who held her arms. Her face was radish red, and spit flew from her lips. She screamed a third time. All the hair on my arms stood up. I didn't know what to do. The people fighting with her made me think of the police, of being put in handcuffs, but they weren't police. I couldn't tell if they were hurting her or not. I wanted to help but had no idea what to do.

The girl wrenched an arm free from the woman and punched the man in the face. He staggered back, holding his nose. Blood spattered the floor. Without a trace of fear, Peter rushed up to the girl.

"Em," he said. "Emily! It's me. Calm down. It's okay." He wrapped his arms around her. The woman let Emily go and checked on the man, whose nose was still bleeding. "Em, it's all right."

"Peter Finn!" Emily's tear-streaked face calmed down. "Peter Finn! They gave me Wednesday shoes!"

"It's okay," Peter soothed. "We'll get you Thursday shoes. Can we go back to your room? The rules say you have to go back to your room." He turned to the woman. "Is Mom or Dad here?"

"Mr. Morse is at headquarters, sir," she said. "Mrs. Morse is on her way now. Would you like me to call one of them?"

"No. Just make sure Mom finds out when she gets home. Get some ice for Allen's nose." He kept one arm around Emily and led her down the hall.

Uncertainly, I followed. Emily, I remembered, was the name of Peter's sister, the one he wouldn't talk about. Was this why? What was wrong with her? Peter kept up a steady stream of chatter in Emily's ear as he steered her through the open door of a bedroom.

The bedroom was as huge as Peter's, but where Peter's room was done up in early American bachelor, this room had your basic bed, your basic desk, your basic wide-screen TV, your basic couch. But two sets of floor-to-ceiling shelves were filled with comic books, those black-and-white ones from Japan that you have to read from right to left—manga. The walls were covered with drawings of manga characters, some in color but most in black-and-white. They were good, like they'd come straight from the artists. Most of them were girls in short skirts with long braids and samurai swords, or boys in armor who cast lightning bolts from their hands. I don't read manga much, so they all looked the same to me.

The closet door hung open, and through it I caught a glimpse of a rack of tennis shoes. More shoes were scattered on the floor in front of it. Emily wore only pink socks.

Peter sat Emily on her bed, and she flopped dramatically onto her back. It reminded me of the way Peter had done the same thing in his room a few minutes ago. "Why did you take your shoes off, Em?" he asked. "It's the middle of the day."

"I didn't like them," she said. "They were pushing on my toes."

Her voice had a singsong note to it. All the words were there, but she said them differently than most people would. She put the accents in the wrong places, and I couldn't put my finger on where. She also looked into the distance when she talked, instead of at Peter.

"So when Kelly tried to put your shoes back on?" Peter prompted.

Emily clapped her hands to her ears and rolled back and forth on the bed. "Wednesday shoes! Wednesday shoes!"

"Em, it's okay." Peter touched her arm with just his fingertip. "We'll get the Thursday shoes, and everything will be fine again."

He dashed to the closet and quickly stacked the loose shoes on the shoe rack in precise order, making sure to tuck in the laces. Then he selected a pair of bright-purple tennis shoes and took them to Emily.

"There," he said triumphantly. "Purple shoes because Thursday is a purple day. Let's put them on."

Emily sat up and let Peter help her into the shoes. His motions were easy and tender. Neither of them paid the tiniest bit of attention to me. I stood near the door like a mouse trying to hide in plain sight.

"I think it's time to draw a picture now," Peter said. "What do you want to draw?"

Emily wandered over to a drawing table on the toes of her shoes. She opened a pad of sketch paper and a set of colored pencils and set to work. Peter seemed to notice me for the first time.

"Hey," he said. "That's my sister, Emily."

I didn't know if I should say hello to her—she was bent over her drawing and ignoring us—so I just nodded.

"She's autistic," Peter continued. "She can't…. Well, there are a lot of things that upset her, so she stays in here most of the time. She loves to draw."

"She's good," I said.

Emily crumpled up her drawing and flung it over her shoulder. It bounced across the floor and landed at my feet. I picked it up without thinking. Emily sharpened her pencil with a little hand sharpener and started on a new sheet of paper.

"Is she okay now?" I asked.

"She'll be fine," Peter replied. "Let's go back to my room." He raised his voice, but only a little. "I'll see you, Em."

Emily kept drawing. We left, and Peter clicked the door behind us. Neither of us spoke until we got back to Peter's room.

Peter picked up a video game controller and switched on the console. *Rage VII* popped up. I set down the crumpled paper and took up the other controller. In a couple seconds, our battle copters were going at it.

"So now you know," Peter finally said.

"Know what?" I fired a KR-16 at him.

"Why I don't leave town, go to school somewhere else." Peter dodged the missile and readied his machine guns. "Haven't you wondered?"

I guess I hadn't. But now that Peter had brought it up, why *did* he stay? He could go to school anywhere he wanted, even overseas. He wouldn't have to worry about his parents finding out he was gay, and when he was twenty-one, he could do whatever the hell he liked. But he was going to college up the road. When I thought about it all, I guess I assumed it was because he wanted to live here, in the mansion, because... mansion.

"Uh... not really," I admitted. "But I don't get what you staying here has to do with Emily."

"Some autistic people go into fits and rages," Peter said. "No one knows why. Everyone is different. Now Emily, she has a strict schedule, and if something disrupts it even a little bit, she gets upset. Or if the weather is bad, she gets upset. Thunderstorms are a terror for her because the noise hurts her ears, and she never knows when the next thunder strike will come. Or if the food is wrong, she gets upset. And if her nurse puts out the wrong color, she gets upset. That's what happened just now. Thursday is a day for purple shoes. The nurse must have made a mistake, but Emily never forgets."

"What's that got to do with you?" My helicopter took half its points in damage, and I fired back at Peter, but only halfheartedly.

"When she goes really ballistic, like she did just now, I'm the only one who can calm her down. It's been like that ever since we were little. We don't know why. It just is. She likes me best in the family, and people with autism don't bother to hide stuff like that. She's okay around Mom, but she barely tolerates Dad, even though they both love her. She'll

111

scream and kick herself into exhaustion if I'm not around. That's why I'm still here."

"Wow," I said. "That's… rough. Are you going to stay around here forever?"

The controller jerked in Peter's hand, and I blew up his helicopter without even trying. Peter's voice went quiet in a way that made my heart slide down to my stomach. "I don't know. I've got so much else to worry about right now. It's just that…."

"What?" I asked.

"I don't know," he said in that same quiet voice. "I'm trapped. I have to study what my parents want. I can't go anywhere for long because of Emily. Now this murder thing is hanging over me. I'm never getting out of here, or if I do, it'll be because I go to jail."

How can you feel awful for someone who has a billion dollars, especially when you live in a trashed-out east-side trailer? But Peter's pain was my own. I pulled his head down onto my shoulder. He resisted for a moment, then wrapped his arms around my body and clung to me like a monkey. Feeling strangely grown-up, I ran my hands through his hair and kissed the top of his head.

"Ten," I said.

Right then the door burst open and a woman in a suit barged in.

ACT II: SCENE IV

KEVIN

"PETER FINN." The woman strode into the room. "What happened to—"

She stopped and stared down at me. I stared up at her, my arms frozen around Peter. Peter's muscles were locked in place against mine. His breath came fast against my shirt like a baby bird's.

"Mom," he whispered.

"God," I said.

"Jesus." Mrs. Morse whipped the door shut. The sound broke both of us free, and we yanked ourselves apart. My heart was banging against my ribs like they were iron bars. *Shit, shit, shit!* I didn't know what to do or how to do it. At that moment I really wanted Dad.

"What... the hell... is this?" Mrs. Morse coasted into the sitting area like a thunderhead. Lightning cracked behind every word. She wore a navy-blue business suit, and her hair was pulled back into a schoolteacher bun. "Who are you? What do you think you're doing?"

It took me a second to understand she was talking to me, not Peter. I scrambled to my feet, heart still pounding, while Mrs. Morse towered in front of me like the first rock of an avalanche. Peter slowly got up. Fear crushed me behind steel girders, and I became small inside. Someone else had to be outside, out there to handle this. Without thinking about it, I spun the Algy shell around me. Algy was used to handling irate relatives. He would know what to do. I straightened, put a half smile on my face, and put out my hand.

"Hello, Mrs. Morse," I said with Algy's confidence. "I'm Kevin Devereaux. Peter Finn and I are in the play together. It's nice to meet you."

Mrs. Morse ignored my hand. I shrugged and made a little gesture with it like Algy might have.

113

"That's not what I asked." Mrs. Morse's voice was made of broken glass, and her eyes, the same green as Peter's, drilled into me. Or tried to. The Algy shell hardened.

"Yes, it is," I said brightly. "You asked who I was. I just told you."

"Don't get smart with me," she snapped. "What did I just see here?"

I wasn't going to fall into that trap. "Peter Finn is upset about what happened with Emily just now. I'm sure the help told you all about it."

Mrs. Morse's eyes went to Peter. Her mouth was tight and pale. "Peter Finn, what is this... boy doing here?"

"His name is Kevin, Mom," Peter said quietly. "Like he told you. Like you asked."

"I just saw you two together on the floor," she said, "writhing like a pair of.... I can't even say it."

"There was no writhing," I put in, using my Algy voice. "Writhing was right out."

She flicked another glance over me, taking in my worn clothes, my knotted shoelaces, my bad haircut, and she visibly tried to get her control back. "We have this *problem* with the police, and now you've taken up with something out of an east-side ditch, Peter Finn. You couldn't destroy the family faster if you tried."

"Mom," Peter said. "That's not—"

That did it for me, though. The tiger roared inside me and made me feel tall. The fear girders dropped away, and the Algy shell shattered. Words shot from my mouth like hornets. "I thought the rich had good manners. Maybe you need to buy some from your son."

"How much are you paying him, Peter Finn?" Her voice was low and dangerous, like a gun pointed at your thigh.

"Half as much as your husband pays you," I snapped.

She slapped me. The *crack* rang through the room, and my entire face stung. The shock of it froze me for a second. Red anger pulsed hard, and my arm twitched. I was going to hit the bitch. Then I remembered Robbie and stepped back. I wasn't going to do that again.

"Mom!" Peter moved between us. "What the hell are you doing?"

Two red spots glowed on her cheeks, and for a moment she looked uncertain, like she was afraid she'd gone too far. "I don't understand—"

"I'm gay, Mom!" Peter yelled. "Kevin is my boyfriend, and he was kissing me when you walked in."

Her face hardened again. "I won't have that kind of talk in this house. That isn't you. It won't be you. Bad enough that Emily is the way she is without you making it worse. You're a *Morse*, and you have responsibilities to this family."

Peter ignored her, though I could see it cost him. He was swaying a little, like a tree that was about to topple. "You saw the truth, Mom. You've *known* the truth for years. Remember how you walked in on me and Gary Hayes?"

"You didn't know any better." Mrs. Morse's tone was December sleet. "And Gary was lucky we only fired him. Your father wanted to file charges."

"You can't file charges for kissing, Mom," Peter interrupted. His voice was shaking, but he didn't stop talking. "Kevin could file charges against *you* for assault."

"With what lawyer?" she sniped. "This trailer trash couldn't buy a used cigarette."

The tiger snarled, and red anger squeezed my stomach. My cheek was still stinging from the slap. Not even Dad hit me, and this woman, this stranger, had slapped my face. Outrage shoved the words out of me. "Wow," I said. "Any similarity between you and a human being is purely coincidental."

"Kev." Peter put a hand on my shoulder, which made his mom's face go from volcano red to snowstorm pale.

"No, seriously," I said with false brightness that sounded a lot like Algy. "Whatever's eating her got diarrhea."

Her hand shot back. I lifted my chin.

"Go ahead—hit me again. I could use the money."

Face white, she lowered her hand. "Yes." Now she used a venomous whisper that would scare a snake. "I can see that."

"Mom," Peter said, "You just said I'm a Morse, and you said being a Morse means I get respect."

"Even when it's not earned?"

I glanced between them. There was something going on there that I wasn't following, and I wasn't sure I wanted to.

"You *are* a Morse, Peter Finn," she said, visibly trying to stay calm. "You will *be* a Morse—a proper Morse. You will get married, you will take over this company, and you will drop these adolescent experiments before this family gets hurt. Before *you* get hurt."

Peter swallowed, then said firmly, "I'll still be a gay Morse."

"I'm your mother!" she burst out. "You don't speak to me that way."

"Then I won't speak to you. Let's go, Kev." Peter strode for the door. I shot his mother a hard look and followed.

Peter didn't speak all the way down to the front door, but I could see how stiff his walk was. I became more unsure by the moment. Was he going for a walk or leaving his house forever?

One of the help guys met us at the door, and I wondered how much they had overheard. Text messages were probably flying at the speed of gossip. "Shall I call Mr. Dean for you, sir?"

"Fuck no," Peter said and stormed out.

He almost ran into another guy coming in. The man was an older version of Peter—same broad shoulders, same height, same night-black hair. Except this guy was going silver at the temples, and he had a carefully done scruffy beard. His eyes were also blue instead of green. The suit and tie he wore probably cost more than my dad had ever seen in his entire life. Peter's father—the co-owner of Morse Plastic. That's what Peter would look like when he got to be that age. Still handsome. Jesus.

"Peter Finn," Mr. Morse said. "I got the message about Emily. Is everything—"

"I just told Mom I'm gay, and Kevin here is my boyfriend," Peter said. "Mom'll give you an earful."

We left him standing in the doorway. Peter's car was nowhere to be seen, but Mr. Morse's car—a sleek black Benz with tinted windows— was at the bottom of the steps, and a driver was just climbing in.

"I'll take it." Peter took the keys from him. "Get in, Kev."

I got in. Peter peeled down the driveway. In the rearview mirror, his dad stared after us.

"Uh... where are we going?" I asked. We had exited the Morse estate through a back gate that looked like it was used for deliveries and didn't have any reporters guarding it, and now we were driving around Ringdale. August sunshine poured over the car like molten gold, but icy air blasted from the AC vents. Peter's face looked carved from a glacier. We ran hot and cold.

"I don't know," Peter said and pulled into a strip mall. "You want some ice cream? I want ice cream."

"Okay."

"There should be a ball cap and a pair of sunglasses in the glove compartment. Give them to me, would you?"

I did. Peter, his eyes and hair now hidden, paid for two huge salted-caramel sundaes at Jim 'n' Joes, and we got a shady umbrella table outside. The heavy, stifling air pressed in around us. People passed us by on the sidewalk, no idea the two guys at the cast-iron table were a couple of... well, were a couple. I poked at my ice cream a little and pushed it into the sunlight. You have to let a sundae melt a while before it tastes good. Despite what I'd told Peter, I wasn't really in the mood for ice cream, but I never got the good stuff, and I wasn't going to screw it up just because I was in a harsh mood. Peter didn't touch his either. The whipped cream was already sliding off the top, toward the table.

"Fuck," he said at last.

"Yep," I said.

"Shit," he said.

"Damn," I agreed.

"Balls."

"Hell."

"Boobs."

I looked up. "Boobs?"

"All the other ones were taken." A smile cracked Peter's face. It widened into a grin, and then he was laughing. He rocked in his chair and slapped the tabletop. A blob of whipped cream dropped through the iron grill, and his cherry rolled away.

His cherry. That broke me, and I laughed too. I couldn't help it. We sat in those uncomfortable metal chairs, snorting and laughing into our fingers while our sundaes drooped into mush and people stared as they passed.

"Oh my god." Peter scrubbed at his streaming eyes with the heels of his hands. "I can't believe I did that. My parents know. I'm screwed, Kev."

"It feels good, though, doesn't it?" I said, breathing a little hard. "Nice not to have to hide from them."

"How would you know?" he gasped.

Oh. Right. We hadn't had the chance to talk about it. "I told my dad yesterday. He got me drunk, and it sort of slipped out."

"Drunk?" Peter repeated. "No fucking way."

"Yeah. It was after the cops came over."

The smile dropped off his face. "What cops?"

I told him about Detective Malloy's visit and how Dad had finally made her leave. "I didn't tell her anything except that we're in the play together and we rehearsed lines at your house," I finished. "She bought it. Afterward, though, we were both freaked out, and Dad let me drink some whiskey. It tasted awful, but it calmed me down so much I sort of told him about you and me."

"How did he take it?" Peter leaned toward me. He seemed almost hungry.

"He hugged me and said it was okay."

"Wow." Peter's sundae had melted into a caramel puddle. "Wish I had your dad. Mine is probably working out how to kick me out of the family forever."

"My dad isn't perfect." I scooped up some melty sundae and let it play over my tongue. Salt and caramel. Meltier than I liked it but still good. "Though he's never slapped me."

Peter winced. "I'm sorry about that. I never saw Mom do anything like that before. It's seriously not her."

"What *is* her, then?"

"She's...." He drifted away for a second. "She married my dad when Morse Plastic was going through a rough time. Mom is old money—really old. Rich-before-Shakespeare old. Her family saved Morse Plastic, and she's superfocused on making sure the company survives—her and Dad both."

"You think they'll cut you off forever?" I asked.

"Oh Jesus. I don't know. It's not that simple. There's Emily, and they'll be worried about me going to the media if they cut me off entirely."

"Would you?" I said. "Go to the news?"

"I don't know." He jabbed at his ice cream. "The Morses aren't like the Kennedys or the Hiltons. We don't live in the spotlight. But a family fight over the Morse heir being gay? That'd be a bloody steak in a piranha tank. The company's reputation would suffer, and my parents don't want that. It's always about the company."

"I'm nobody," I said. "So no one would care about me being gay except maybe at school, but I'm already a loser there who—"

Peter grabbed my shoulder. "You don't understand, Kev. If this gets out, they *will* care because you're *my* boyfriend. They'll want to know all about you. How you got on probation, why your dad went to jail, where you live, what kind of grades you get. They'll want to know how we met, why we're together, and they'll talk about whether or not it's okay for me to see someone who's only sixteen. And they'll want to know if you had anything to do with Les."

A chill went through me. The thought of my picture behind a newscaster with the word *Raped* scrawled across my face rushed through my head. I felt dizzy, but I only said, "I thought you said it was legal for us to—"

"It *is*," Peter said. "But lots of people won't care what the law says. They'll make judgments about you, about us. And they'll let you know. I've already gotten hate mail over Les."

"You have?" I said, startled. "How? That only happened yesterday."

"People post it on the company's social media pages. I haven't read much of it." Peter let me go and slumped back in his chair. "My lawyers go through it, hoping they'll find some clue to the real killer. It's a lot of 'you're a rich snot who thinks he can buy his way out of trouble' stuff."

I looked guiltily down at my sundae. That was pretty much what Dad and I had said to each other last night... and a small part of me still wondered if it was true. I glanced around uneasily. "Aren't you worried that reporters will recognize us now?"

"Nah. Hat, sunglasses." Peter pointed to his own face. "Besides, they aren't expecting to see me here. And I'm not a movie star or anything. I mean, the average guy on the street wouldn't recognize Bill Gates or Sam Walton."

"Who's Sam Walton?"

"See? He's the guy who owns Walmart. The reporters think I'm at home. A strip-mall ice cream shop isn't on their radar. I've got bigger shit to worry about than random reporters."

I shook my head. Peter lived in a totally different world than me. It wouldn't occur to me to keep a cap and sunglasses in the car as a disguise. It wouldn't even occur to me to have a car.

"You've got one less thing to worry about," I said. "You don't need to worry about your mom and dad finding out about us."

"Kinda," Peter snorted.

It took a minute to make myself brave enough for what came next, but I did it. With a deep breath, I slid my hand across the table toward him. The rough cast iron grazed my fingertips. "How about we try this?"

I took his hand. There, in shade and sunlight on a public sidewalk, I took it.

Peter started to pull away, but I gripped harder. "Don't let go," I whispered. "Just... hold on."

Half a moment passed. I tried to read Peter's eyes, but they were hidden behind the sunglasses. Then Peter squeezed my hand and kept holding it. With his other hand, he went back to eating his sundae. I swallowed once and did the same. People passed by us on the sidewalk, and I flinched, expecting a nasty word or worse.

Nothing happened. Most ignored us. Peter continued to hold my hand, and I held his. A few people flicked their eyes our way, then went straight ahead as though they hadn't seen anything. Nothing to see, nothing to notice. None of their business. It was tremendous and terrifying at the same time. I felt like I might fly away, soar into the bright sky with Peter, both of us weightless as feathers made of air and sunlight.

We sat like that, hand in hand, eating cold ice cream on a hot summer day, hiding from reporters in plain sight, scared about the future and happy with the present, poor rich guy and rich poor kid. Peter and me. Me and Peter. I didn't want it ever to end.

But it finally did. We reached the bottom of our paper sundae cups, and Peter checked his phone for the first time. I suddenly remembered I still had Les's phone in my pocket. After everything that had happened with Emily and Peter's mom, I'd forgotten I'd grabbed it—and that I hadn't told Peter. Now I felt weird about saying anything. After that perfect moment, I didn't want to bring up the murder again. It would just make us both unhappy. Besides, the whole point of the phone was to get rid of it, something Peter hadn't had a chance to do with everyone watching him. But no one was watching me. Later I'd have lots of chances to dump it, and I could surprise Peter by telling him I'd taken care of it for him.

"We've got a couple hours before evening rehearsal," Peter said. "I don't know what to do."

"Let's go to my place," I said. "My dad's working, and we can be alone."

That came out a little different than I'd meant it, but the words were already hanging there between us. We *could* be alone. Peter nodded, and we got into his car.

ACT II: SCENE V

KEVIN

THE TRAILER exhaled hot air and the smell of paper. I flushed as Peter came in behind me. Home was hot, stuffy, and embarrassing, especially after Peter's marble palace, and I suddenly didn't want him here, seeing it again, reminding him this was where losers lived. But he was already inside, acting like I didn't live in a puke pile.

"I like all the books," he said. "Reminds me of Emily's room."

"Thanks," I muttered. "You want something to drink?"

"I'm good." His hands were in his back pockets, and he was examining some of the titles on Dad's junkyard shelves. "Man. John le Carré. Ian Fleming. Alice Walker. Hal Borland. Whoa." He took down a thin book and flipped through it. "*Encyclopedia Brown*. I remember these books from third grade. I don't think I ever figured out a single solution, but I always tried."

I turned on the box fan and tried to crank the windows farther open. The room cooled a little. "Yeah, Dad reads everything. He picked up the habit in… when he was away, and he kept it up after he got back."

"Huh." Peter put the book back. "So."

"So," I agreed and touched his face. It was nice to do that. My boyfriend. He was my boyfriend. I kept coming back to that thought, like a puppy finding the same treat over and over. "How are you holding up?"

"Been a hell of a day," he said with a little laugh.

"Your parents had no idea you're gay?" I said.

"They knew, but they didn't want to admit it, and I didn't want to talk about it. Did yours suspect before you told?"

"I don't think so," I said. "But my mom left like four years ago, and my dad was… gone… so they didn't know me very well."

"Why did your mom leave?" Peter asked.

"Fuck if I know." I dropped onto the couch, and Peter dropped beside me. He was wearing shorts, and his knee rubbed warm against mine. I remembered the last time we sat there, half wrestling, half making out. That was a memory I would keep forever and take out for walks on lonely winter nights. "I sort of want to ask her and sort of don't want to know. In case it was... you know... something I did."

Peter stroked my hair in a way I liked a lot. Every time he touched me, I shivered a little. "You're a sweet guy, Kev. It wasn't anything you did. It was her. Adults are stupid sometimes."

Weirdly, I wanted to defend my mother. She wasn't stupid—I was. But she wasn't here. Most of my memories of her were when she was angry at me or at Dad. How could I miss her or care what she thought about me? But I did. For some reason right then, I remembered sitting in the living room of the little apartment she'd rented after Dad was sent away. A hot bowl of microwaved SpaghettiOs sat in my lap. The bowl was green with a chip in the rim. I ate from that bowl almost every day. I was watching cartoons while Mom was talking on the phone in the kitchen. Gray rain pattered against the windows, but I felt warm and safe with my bowl and my cartoons and my mom in the next room.

Now she was gone. She didn't know I was gay, and she would never know. Screw her.

"Anyway," I said with my leg still pressed against his, "you kinda changed the subject. Your parents didn't really know you were gay? Sure sounded like your mom knew."

His face became sober. "Mom and Dad pretended not to know and hoped the whole thing would go away. I mean, you aren't my first boyfriend."

I sat up straighter. "You told me about that. The older guy. He was a gardener?"

"Gary. Yeah." Peter sheepishly rumpled his hair. "We didn't do more than hang out and kiss a few times. It probably would have gone a lot further. I sure wanted it to. But my mom caught us. The next day he was gone. Mom wouldn't talk about it, and I was too scared to ask." He gave a weird little laugh. "I guess it's not something you talk about with your current boyfriend. You've had boyfriends, haven't you?"

"No." This conversation was getting weirder by the second. My chest constricted again. Peter had kissed other guys besides me. I knew that, but I hadn't *known* it. Not until now. It was easier to pretend there hadn't been anyone else but me, even though he'd talked about dating someone else during Two Truths and a Lie on the very first day of rehearsal.

Maybe that's how Peter's parents felt.

The thought that I had something in common with Peter's mom, the bitch who'd slapped me, creeped worms all over my skin. I wasn't anything like her.

"You're shitting me." Peter turned sideways on the couch and stared at me. "No boyfriend ever?"

I wished he would drop it. "No."

"Jesus." He ran the back of his finger down my cheek, and it made me shiver again. That I liked. God, I was all over the globe. "You're the most gorgeous guy I've ever seen, and you've never had a boyfriend."

That made me feel better—until I saw the bruises on his knuckles. Those hands had smashed Les's face. The memory of skin and bone smacking together echoed like dropped stones on my head, and for a tiny moment, I was swinging my own fists and feet against Robbie, watching his scared face. Hot-and-cold shudders went over me. I tried to push the stony memories aside, but they weighed me down and mingled with thoughts of Peter going to jail. The pressure pushed me deeper into the couch, made me heavier than granite. I was sinking, dropping, falling into the center of the earth.

"You okay?" Peter asked. His voice came from far away.

"Sure," I said, but a long pause followed. My tongue was heavy, and I wanted another gulp of whiskey. Then I got pissed off… I mean *really* pissed off. Anger burned red and scarlet and crimson hot. I slammed my fist on the cushion. "Fuck no. I'm *not* okay!"

Peter jumped a little but didn't move away. I didn't look at him. My jaw was clenched, and I kicked at a pile of books on the floor. They scattered like frightened butterflies. The tiger was roaring in full voice.

"I'm fucking scared, Peter Finn!" I snarled. "I'm scared all the time. No, I'm ball-shriveling terrified. Aren't you scared about going to jail?"

Peter closed his eyes. "Every second. I can't stop thinking about it. Even when I'm onstage, pretending to be Jack, I can't stop thinking about it. Jesus, don't shout at me. I'm freaking out as it is."

Those words cracked me, and the red anger drained out. Mostly. A coal of it still glowed inside, but deep enough that it wouldn't burn Peter. I didn't want to burn Peter.

"Sorry," I said. "I'm just…. Do you think you'll end up in prison? I mean, you're rich, Peter Finn. Can't you… bribe the judge or something? Get him to drop the charges?"

Peter gave a weird bark of a laugh. "Everyone expects that. And man, I've thought about it. My parents talked to the lawyers about it. And if you ever repeat that, I'll deny I said it, no matter how I feel about you. But we can't buy our way out of this one. It's *because* we're so rich."

"You'll have to walk me through that," I said.

"Look," Peter said, "if we were middling rich, nobody would care what happened in a trial. But because we're the Morse family, everyone figures we'll try and buy my innocence, and *that* means a bazillion people will microscope-watch every step of this process. If I go on trial, we won't have a chance to bribe the janitor, let alone the judge."

"Would you do it if you could?"

"Fuck yeah." Peter crossed his arms. "Hand over a pile of money and all this goes away. Wouldn't you?"

It sounded more and more like Peter *had* done it and was forgetting to lie. "I don't have a pile of money to hand over."

"It's unfair." Peter pulled his knees up to his chin. The saggy couch creaked beneath him. "He deserved to die after what he did to you, and now that he's dead, I'm going to prison, even though it wasn't me. Les gets away with another crime."

Or not. God. The whole thing was killing me. Which wasn't the best way to put it.

With a sigh, Peter pulled out his phone and checked it. "Nothing."

"From your parents?" I guessed.

"Yeah. Mom must've told Dad by now, but they haven't texted or called or anything."

"How pissed do you think they are?"

Peter gave that bark-laugh again. "Dad's probably throwing shit against the wall. Mom is walking in circles, waving her arms and trying to come up with a plan. Mom always has to have a plan."

"What kind of plan?"

"I don't know. I'm not there." He sat up straight, and a wild look came into his eyes. "What if they really throw me out forever?"

"That'd be super shitty," I said slowly. "Do you think they would?"

Peter put his head in his hands. "Mom was mad enough to slap you. She could do anything."

It put swiss-cheese holes in my heart to see him that way, and I hurt for him, even though his mom had slapped me. In the short time I'd known him, Peter was always the powerful one—tall and strong and untouchable—but here he sat, small and scared and not knowing what to do next.

"Hey." I put my arm around him. "You've got me, Peter Finn. I know it's not much. Hell, it's nothing. But we're together. Right?"

Peter's head came up. "You're not nothing, Kev. God, I don't know what I'd do without you." He leaned over and kissed me, and all my breath slid away. Would that ever change? I hoped not. "Eleven."

"If your mom has a plan, we should have a plan," I said at last. "Do you have money?"

"Some."

"How much?" I asked this partly out of practicality and partly out of curiosity.

He looked genuinely mystified. "I don't know."

"How do you get ahold of it?" I pressed. "Can your parents stop you from getting it?"

"Oh. I don't…. Let me think." He took out his phone. "I have a debit card for the household account when I need stuff, but there's my own account too. Let me check."

This was clearly something he had never thought about. It was weird—I never had more than a dollar at a time, but Peter had so much he never thought about it. How could you lose track of everything you had?

Peter tapped at his phone and swore. "They've locked me out of the house account," he reported. "And my credit card has been canceled. I can't touch the family money at all."

That made me a little cold inside. "But they haven't cut your phone off," I pointed out.

"Not yet," he agreed. "Does yours still work?"

I reached into my pocket and touched Les's phone by mistake. A little bee sting went through me. For a second I thought about pulling it out and showing it—without Dad there, we could do whatever we wanted with it—but my fingers moved like little robots over to the phone Peter had given me. I didn't want to talk about Les's phone right now. Peter might get pissed off again—this time at *me*—and I didn't want to deal with that right now. It'd be easier to chuck the phone and tell him about it afterward. Better I had it than him, that was for sure, in case the cops got a warrant to search his house.

I pulled out my new phone and texted Peter a heart emoji. The symbol popped up on his screen with a happy little *ping*.

"Still works," I said.

"They probably don't know that I gave it to you yet," he said. His face was growing hard, like setting cement, and I was glad I had kept Les's phone to myself. He didn't need the stress. "Hold on."

I leaned over, trying to see. My stomach clenched for him. "What's wrong now?"

He frowned at the screen as his thumbs moved over it. While he was doing that, I slipped Les's phone out of my pocket and shoved it under the couch.

"I'm checking my own bank account," Peter said. "It's only in my name, and I'm an adult, so—ah-ha! I'm still in. They haven't found a way to touch it."

"How much is in there?"

"Not a lot," Peter said with a grimace.

"How much is not a lot?"

"Couple hundred thou," he said. "Counting the bonds and CDs I got when I turned eighteen."

I couldn't help it. I burst out laughing.

Peter gave me a look. "What's that for?"

"Couple hundred thou," I echoed. "Fuck me."

"Okay, okay." Peter flushed a little. "But you know what I mean."

"I can show you how to live until you turn twenty-one," I promised. "A couple hundred thousand will buy three or four of these trailers and a lot of ramen."

He laughed. "Long as I can have a Quarter Pounder once in a while and internet with gay porn on it."

Silence fell between us. I said, "Uh… what do we do now?"

Peter checked his phone again. "It's an hour before evening rehearsal. When does your dad get home?"

"I dunno. He got a job hanging Sheetrock or something, and they pay him by the hour, so I hope he's out there until sunset."

"Look, if you guys are short, I've got a couple hundred th—" Peter began.

"No." I put my hands up. "It's hard enough to take the phone. Okay? And you paid for the ice cream. I don't…. I can't take money from you. It would be too weird. Like I was a hooker or something. That's what your mom said."

Peter looked like he wanted to argue for a second, then shrugged. "Okay. But can I give you something that's free?"

"What?"

I should have seen it coming. Peter kissed me. The kiss went on for a long time, like Peter was trying to devour me or pull something out of me. My skin was a little sweaty against his in the stuffy trailer, but I didn't care. I let myself mold against him, let the world and its problems fade away for just a while. My insides both melted and swelled, and in that moment, I knew I would be happy forever if I could be with him, and only him. Peter put his arm around my back. His face was a little scratchy, and his breath warm against my face. I sighed inside, lost in him, lost in *us*. This was how life was meant to be.

"Twelve," he whispered.

"Yeah," I said.

Peter slid his other hand over my chest. His touch made me ache and quiver at the same time. He kissed me again, and at the same time, he slid his hand lower, across my ribs and to my stomach. My nerves were on fire. I was aching and ready to break open and scream all at once. I wanted him to keep going, to touch me and grab me and—

And Les was grabbing me and shoving me. His voice came harsh in my ear while pain pierced me. Fear ripped me in half. My heart stopped, and for an awful moment, I couldn't draw breath. I pushed Peter away hard.

"Stop," I said. "You have to stop."

Peter pulled back. The couch creaked again, and it cut loose a little puff of dust. The stupid box fan whirred endlessly in the window. "It's Les, isn't it?"

"Every fucking time," I said. Anger ate the fear away and left fangs behind. "Anytime you and I... do stuff, he pops up like a jack-in-the-box. I can't forget him. What if this happens for the rest of my life? I can't ever.... I won't be able to...." I wanted to destroy something— smash and crash and break. My hands shook.

"I don't know what to do," Peter said. "Maybe you should talk to a therapist or something."

"Talk to a stranger? About this?" My face grew hot at the thought. "You're crazy."

Peter shrugged. "I see a shrink—a counselor—every week."

"You do?" I sat up.

"Yeah. She comes to my house and we talk about stuff."

I blinked. "Like what?"

"Lots of stuff. Emily and my parents, mostly."

"Anything about me in those sessions?"

"I haven't seen her since I met you, so that would be difficult. Maybe you could see her too."

"With what money?" I laughed harshly. "They charge like a billion dollars an hour, and we don't have insurance. Dad's a felon, so we don't get any help from the state." I pointed at him. "And don't you say anything about paying for it."

Peter held up his hands. "Wouldn't dream of it." But he put his hands back down and subtly adjusted himself in his shorts. It made my own equipment tighten again, and even that little bit brought Les pressing in at the edges of my mind. I bit my knuckles to make him stop.

"Hey, look at me, bro," Peter said, and I did. "I'm not Les. I'll never, ever ask you to do something you don't want to do. Everything we do will happen because you say so."

"Yeah?" I said, not wanting to admit how much those words made me want to cry. The anger faded down to a dull-gray coal. "What if I say we go skinny dipping at the golf course in broad daylight?"

"Let me grab a towel."

I moved a little closer to him. "What if I say we get our nipples pierced and we wind the needles up like propellers and let them spin four or five times and the first one to scream has to run naked through the nettle patch behind the trailer?"

"The piercing place down on Franklin Street takes walk-ins."

I moved closer still, close enough to feel the heat in the air between us and smell his skin. Tentatively I touched the hard muscle of his leg. It was the finest thing I'd ever put my hand on. Peter sucked in air but didn't move, not an inch. He was a Peter statue. Was I really doing this? What, exactly, was I doing?

"What if I said we had to cover ourselves in melted cheese and roll around in pine needles in the front yard?"

"My family owns stock in Cheez Whiz," Peter said. His voice was a little hoarse, but he still hadn't moved.

I slid my hand up his thigh under the fabric of his baggy shorts, but I paused when that coppery taste came back to my mouth. Peter sat like a marble god, and I could feel the warm skin and fine hairs on his leg. How much hotness could one guy contain without going Vesuvius? And maybe that wasn't the best metaphor, but from where I was sitting, no others worked better.

With my other hand, I touched his face again—his ears, his cheek, his chin, his lips. He closed his eyes and let out a shuddering sigh. He was shaking a little. I was doing that to him. Still he didn't move. My crotch was tight, but I didn't want him to touch me, not with Les ready to pounce in the background. Right then I just wanted to touch Peter, see what another guy felt like.

I pushed my hand farther up his thigh. He was wearing boxers, and I had a choice between going between or going for broke. Peter's breath stayed tightly controlled.

I lost my nerve and went between. With my other hand, I stroked Peter's hair, soft and black under my palm. Was I really doing this?

My lower hand slid higher, and he gasped, even though I was touching him through his boxers. He was hard, and so was I. My heart jerked around my chest like a bird in a cage. I was really touching another guy! Sort of.

"God," Peter muttered.

"Is it okay?" I asked. He still wasn't moving, but my hand was. I had done this thousands of times to myself, but never to someone else, never with someone whose skin I could smell and whose hair I could touch.

"It's good." Peter's voice was a grunt. "I'll be…."

He gasped, and I yanked my hand away, suddenly scared. For a crumb of a moment, I flickered to Les. Then I was back with Peter. He was trembling and breathing hard, and my hand was damp. I pulled it away.

"Are you okay?" I asked stupidly.

"I'm good." Then he laughed and leaned over to kiss me. "Really good. Thirteen. Or was it fourteen? I think I lost count."

"I don't want to count anymore," I said. "I want them to be infinity."

"Infinity," he agreed. "I think love is like that. There's always more."

"Is that what this is?" I asked. "Love?"

"God, I don't know," Peter said. "I've never been in love before. I've only known you for a few days."

"What's a few days against infinity?"

"Against infinity, everything is just a few days," Peter said. He put his arm around me. My ear was pressed against Peter's side, and I heard his heartbeat. It was fast at first, but slowing. We talked about nothing and everything at the same time. I felt safe.

"You did that," Peter said. "It was all you. How you feeling?"

"A little weird," I admitted. "I've never done anything like that before. Except for… you know. Les said he would always be my first."

Little pervert.

"Les lied," Peter said firmly. "He doesn't count. This does." He leaned down and kissed me again. "Infinity."

"Okay," I said in a small voice. "Infinity." But I didn't really believe it.

ACT II: SCENE VI

KEVIN

THE FIRST part of rehearsal had Peter as Jack onstage with Melissa as Lady Bracknell. Wayne got the rest of us to paint more flats until Iris needed us. Joe and Thad built a staircase out of pale lumber. Their hammers banged as loud as gunshots, and I thought Iris would tell them to stop, but she said it was good concentration practice.

Bang bang bang.

"The stage won't be silent during the show," she said. "The audience will laugh or even applaud. A prop might tip over backstage. A light might explode above you. Someone might trip and fall. You never know what'll happen to distract you behind the scenes," she said.

Bang bang bang.

Peter and Melissa—sorry, Jack and Lady Bracknell—dug into their scene under Iris's watchful eye. The hammers pounded. The rest of us painted with brushes and rollers. But Peter—Jack—kept pulling at the corner of my eye. Damn, he was handsome. And sexy. And my boyfriend. I wanted to tell everyone.

And let them know I was seeing a suspected killer. Who had killed for me. Whose powerful billionaire parents hated me. Shit.

"Watch what you're doing there, bud," said Wayne behind me. "The paint needs to be even."

I jumped and dropped the roller onto the wet flat. Wayne squatted next to me and plucked it from the canvas. Paint flecked his fingers, and his bowling-ball biceps bulged under his sleeves.

"Sorry," he said. "I should've remembered you'd be wound up."

Bang bang bang.

"Remembered?" I said.

"Iris told me you got jumped in the park. Can't blame you for being nervous after something like that." He sloshed the roller through

132

the paint pan and ran it over the canvas. "Smooth and even, like this. We don't want thin spots."

I took the roller back from him. "She told you about that?"

He shrugged. "Was it a secret?"

"I guess it's… not," I said slowly. "I just don't want to talk about it much."

"Sure, sure." Wayne picked up a roller of his own and set to work beside me. "Must've been scary. I'd be pretty pissed off at the guy who did it."

"Yeah," I said, not sure where this was going. I didn't want him to ask for details.

"And now Peter's a suspect in Les's murder," he continued. "That's rough on you."

"Back up," called Iris from the house. "Lady Bracknell, come a step downstage at the previous line and turn."

Bang bang bang.

I froze for a tiny second. My heart jerked sideways, and I couldn't help shooting a zap glance at Peter. Then I kept painting with my chest all tight. "Rough on me?" I repeated. "Why would it be rough on me? I mean, we have a lot of scenes together and stuff, sure, but—"

"But you and him have something going," Wayne interrupted in a voice that carried no farther than the two of us. "Ain't that right?"

"*I have always been of opinion that a man who desires to get married should know either everything or nothing*," said Lady Bracknell. "*Which do you know?*"

I paused with my heart at the back of my throat. "We don't have anything going."

"*I know nothing, Lady Bracknell*," said Jack.

"Sorry. My mistake."

Wayne dipped his roller again. The soft sound it made as it glided over the canvas made my skin itch. I wanted to drop my roller and take off, but that would look like I was hiding something, so I kept on painting without looking at Wayne. Shovel-beard Wayne. Jesus, why would he say something like that? Had he seen us together, like Les had? Was he going to make me do something too? My breath came shorter and faster.

133

Bang bang bang.

"Kid," Wayne said quietly, "don't freak out on me. It's okay. I'm like you."

"*Ah*," said Lady Bracknell. "*Nowadays that is no guarantee of respectability of character.*"

Now my head snapped around. I felt balanced on the head of a pin. "What do you mean you're like me?"

He shrugged again. "I have a boyfriend too."

"You're gay?" The words popped out before I could stop them.

"Sure." A grin split his beard, but he kept his voice low. "There are more of us around than you think, even in this town. Don't you watch TV?"

"I don't…. My dad doesn't have a…. We read a lot at my house," I said lamely.

"*Mr. Worthing, I confess I feel somewhat bewildered by what you have just told me*," said Lady Bracknell.

"Good for you." Wayne glanced pointedly at the others, who were painting and chatting only a few steps away, and set down his roller. "I need a walk. Want to come with? We can talk where it's quieter."

"A walk?" I followed his glance to the others. Overhearing. "Oh. Okay, yeah."

We wandered backstage to the maze of hallways and rooms behind the theater itself—dressing rooms, prop storage, the green room. It was cool and dimly lit, with half the lights out.

Wayne waited until we were out of earshot of everyone else and then said, "I figured you and Peter had something going. The way you look at each other set off my gaydar in a big way."

"Gaydar," I repeated.

He laughed. "You develop an instinct for spotting guys like us after a while. Mine's pretty good."

I felt weird. Was he going to hit on me or something? I flashed on Les—

Bang bang bang.

—and backed away.

"You okay, buddy?" Wayne's face changed. "Oh, hey—I didn't ask you back here to…. Jesus, you're half my age, even if I didn't have a boyfriend. I just figured you might want to talk to someone who's been through it."

My face turned red. "Oh yeah. I wasn't worried." I changed the subject fast. "You said you have a boyfriend?" It was weird asking another guy that question.

"His name is Jake," Wayne said without blushing or stammering. "Our first anniversary is coming up in a couple weeks."

"You're married?" Yeah, I know it's legal for guys like me to get married, and I know there are lots of places where it isn't a big deal. Ringdale isn't one of those places. There was supposed to be a judge at the courthouse who wouldn't marry two men or two women, even though the law said he had to, but no one had sued about it. Not around here.

"He's my boyfriend, not my husband," Wayne said. "We kinda dance around getting married. Maybe we will and maybe we won't."

I imagined me and Peter in tuxedos, standing in front of a minister saying, "I do," while my dad cried into a Kleenex. That was weird too. Online at the library, I'd seen pictures and videos of guys marrying each other, but they always looked like something out of a fairy tale—long ago and far away. It wasn't anything to do with me.

Actually Peter would look really good in a tuxedo.

Bang bang bang.

"Where did you meet?" I asked, and more questions poured out. "How did you know he was gay too? Were you scared? How do you go out? When did you know you were gay?"

Wayne leaned against the wall. "Well, let's see. We met online at a dating site, so that's how I knew he was gay too. He asked *me* out. I was a little nervous the first time we met. That's the way it always is on a first date, right? But when I met him—wow. He was cute! And funny. And smart. With a tight little...." He laughed. "Anyway."

"What else?" I said. It was the first time I'd talked to someone about this besides Peter, and this was different. It was like talking to a big brother who knew a lot about girls. Boys. Whatever.

"We started talking, and coffee turned into dinner, and dinner turned into clubbing. And we've been together ever since."

"Do you have a picture?"

"Sure." He pulled out his cell phone and thumbed through it until he came to a headshot of guy with bright red hair, longish on top and shaved on the sides. He had vivid green eyes, lots of freckles, and a long jaw. A blue sun symbol was tattooed on his chest so it just peeked above the neck of his tank top. He was good-looking. Sort of.

"I have a thing for ginger guys," Wayne said.

"Does your family know?" I asked.

"Well, yeah," he said. "Most of them."

"How'd they handle it? Did you tell them, or did they find out?"

"Iris knew when we were in high school, but I didn't tell my parents until way later. Mom was okay with it. My dad pitched a shit fit. It's why I waited until I was out of the house. He's kind of come around, but we don't talk much these days. I think if Jake and I ever get married, he won't come, you know?" Wayne looked sad. "His loss, I guess."

"I told my dad yesterday," I said.

"Really? Congrats. You're brave. Course, these days, a lot more teens tell their parents. How'd he take it?"

It was a relief to talk about it. I hadn't realized how much I'd been holding in. "He was fine with it. Kinda surprised me. He's met Peter, and he likes him. That surprised me too."

"How'd you and Peter meet? Here at the play?"

"Yeah." I gave him a thumbnail sketch. It was stuff I hadn't even told Dad yet.

"So Peter's your first boyfriend." Wayne sighed theatrically. "First time. You always remember your first."

Les kissed my temple again in my head, and I looked away.

Wayne misread what was happening. "It's gotta be hard with you getting beat up and Peter under suspicion for murder and you just figuring all this gay stuff out, right?"

"Kinda," I said.

Bang bang bang.

"Look," Wayne said, "you said you don't have internet at home, and there's no real gay scene here in Ringdale. It's isolating. I know. I grew up here too. There's a Pride festival down in Detroit. Starts tomorrow. Jake and I are doing a day trip. How about you come with us? You can see the community up close."

I balked. Me at a Pride festival? And it was all the way down in Detroit. I said, "What about the extra rehearsal tomorrow?"

"Your scenes aren't in it," Wayne said. "You're only on in the evening. Peter's onstage all day, though, so he wouldn't be able to come with us."

"He wouldn't be able to anyway," I said. "Not if news cameras are going to be there. But I don't know."

"You're thinking it's all drag queens and leather costumes and dancers," Wayne said with another smile. "It's more like a street fair, with booths and music and lots and lots of the LGBT crowd. You'll meet some cool people—people just like you."

"Oh." I didn't know what to say. It was a big offer, and saying no seemed rude. But it was weird.

"Think about it," Wayne said. "And ask your dad. Do you have a phone?"

"I just got it." I gave him the number, and he sent me a test text.

"Look, no pressure." Wayne held up his hands. "Yes or no is cool. Have your dad call me if it's a yes, and me and Jake will pick you up tomorrow at seven."

"In the morning?" I squawked.

"It's a long drive." Wayne clapped me on the back. "Let me know."

"Algy to the stage!" Iris shouted.

"Your cue, buddy."

Bang bang bang.

I WAS loving theater. I loved the stage. I loved the lights overhead. I loved the smell of paint and wood. I even loved the director shouting at me. And Iris worked us hard.

"Don't lose your accent!"

"Stay in character, even if something goes wrong!"

"Your words say you're an English snob, but your body language says you're an American teenager. Stiffen up. Posture, posture, posture!"

"Stage left is *your* left as you face the audience. And upstage is *that* way—away from me. Do it again."

Peter and I glided and danced our way through the words of Oscar Wilde. I couldn't keep my eyes off Peter, even when I wasn't supposed to look at him, and Iris barked at me about it. Wayne stood offstage with his big arms crossed and waved a finger. I blushed and concentrated harder. My Algy shell spun tighter. For a moment the scuffed black floor, the harsh overhead lights, and the *bang bang bang* of hammers disappeared, and I was standing in the rose garden of a mansion with high windows. Peter was dressed in a long black coat.

"This Bunburying, as you call it, has not been a great success for you," he said and stomped away.

"Good," called a voice.

The moment faded and I was me again, inside my Algy shell. My mouth fell open for a moment, and I clapped it shut. That was awesome. I didn't know theater could do that.

"Line, Algy," Iris said, back where she'd been sitting from the beginning.

Don't break character, no matter what. I kept Algy going and scrambled for the line.

"I think it has been a great success," I said aloud to myself. *"I'm in love with Cecily, and that is everything."*

"Enter Cecily!"

Meg came onstage with a watering can and mimed watering nonexistent roses. She was short and pretty, and I barely knew her. Then I remembered the script said I had to kiss her at the end of the scene. I shot Peter a glance. He had wandered offstage to watch, though Wayne would probably hand him a paint roller in a minute.

"Don't break character, Algy," Iris reminded.

Damn it.

"Remember, Cecily, you're in love with Algy, but you think he's someone else," Iris said.

"Earnest," Meg said. "I know."

Peter looked away.

"Okay," Iris said. "The script doesn't say anything about how to play this scene, so let's try it this way—you two are young kids newly in love. You haven't even kissed yet, but you hate being apart. Jack doesn't like you two being together, remember, so he's trying to send Algy away, and this is an awful moment. But you're still crazy about each other. Awful moment, crazy love. The words in the script don't say that, so you have to punch them up with body language and tone."

"And then you get to kiss," Joe called from the painting area.

"Lucky," said Ray.

Great.

The scene didn't go well. Iris wanted us to be in love, but I couldn't see how lines like "*Your Rector here is, I suppose, thoroughly experienced in the practice of all the rites and ceremonials of the Church?*" could be said like I was in love. It didn't help when I was supposed to say, "*He's gone to order the dog-cart for me*," and I said dog-fart instead. Everyone within hearing died laughing, and it took forever for me and Meg to get back in character.

"I'm not hearing the love, Algy," Iris called for the fourth time. "Look at Cecily."

I did. She looked up at me, and I had to force myself not to squirm. It was hard enough to imagine a short Asian girl in England in the 1800s. I was—Algy was—supposed to love her. But when I read the script, I wanted Algy to run off with Jack. I'll bet Oscar Wilde originally wanted to write it that way. The "About the Author" thing at the back of the script said he was sent to prison for being gay, which pissed me off.

Anyway, I looked at Meg—Cecily. She wore little pink shorts and a low red T-shirt and plastic sandals. Thad had a thing for her. What was *that* like?

"Now think of the greatest thing in your life," Iris said, "whether it's a person or a thing or a hobby. If you love baseball, think of baseball. If you love puppies, think of puppies."

"Hey!" Meg said.

"Run with it," Iris said.

"I don't know what to think about," I complained.

"You'll find something," Iris said. "We have an hour."

Out of the corner of my eye, I saw Peter watching us. Jeez. The answer was obvious. I looked down at Meg and pretended she was Peter.

"That's it!" Iris said. "Perfect! Hold on to that expression. Now— you only have ten seconds before that… dog-cart is leaving. Don't break character. Lean down, kiss her quickly and shyly, and dash out stage left. Go."

I grabbed Meg's face with my upstage hand, took her shoulder with the other, and kissed her quickly. But in my head, I was kissing Peter. Peter, who was handsome and kind and wanted me to be happy. Meg's eyes widened, and she made a little sound. I had time to notice her lips were softer than Peter's. Then I broke free and dashed away like Iris had said.

Meg stared after me for several moments like she'd been smacked on the head with a board. She said, *"What an impetuous boy he is! I like his hair so much."*

"Yes!" Iris whooped.

And everyone else broke into applause.

"Where did you learn to kiss like that?" Melissa asked me offstage. "Jeez, Kevin. You floored her."

"I did?" I glanced at the stage, where Meg-as-Cecily was continuing the scene with Jack's girlfriend, Gwendolen. "She was acting, right?"

"Yeah," Melissa scoffed. "Acting. Meg's good, but she's not *that* good."

"Kevin's talented." Peter wandered up at that moment and clapped me on the back. "He brings it out in everyone else."

"So what did you think about?" Melissa said.

"Think about?"

"Yeah. Iris said to think about something you love so you could look like you love Cecily. You pulled it off. What were you thinking of?"

"Oh. Uh…." I looked at Peter, and right then he knew the answer. His face turned red. I said, "Ice cream. Lots of ice cream."

ACT II: SCENE VII

KEVIN

REHEARSAL ENDED way early, and Iris kicked us out of the theater. "You need a break. I don't want you burning out. Don't study lines either."

"Cast party at my place!" shouted Meg. "Bring suits—we have a pool."

"What about your parents?" asked Krista.

"They won't mind." Meg was already texting. "Long as we don't make a mess. Be there in half an hour."

Everyone scattered, leaving me and Peter in the parking lot. "Should we go?" I asked.

"You got something else to do?" Peter hopped into his car. "Come on."

"I don't have a swimsuit," I objected.

"We'll get a couple." He eased out of the lot. Now that he'd been arrested, Peter drove a lot slower. "I still have *some* money."

My no-money instincts kicked in. "Shouldn't you save that?" I asked. "We already had ice cream today."

"It's just a couple of swimsuits." His face was tight and his mouth was hard. "We'll stop somewhere cheap. Let me do this for us, Kevin."

"Peter, I'm not—"

"Let me do this, dammit!" he snarled.

I shrank away from him. "What the hell?"

"Just do this, Kevin." His knuckles were white on the steering wheel. "Right now I need normal, okay? I'm accused of murder, my parents have disowned me, and I don't know what's happening next. So right now I need to rehearse for a summer play and go to a pool party and buy a fucking swimsuit for my boyfriend. Okay? Can we do that?"

"Sure," I said softly. "We can do that."

He drove for a while, then said, "I'm sorry. I didn't mean to yell. I'm just... I don't...." His voice got thick. "I'm holding it together all during rehearsal, and now it's all coming out. I'm sorry."

"I know." I touched his knee. "It's bad here behind the scenes. Just like Iris said."

He rubbed at his eyes with one hand. "Yeah."

"So... let's get bathing suits with orange palm trees on them or something," I said. "The last thing a couple of gay guys would get."

"What kind of swimsuits would gay guys get?"

"I don't know. Something with tidy little dolphins on them."

Peter snorted. Then he snickered. Finally he laughed harder and harder until he was pounding the steering wheel and the car swerved a little.

"Hey!" I said, clutching the Jesus handle. You know—the handle you grab when you shout *Jesus*!

"Tidy little dolphins," Peter snarked. "Oh my god! Awesome."

"Okay." I laughed with him. "It's cool."

"No matter what, we'll always have the tidy little dolphins," he said with a grin that melted me all the way through.

We looked for suits at a twenty-four-hour SavMart. They didn't have tidy little dolphins, but they did have violent-orange palm trees that gave you a sunburn from looking at them. They were hideous, and we had to get them. Peter also grabbed stuff like a toothbrush and a comb and all that, along with some underwear and a couple of cheap changes of clothes. Neither of us mentioned why he needed these items.

"Did you know Wayne is gay?" I asked as we drove to Meg's house.

"No shit! How did you find that out?"

I gave him a little summary of our conversation. Peter took it in silently. "He said there's a Pride festival near Detroit tomorrow, and...." I hesitated, a little unsure of how Peter would react. Then I thought, what did it matter how Peter reacted? He didn't own me. If I wanted to go somewhere, I could go, right? "He invited me with him and his boyfriend, Jake. To see what it's like."

"Isn't that a little weird?" Peter asked.

"What do you mean, 'weird'?"

"He barely knows you, but he's asking you to a gay event with him."

"With his boyfriend," I said. "And he said himself he's twice as old as I am. He's not going to try anything."

"Hmm." Peter turned a corner.

I fiddled with my new bathing suit. The tag said Made by Slaves in China or something. "You still think it's weird, don't you?"

"I was wishing I could go," Peter said. "But I can't because I have rehearsal, and those Pride things always have reporters at them. 'Come look at the fags!'"

"Is that what it's about?"

He sighed. "No. At least I don't think so. I've never been to one. You should go."

"Really?" I coughed. "I mean, yeah. Why shouldn't I?"

"Why not? Bring me back a souvenir." He grinned again. "And stay away from the kissing booth."

"They have a *kissing* booth?"

"You're totally adorable when you're naive." He rumpled up my hair, and I leaned into his touch. "But text me pictures. If I can't go, I can at least live through you."

MEG'S HOUSE wasn't as big as Peter's, but it was big enough. Was everyone rich but me? I was kind of nervous. The last party I'd been to was the mailbox bash Hank had called. I didn't want to be around beer and stuff again. It only made me think of Robbie.

Music thumped from behind a big privacy fence that surrounded the backyard, and a hand-lettered sign on the gate said Cast Party Come In!!!, so we went in.

It looked like just about everyone was there. Melissa was talking to Meg and Krista while Thad drank a Coke and watched Meg out of the corner of his eye. Even though it was evening, Charlene spread on sunblock. Joe and Ray splashed around in the pool, and I automatically sneaked a look at their builds. Ray was kind of soft, but Joe was kind of hot. There was a relaxed feel around the pool. Michigan summer days are really long, and we had lots of time to swim before sunset. Everything smelled of chlorine water and mellow sunscreen.

Meg waved at us. "Changing rooms are over there."

We changed in a little booth. When Peter undressed, I glanced at what I'd been handling a little while ago. It made me feel fun and funny at the same time. Peter caught me at it and gave a silent grin. Then he elaborately turned his back.

"Unless you want me to watch," he said.

I kind of did and kind of didn't. I changed fast and tapped Peter on the shoulder. When he turned, I gave him a fast kiss and said, "Thanks."

Outside the changing room, Meg called us over. She was wearing a teensy two-piece, and I had to work not to stare. Next to her on the ground was a cooler filled with ice and pop bottles, and one of those giant subs from a takeout place was carved into chunks on an umbrella table. I suddenly realized I was starving.

"Help yourselves," Meg said. "We're not formal in our *Earnest* little family."

I grabbed a sandwich chunk. "Thanks. This is awesome, Meg. I love your house."

"We'll have a megaparty here later," she said, "when we have more time to plan. My parents actually love having people over. They figure if I'm getting into trouble here, I won't get into trouble somewhere else."

"Got that right." A woman with Meg's features but with graying hair came out of the house with two big bags of chips. "I have enough trouble in my life."

Meg elaborately stuck her tongue out at her mom, who tore the chips open and set them on the table.

"Where's your lawyer?" Melissa asked Peter.

Peter cracked open a bottle. "Even lawyers need downtime."

"I thought you weren't supposed to go anywhere without him or something," Melissa said.

"Ducking!" Peter shouted. He grabbed me by the waist, flung me over his shoulder, and jumped into the pool. Water exploded in all directions and went up my nose.

Peter let go and I surfaced, blowing water like a tidy little dolphin.

"You bastard," I said and splashed him.

"Hey!" said Joe, who was caught in the crossfire. He splashed back.

That touched off a water war with me, Peter, Ray, and Joe. At first the girls didn't want to join in, but finally they did, and we all ended up in the pool, even Thad. It was so much fun. I don't swim much, and it was just awesome being with the cast. They laughed and chattered and talked with me. I'd only known them for a little while, but we were already friends. Wow.

I lay on my back and floated a little. For a while I could just be Kevin Devereaux. Not Kevin who was attacked or Kevin who beat up a kid or Kevin the semisecretly gay guy. Just Kevin.

A while later Thad said to Peter, "What's going on with the murder investigation?"

I tensed, and all the fun went out of the cast party. A cloud even went over the sun.

"I'm not supposed to talk about that," Peter said.

"Aw, come on," Thad said. "This is *us*. Who are we going to tell? Are you going to jail?"

"Thad," Melissa said.

"What?" Thad said. "We have to talk about it. What if he has to leave the play?"

"Thad," Charlene said.

"It's okay." Peter hauled himself to the edge of the pool. Water streamed down his back and glistened in the sun. "Look, I didn't kill Les, okay? I'm not lying about that."

"Why were you at Les's apartment?" Thad pressed.

A cold fist punched me in the gut. I hunched down until I was neck deep in the water. "Don't talk about it, Peter. You might get into trouble."

Peter opened his mouth to say something, and the fist in my stomach turned colder. Then he seemed to change his mind. "I really can't talk about it, guys. I wish I could because I'm scared that you don't trust me or like me. But the evidence the cops have is totally circumstantial. They don't have any proof—because there isn't anything to prove. I didn't kill Les. Come on. You guys have been in a dozen plays with me. You *know* me."

"We didn't know you were a Morse," Joe said.

145

Peter kind of laughed. "Okay, you got me there. I kept that back because I didn't want people to think I got cast because my family basically built the Art Center. Not even Iris knew."

"So how rich are you?" Thad asked intently. I wondered at the interest and realized I didn't know all that much about Thad. He and Joe were brothers, and they lived with their mother—I knew that—and Thad had a thing for Meg, but that was about it.

"Being the rich guy is what I'm trying to get away from." Peter kicked some water in Thad's direction, and everyone laughed a little.

"So all you guys have been in plays together before?" I asked to change the subject.

"Pretty much," Melissa said. She looked very pretty—the blonde pool bunny—and it seemed weird she was playing an old lady in the play. "Except Ray. He's new."

Ray waved.

"And you, Kev," Meg added. "This is your first play, right? How come you never auditioned before?"

A lie formed in my head and showed up at the back of my throat. But suddenly I was tired of lying, tired of keeping secrets from people who were supposed to be my actual friends. The truth leaped out ahead of the lie. "I beat up another kid, and my parole officer said I had to get a job or do volunteer work this summer. So I tried out for the play."

A second of silence followed. "No shit?" Ray said.

"No shit," I said.

"Why'd you beat up the kid?" Melissa asked.

Because I had a crush on Hank. Because I hated myself. Because I still can't make myself say the word gay *out loud to you, even now.* Apparently the truth only goes so far.

"Because I was hanging out with some really shitty guys, and I got caught up with them," I said. "It was stupid, and I feel really bad about it. But I met all of you"—*Peter*—"because of it. So that was a good thing, I guess. I never really had friends before."

"What about the shitty guys?" Thad said.

I snorted. "They're by definition shitty. Not friends. They just wanted to fight and get high and break shit. I only hung out with them because… I was mad."

Melissa said, "At who?"

This was turning into a real therapy session. "At everyone. At the world. Is there any more of that sandwich left? I only had a couple bites before dickwad over there threw me into the pool."

"I'm not a dickwad," Peter said airily. "I'm just a dick."

And we went back to swimming and eating and talking and listening to music. I sat at the umbrella table and ate more sandwich and watched Peter—and the other guys, I have to admit. Thad sat down and grabbed a handful of potato chips from the bag, his dark hair damp from the pool. We talked about nothing much for a while.

"So who do you think killed Les?" he asked suddenly. "I mean, if Peter didn't do it."

The question caught me off guard. I'd been concentrating so hard on Peter *not* being the killer that I hadn't really thought about who it really was. "Some guy, I guess," I said. "I don't... didn't... know Les."

Thad crunched another chip. "Did you know he was dealing?"

"Nope."

"Pills. Pot. Meth. He had it all. Found a lot of customers at the Art Center."

"Like who?"

"Lots of people." He threw a glance toward the pool, where a bunch of the cast were still swimming.

"Someone in the play?" I said. "Who? You gotta tell."

"He was all beat up, right? He probably pissed off one of his customers, or maybe the guy he bought his shit from."

"Who supplied him?"

"Hell if I know."

I took a swig of pop. "You tell the police about any of this?"

"The cops?" he scoffed. "They'll arrest you soon as look at you."

"Amen, bro," I said, tilting my bottle toward him. But I still wondered.

A ways after ten, Mrs. Kimura gently kicked us all out. Me and Peter headed for his car. I was still kind of trippy over the awesomeness of the party, and Peter must've noticed.

"You've caught it," he observed as we climbed in.

"Caught what?"

"The theater bug," he said. "You've had your first cast call, your first rehearsal, your first set building, and now your first cast party. And you're loving it."

"Yeah," I said with a smile. "Sometimes I think I could live here."

"Wait'll your first performance," he said. "It's total magic when the house is full of people and you're in costume and makeup and the lights go up and you go out there. Nothing like it."

"Why don't you try it? You know, professionally?"

"Me?" Peter snorted and pulled into the street. "I'm not good enough. It's fun, but I like building stuff. Before the play even started, I was helping Iris with the set design. I want to be an architect."

"You're an awesome actor," I protested.

"Nah. I'm just good. You're the one who could go all the way. All of us have seen it. It's rough breaking into acting. Lots of guys just as cute with just as much talent want in just as bad. But you could do it, Kev. When you walk on that stage, everyone looks. They can't help it. I'm serious."

I was flushing red-hot by now. The compliments were coming fast and furious, and I didn't know how to handle them. "Uh…."

"Say *thanks*," Peter said with that killer grin.

"Thanks," I said with a grin of my own.

Peter turned down good old Six Mile Road. "You know, I hadn't thought about where I was going to stay."

"Yeah," I said slowly. "You know, my dad might let you stay with us. For a while. He turned out to be pretty cool about me being gay. And being with you."

"That wasn't a hint," Peter said. "I didn't mean to—"

"Just shut up and say yes," I interrupted.

Peter thought a moment. "Let me take you home, and we'll talk about it."

Dad was on the couch, the one Peter and I had been messing around on earlier that day. The one that had Les's phone under it. So much kept happening, I never had the chance to dump the stupid thing. Dad was barefoot and reading, like usual. He looked up when we came in.

"Hey, guys. Rehearsal run late?" His tone was super casual, and suddenly I was nervous again.

"Little bit," I said, not quite lying. I didn't want to go into the cast party. Even though there hadn't been any drinking or stuff, Dad might get suspicious anyway because of the shit I used to get into, and we'd get into a fight. "Can I talk to you?"

Dad closed the book. "Is this about the two of you? Kevin told me you two are… dating, or whatever you guys call it, Peter."

"We are, sir," Peter said. "I hope that's okay."

"It's complicated," Dad said seriously. "I mean, you're a Morse, and we're… not."

"*Dad*," I said.

"How old are you?" he said, ignoring me.

"Nineteen, sir."

"A little older than Kevin," he said in a voice you could have bent an I-beam around. "He's technically age of consent, but he's still a minor, and I'm his father."

"Yes, sir," Peter said.

"Are you having sex?" he said bluntly, even though he'd already asked me about that.

"*Dad*!" I said again.

Peter slid his hands into his back pockets. "No, sir."

Was that a lie? *Had* Peter and I had sex? I wasn't sure if what we'd done on the couch counted. What did count?

But Peter wasn't finished. "Can I ask you something, sir?" he said.

"What's that?"

"Would you have brought up that last question if I were a girl?"

Dad thought about that for a second. "I don't understand how it's relevant."

"When people see a guy and a girl holding hands, they think, 'Oh, they must be boyfriend and girlfriend,' or 'They must be married.' But when two guys are holding hands, they think, 'They're having sex.' Isn't that right?"

Dad thought another second. "I guess so." He thought again. "Not really fair, I suppose."

"Yeah," Peter sighed. "It's been an unfair kind of day."

"I just found out my son was gay and that he already has a boyfriend," Dad said. "And *he's* the son of a billionaire and accused of murder. You'll have to give me some time to catch up. At least Kevin is positive you've been falsely accused. I trust his judgment, and I don't trust the police, so you're welcome here."

This was weird, my dad talking to my boyfriend. It was weird enough that I had a boyfriend at all.

"Uh… speaking of that, Dad." I sank to the couch next to him while Peter took up the only chair. "I wanted to ask a couple things."

He took on that narrow look all parents do when they know they're in for an argument. "Like…?"

I decided to start small. Smallish. I told him about Wayne and Jake and the Pride festival. The more I talked, the more my earlier worry about it faded, and the more excited I got. "Can I go? Please? Wayne said it would only be okay if you called him."

"Are you going?" Dad asked Peter.

"I can't," Peter said. "I have rehearsal during the day. Kevin doesn't." He left out the news cameras.

"Please?" I said.

"Kevin, this is… a lot," Dad said slowly. "I just found out about you yesterday, and now you're already asking to go to this Pride parade thing. It's all moving so fast."

"There's no parade," I said. "No parading. Parades are right out. I just want to go and look around."

"Kev—"

Words spilled out, words I didn't know were inside me. "Dad, my whole life I've wondered what it was like to see other people like me. I knew they—we—existed, but never actually knew anybody. Peter's the first one I met, and it was incredible. There's a whole… community out there, and I want to see it so much, see if they're like me. Wayne and Jake will be chaperones, so nothing's going to happen. Please, Dad." I made my biggest, best puppy face at him.

A long moment passed, and then Dad sighed. "What's Wayne's number?"

Yes! I pulled out my cell. "I've got it here."

"What? When did you get a cell phone?"

Shit. "Oh. Uh—"

"I gave it to him," Peter said. "A gift." Then he flashed his most disarming smile. "It's what the Morse family gives instead of flowers and chocolates."

"Oh Jesus," Dad grumbled. He poked at Wayne's number, strode into the kitchen to speak for a few minutes with his back to us, then came back into the living room. "It's not happening," he said flatly.

My heart sank. "What? Why?"

"Because you'll never get up by seven in the morning."

I attacked him, but it turned into a hug. He slapped me on the back, and Peter looked jealous.

"Thanks, Dad. Uh… can I ask something else?"

"Oh god. Hit me." He plopped back onto the couch.

"Peter's parents kind of saw us kiss." I held up my hands. "That's all we did. But now they know Peter's gay. They didn't take it really well. Not like you."

"They freaked?" Dad said to both of us.

"Big-time," I said as Peter nodded. "That's kind of why Peter's here. He didn't just give me a ride home."

"They threw you out?" Dad said incredulously.

"Sort of," Peter said. "My mom yelled at me, and I left, and they cut off my debit card and stuff. I haven't talked to them."

"So… you're asking if Peter can stay here?" Dad hazarded. "Oh, Kev, I don't know."

"Just for a while," I said quickly. "Until—"

A harsh knock banged on the door. Dad sat up and glanced at the clock. It was nearly eleven. "Who the hell?"

Cops? I mouthed at Peter, who paled. But how would they know where Peter was?

Dad strode to the door and yanked it open. On the other side were Mr. and Mrs. Morse.

ACT II: SCENE VIII

KEVIN

"Mom! Dad!" Peter said. "What…? How did you know where I was?"

"There aren't a lot of Devereauxs in Ringdale," Mrs. Morse said. "When you didn't come home from rehearsal, we looked up this address."

"There's also a GPS on the car." Mr. Morse stuck out a hand at Dad. "I'm Scott Morse. This is my wife, Helen. You must be Jerry Devereaux."

I stared hard at Mrs. Morse. Earlier today she had slapped me and thrown Peter out of the house, and now she was coming *here*?

"You got me," Dad said. "Looks like we have stuff to talk about. Do you want to come in?"

I so didn't want them to come in. But they did. Mrs. Morse looked around the trailer and at the book piles with iron eyes. I didn't like her judging where I lived. Who made her queen of the sun?

Dad ushered the Morses to the couch. Peter gingerly took the armchair, and I brought in two kitchen chairs for me and Dad. The box fan whirred in the window, trying to keep things cool, but it was a losing battle with all these people in the trailer.

"So, Scott and Helen," Dad said, and I liked the way he called them by their first names, "where do we start?"

"We're really here to see Peter Finn," said Mrs. Morse.

Mr. Morse coughed. "Helen."

Her face tightened. "And Kevin."

"Me?" I said. "What for?"

She didn't say anything until Mr. Morse touched her arm. At last she said very fast, "I'm sorry about my outburst today. I wasn't thinking, and it was wrong. Please accept my apology."

That caught me off guard. I could tell she didn't really mean any of it and Mr. Morse had probably pushed her, but she still said it. I didn't know how to respond.

"Way to go, Mom," Peter said, but he was clearly still mad.

"What outburst?" Dad asked.

"Apparently Helen and Kevin got into it at our house today," Mr. Morse said. "She said some things, and there was some... behavior on both sides. But she's apologized. I hope that can be the end of it."

"What did *I* do?" I burst out.

"You were engaged in inappropriate activity with my son," Mrs. Morse said tightly.

"Inappropriate how?" Dad asked.

"We were hugging," I said.

"Peter's over eighteen," Dad said. His hands lay flat on his thighs. "I don't know why the two of you are involved here. He can hug who he wants."

"What do you want, Mom?" Peter asked. His face was tight, and I could see he was being pulled in different directions. He was pissed off, but he was scared too. I knew the feeling.

"I—we—want you to come home," said Mrs. Morse.

"You threw me out."

"I did no such thing," Mrs. Morse said. "You left."

"And you canceled my cards. Did you try to get your hooks into my personal bank account too?"

"That's unfair, Peter Finn," said Mr. Morse.

"I could have reported the car stolen," Mrs. Morse said. "I could have shut off your phone."

"Is that supposed to make me feel better? That you have all the power? After you called my boyfriend trailer trash? After you slapped him?"

"Oh Jesus," Mr. Morse muttered.

Dad's head came around. "What's that now?"

My mouth was hard despite Mrs. Morse's earlier apology. "She slapped me in the face, Dad. That was her 'outburst.'"

"You insulted me," she shot back, trying to rally.

Dad leaned forward, his face a quiet thunderstorm. "So you're telling me Kevin called you a couple names, and you *slapped* him? That's assault."

"You would know," said Mrs. Morse.

"What's that supposed to mean?" Dad asked in a low voice.

Two red spots appeared on Mrs. Morse's cheeks now, the same ones I had seen before in Peter's room. "We had our people run a background check. You served time for murder. Kevin is on probation for beating that boy. What kind of people are you getting involved with, Peter Finn?"

Dad's face was red too. "You come into my home and—"

"We're only fighting about this because you don't like me being gay," Peter interrupted. "You can't handle your perfect son being a ho-mo-sex-shul." He drew the word out with a drawl.

"You aren't gay, Peter Finn," said Mr. Morse. "You're just... experimenting. One day you'll meet the right girl, and—"

"You think I haven't tried, Dad?" Peter interrupted again. "You've seen me go out with girls. It doesn't work. But with Kevin... it's different, okay? You can't change it, and I don't *want* to change it."

"You *have* to," Mrs. Morse snapped. "This isn't a good time for any of this. We have the court case to deal with, and god only knows what'll happen there. Detective Malloy has already decided you killed that man, even though our own investigators are—"

"Helen," Mr. Morse said warningly.

She glanced at me and Dad and clamped her mouth shut.

"Look," Dad said, "I know this isn't easy. Shit, it shocked the hell out of me when Kevin dropped the bomb. But Peter's your *son.* Who cares what other people think?"

That made me feel all warm inside.

"Where is this going?" Mr. Morse asked.

I realized he was talking to me. "Where is what going?"

"Your relationship with Peter Finn," he said. "Where's it going? Casual dating? Long-term relationship? Are you getting married? Do you want kids?"

I was swimming in a whirlpool, no control over where the currents yanked me. "I—what?"

"Hey, they've only known each other for a few days," Dad said. "Give them a break."

"You have to come, Peter Finn," Mr. Morse said. "You have to come home, you have to study business, and you have to give up this... stuff."

Peter worked his jaw and looked pointedly away. I wanted to take his hand, but I was sitting on a powder keg, and I was afraid it would explode if I moved.

Then Mrs. Morse smiled a little, cocked her head, and leaned forward. "You know," she said in a sweetie-pie voice, "we're putting up a new facility in Toledo. Big project, lots of workers. They could use a foreman. Very easy to arrange. We can overlook the background check."

Now Dad blinked. "Sorry?"

"Salary. Sick leave. Medical benefits. Moving expenses. And a ten-thousand-dollar signing bonus."

Jesus. I looked at Peter. His face was a white stone.

Dad swallowed hard. He flicked a glance around the shitty little trailer. A foreman's salary. A signing bonus. No background check.

"You move down there. Peter stays up here," Mrs. Morse continued. "Everyone is happy."

Dad stood up. "I think it's time for you both to leave. Thanks for coming by."

"Twenty-thousand-dollar bonus," Mrs. Morse said. "Thirty."

"This isn't an auction." Dad held the door open. "Goodbye."

Mr. and Mrs. Morse headed outside, their expressions flat. Me and Peter got up too. At the last minute Mrs. Morse said, "Emily has been asking for you, Peter Finn."

Peter looked like he'd been gut-punched. He took a step toward the door and started to say something, but then his mother nodded, and I touched his hand. He bit his lower lip and turned his back on the door. Mrs. Morse glared at his back, and then she and Mr. Morse marched off into the night.

Dad shut the door and leaned his head against it for a second. He looked really tired. He had just stood up to Scott and Helen Morse, two of the richest, most powerful people in the country. And he had turned down all that stuff for me. Holy shit.

He turned around, and I gave him a hug then. "Thanks, Dad."

"I won't let them control us," he said hoarsely. "I won't let them control *you*. That's what dads are for, right?"

"Thank you, sir," Peter said.

"Come here." Dad pulled him into the hug too. "It'll work out."

I felt Peter shake a little. "Sure."

Finally we stepped back, all of us blinking hard and pretending we weren't tearing up.

"I guess we've decided Peter is staying here," Dad said.

"Yes!" I said. "Where will—"

"Couch," Dad answered. "And don't forget whatshisname is picking you up at seven tomorrow morning for that Pride-y thing. I can't decide if I should be made father of the year for this or get sent back to prison."

ACT II: SCENE IX

KEVIN

IN THE morning I stumbled out of my room still pulling my shirt on. No one should have to get up at seven a-freakin'-m in summer, no matter how proud they are. Peter was sleeping shirtless on the couch with one arm flung over his eyes and the sheet bunched around his waist. For a long moment, I stared at every inch of smooth skin and etched muscle. Woke me up better than coffee.

Silly idea! I pulled out my new cell phone and posed myself with a huge grin and a thumbs-up while chiseled Peter slept in the background. My first selfie! My first boyfriend pic! Then I took another picture of Peter because he was so damned handsome and I wanted to be able to see him on my cell phone whenever I wanted.

Cell phone. Les's cell phone was still under the couch. I had totally forgotten last night. Even if I remembered, I wouldn't have had a chance to do anything with it. Maybe I could toss it in Detroit, far away from the Ringdale cops. Or when I got back, I could smash it with a hammer, if I could find time alone.

I crouched and tried to feel around under the couch, but Peter stirred and rolled over. I yanked myself away.

"Hey, Kev," he said sleepily.

"Morning, Peter Finn." So much for the phone. I'd get it later.

I touched his black hair, all mussed from sleep. I'd never done that with anyone before, and it was new and exciting and just a little scary, even though we weren't sleeping in the same bed.

"What time is it?" he asked.

"Almost seven. Wayne'll be here soon. Dad has a job hanging Sheetrock today, so he'll be up soon too. Uh… you okay by yourself? There's coffee and bread for toast in the kitchen. I think there's some peanut butter too."

Jeez, we didn't even have decent food for him. He was used to servants bringing him little hors d'oeuvres and sausages, and the best I could offer was stale bread and old coffee.

"I'll be fine." Peter gave me a morning kiss. "Infinity. Text me pictures from the festival."

Gravel crunched outside then. I gave Peter a fast hug. I smelled his skin and touched his hair, and for a moment, I couldn't think how to leave him. So I made myself dash for the door. Peter gave me one more wave as I shut the door, and then he was gone and the world beyond the front stoop was all pain without him.

A sunshine-yellow Jeep Wrangler scooted up the drive and stopped under the pine trees. Wayne got out of the driver's side.

"Hey, Kevin." He waved at me. "I'm glad your dad said you could go. Ready?"

In the passenger seat was the red-haired guy I'd seen on Wayne's phone. He stuck out a broad hand for me to shake. "I'm Jake. Hop in back. You like McDonald's?"

"Sure."

"You be food fairy, then. I have to navigate." Jake brandished his phone.

"Food fairy?" I hopped in back and found two fast-food bags and a tray of drinks on the seat. The Jeep smelled like coffee, sausage, and toasted bread. I hadn't eaten since the sandwich at the party the day before, and suddenly I was starving.

Wayne pulled out of the driveway and headed down the road. The Jeep was a sweet ride, even if the back was cramped. I checked the bags. A pile of greasy egg-and-sausage sandwiches, deep-fried hash browns oozing oil, fakeass blueberry muffins. The perfect breakfast. I handed food around, then did the same with cups of coffee.

"Thank you, food fairy," Jake said around a mouthful of muffin. He tossed a wrapper at me. "Make this disappear."

I laughed a little and stuffed the wrapper in a bag. Jake calling me *fairy* didn't feel like an insult—it was like being accepted into a club.

"So you're the gay boy from Wayne's sister's theater project," Jake said, then to Wayne, "Turn left up here."

"I guess."

"And you scored a boyfriend already. Nice. I didn't get a boyfriend until I was twenty. You got a picture? Wayne says he's cute."

I called up the picture of Peter I'd just taken on my phone and passed it forward.

"Woo-woo!" Jake said, pretending to pant. "Shirtless! You keep hold of him, honey, or I'll steal him away."

"You better not." Wayne thwapped him on the shoulder.

"Ow! My tender flesh!" Jake flinched too dramatically. "You said you don't like the rough stuff."

"Not in front of the kid," Wayne admonished.

"Oh please," Jake laughed. "We're going to a Pride festival with leather boys and drag queens who let it all hang out, and you're worried about a little joke?"

Now I was getting both interested and nervous. "Leather boys?"

"First, ignore my boyfriend. He's harmless and doesn't mean half of what he says," Wayne told me, his eyes on the highway.

"The half I do mean is really fun, though," Jake put in.

"Second," Wayne continued, "we already talked about this. Yes, there will be drag queens and guys in leather, but they're a small part of the crowd. And everyone wears street clothes. Almost everyone."

"Guys in Speedos!" Jake whooped. "Speed up!"

"Eat your muffin," Wayne said.

It took almost two hours. I alternated between dozing in the back seat and talking with the guys. Jake was a little strange. One second he'd be all... flamey and stereotypical gay guy, and the next he'd be serious and masculine. I finally asked him about it.

"Flame on, flame off," he said, snapping his fingers. "Lots of us do it, honey."

Us. Did that mean I had to act that way?

We finally got down to Detroit. I was expecting bombed-out buildings and gun gangs roaming the streets, their pockets bulging with drugs. Instead Jake and his phone guided us through a superconfusing maze of highways to an area where the tall buildings and plazas looked more like New York. We left the car in a giant parking structure and hiked a few blocks down a hot sidewalk. Music blared in the distance, and lots of people milled around ahead of us. Signs all over the place said Detroit Pride and Pride Power and Celebrate Pride Month.

"Here it is," Wayne said. "Your people."

I couldn't quite take it all in. Ringdale was almost all white, and the first thing I noticed about Detroit was the mix of races. There were men and women walking everywhere, not just guys like I had imagined. There were kids too, toddlers and babies in strollers and little kids holding hands with their parents—mom-mom and dad-dad parents. I tried not to stare. What would it be like to have two dads? Hell, what would it be like to have two parents?

And there were straight people too. I knew because some of them wore T-shirts that said stuff like Straight Ally and Not Queer But Here. That surprised me.

And yeah, Wayne was right—most people wore normal shorts and T-shirts and tank tops and baseball caps and tennis shoes. But lots of people didn't. We passed three guys in black leather from head to foot, including jackets, boots, and hats. It was kind of hot out and they must have been roasting, but they didn't seem to care. And another guy wore nothing but a mesh shirt and a Speedo that let you see pretty much everything. His body was incredible. Two older women in bikini tops and harem pants were holding hands, and so were two guys dressed like cowboys. And over there were two guys kissing, and over there were two girls kissing, and over there were two frazzled-looking guys chasing after a little girl in a pink dress who was running away and laughing. It felt strange and forbidden and all out in the open at the same time. It seemed like everyone knew I was there, and they were all staring at me. *Here's the queer kid! Look at the little weirdo!* I half expected a strolling cowboy to ask how long I'd been gay.

Lots of booths sold food—grilled sausage and meat skewers and egg rolls—and tasty smells were everywhere. Wayne bought three cans of pop from a booth and handed them around. I thanked him.

"Drag queen," Jake said, nodding to a big woman in a huge blond wig and a purple dress with spangles on it. That was a man?

"Oh!" Wayne said. "That's Eutha Nasia! She's famous."

She turned, and now that I knew what I was looking at, I could see she was definitely a man underneath. It made my head twist for a second.

"Do you know him?" I asked.

"Her," Wayne said. "And I'm about to. Eutha! Hey, Eutha!"

My face went hot. *Oh my god! Please don't come over here please don't come over here please don't—*

"Darlings," Eutha said as she glided over. She held out a hand, and Wayne kissed it. I shrank into a little ball. Everyone was staring. Wayne introduced himself and Jake.

"I'm a huge fan," Wayne said. "Can I get a picture?"

"Love to, hon." She posed with Wayne while Jake grabbed photos with his phone. When he was done, she asked, "And who's this tender morsel?"

She was talking about me. I wanted the sewer to open up and suck me down.

"This is Kevin," Jake said. "He's just come out, and it's his first Pride Fest."

"Congratulations, darling." Eutha batted giant eyelashes at me. "Welcome to the tribe. How are you loving it?"

"It's only been a few minutes," I mumbled.

"Hm." She held me at arm's length, and I smelled her perfume. "It's a lot easier to be yourself than hide yourself, honey. Take it from a big old queen—life gets better when all your fabulousness comes pouring out. Kiss, kiss, darlings!"

Eutha sauntered away to talk to a thin woman in a tank top and flip flops. The tank top said Don't Assume My Gender. I stared after Eutha for a long moment, the pop can forgotten in my hand.

"I met Eutha Nasia," Wayne sighed, "and totally forgot to get her autograph."

"What's bugging you, Kev?" Jake asked. "Your face is red as a Roma."

I didn't want to say. They'd brought me here, like a puppy to a new home, and I wasn't going to tell them I thought it was weird and bizarre and I just wanted to go home and see Peter. Instead I made myself smile a little. "It's just so new. I don't know how to take it in."

Jake clapped me on the shoulder. "We'll have you queening around in no time."

161

But that was the thing—I didn't *want* to queen around. Or snap my fingers. Or flame on, flame off. If other people wanted to, that was fine, but I didn't want any of it. This was kind of why I hadn't wanted to talk about being gay. Not until I'd met Peter, anyway. I was afraid I'd turn into this.

There was music too. Wayne and Jake took me past three stages where different musical acts were performing. None of them were in drag. One group sang country songs, another sang rock, and one guy in a flannel shirt and jeans did little folk songs and told jokes in between.

"When I was fifteen," the guy said, "my dad asked me, 'Son, are you gay?' I got really scared, but I pulled my courage together and said, 'I am.' And my dad said, 'Your generation has it lucky. I've been stuck in the closet my whole damn life.'"

Everybody laughed but me.

Booths lined the streets and sidewalks too. The big square ones you see at art festivals and stuff. They showcased a church that took gay and lesbian members, motorcycle riders (more leather). Gay Democrats. Gay Republicans. ("Don't understand those," Wayne said.) Free HIV testing, books, magazines called *Out Post Detroit* and *Flame* and *Metra*, LGBT bookstores. There were booths that sold clothes and bumper stickers and hats and magnets and stickers and artwork and sculptures and photographs. Almost everything had a rainbow on it.

One booth was from a Detroit radio station, and they were interviewing people. I avoided that, though Jake strode right up and talked to the reporter. Wayne watched him.

"Man, I got it bad," he remarked.

"Bad?" I said.

"For that boy," Wayne said. "I don't know what I'd do without him. He's funny and smart and cute with a capital *Q*. That the way you feel about Peter?"

"I suppose." It still felt funny talking about it.

"Is he staying at your place?" Wayne continued. "That looked like his car in your driveway."

"Oh. Yeah. He had a fight with his parents, and he's staying with us for a while."

"Was the fight about him being gay too?"

"Kinda, yeah."

He gave me a look. "Still strange talking about this stuff, huh?"

"I've never talked about it with anyone much," I said. "I don't.... It's just weird."

"Yeah. Took me a while too. Jake, now—he's been out and proud since he was younger than you. Got smacked around a lot for it too, but he's never hidden it."

Right then Jake came back and gave Wayne a fast kiss. "They're recording, not live," he said. "Maybe we can catch the show later. I'll be a famous flamer."

Wayne glanced at me as though he was thinking, then said, "Let's head down this way."

As we walked, Wayne bought us hot dogs and chips for lunch from one of the booths, and I thanked him. I was kind of embarrassed that I didn't have money for food, and I hadn't thought to brown bag it.

"Gotta keep the upcoming generation fed," Wayne said gruffly as we neared yet another booth. This one was labeled Affirmations. More rainbows and a table covered with flyers. *Gay Your Way* and *Talking To Your Parents* and *What Jesus Said About Homosexuality*. I picked up that one and flipped it open. The inside was blank. It took me a second to get it.

The booth had a bunch of people inside. Behind the table were an older man and woman, and in the back corner were three kids my age— two girls and a guy. The guy looked Hispanic or Middle-Eastern and was kind of cute. The first girl had short hair streaked with purple. The other girl was heavy, with big soft arms, and she wore a red tank top. They were playing cards. In the corner a box fan was going, which made me think of home.

The woman and man said hello, and they introduced themselves as Ronna and Larry. They made some small talk—were we enjoying the festival, how hard was it to park, that kind of stuff. The Middle-Eastern kid caught my eye and sketched a wave. My stomach flipped, and I felt like I was cheating on Peter.

"Hey," he said. "I'm David," though he pronounced it *Dah-veed*. "That's Sonia"—the purple girl—"and Jess." The tank-top girl.

"Hey," I said uncertainly.

"Are you from around here?" Jess asked over her cards.

"Ringdale. Up north." I held up my right hand with the thumb sticking out and pointed to a spot a little right of center. You do this in Michigan—use your hand as a map to show where you're from. If you turn your left hand sideways, it works with the Upper Peninsula too. People from other states look at you like you're nuts.

"You drove all the way down here for our little party?" David said. "Damn."

"Kinda," I said. "It's my first time at one of these."

Sonia cracked her gum. It was purple too. "We need a fourth player. Sit down and we can play Euchre for real."

She didn't ask if I knew the game. That's because everyone in Michigan knows how to play Euchre. It had been ages since I'd played, and David was getting cuter by the second. I looked at Wayne and Jake.

"Go for it," Wayne said. "You don't have to hang with us geezers all day."

"What?" Jake said. "I thought—"

"We'll text you." Wayne just about shoved Jake out of the booth. "Have fun."

I grabbed a chair. "Deal me in."

"Lesbians against gay boys," Jess said and flipped us the cards.

We ran through a couple hands. I always play careful, never ordering up without at least two trump cards and a right bower—if you don't know what that means, look it up—while David was more willing to run with an ace and an unguarded left.

"Your parents know you're gay?" Jess asked. "I mean, those two guys you were with definitely weren't your dads."

Did everyone lead with that question? "My dad just found out," I said. "He took it pretty good. My boyfriend's parents totally freaked. They kind of kicked him out of the house. He's staying with me and my dad."

They all looked at each other, then laughed and shouted, "Dick kick!"

"Dick kick?" I was kind of pissed off at them for laughing at Peter.

David and Jess traded high fives. "Yeah, man," he said. "When someone's parents kick them out, it's a kick in the dick."

"Even if you don't have a dick," Sonia put in.

"And you gotta laugh," Jess said. "Otherwise you cry. We've all been kicked like fifty times, so we laugh about it. If you cry, they win."

"I hit the motherfuckers back," said Sonia.

"And you laugh afterward," David said. "Who's your boyfriend?"

I felt better. I told them a little about Peter, leaving out the billionaire parents and the murder problem. I even showed them his picture.

"Wow." David whistled. "If you throw him away, can I have him?"

And out of my mouth, from nowhere, came a high-pitched voice like Eutha's. "You couldn't afford him, honey."

A second marched past. I couldn't believe I said that. God, I was turning into Jake! I was such a dumbass.

Then all three of them died laughing. I mean, *died*. They were holding their stomachs and pounding the table. Larry and Ronna glanced at us. People walking past the booth stared. I got sucked into it too. Laughter burbled out of me. Jess whapped me on the back. Sonia swallowed her gum. David ripped a loud one.

"Fag fart!" he shouted, and that set us all going again.

"Hey!" Larry said. "Public face, David."

At last we settled down and went back to playing cards and talking. I took a bunch of pictures and selfies with them. Sonia wanted to study graphic design and get a job at an ad agency, but she didn't know if she'd be able to afford college. "Or maybe I'll draw a comic strip," she said.

Jess played five instruments and worked at a pizza place. "Seriously," she said, "don't *ever* order the sausage special."

David lived with four brothers, a sister, two aunts, and his grandparents. Their house was *never* empty. He didn't know how to make a bed because his mom wouldn't let him. "My family is very traditional. Girls stay home, boys work. I'm thinking about joining the army just to get away."

I told them about trying out for the play and how everything felt like home in the theater. We weren't gay teenagers. We were teenagers who happened to be gay. It was sitting in a living room with instant friends. That was suddenly the most awesome feeling in the world. It was drinking sunlight or dreaming rain.

Outside the booth, four guys in identical red polo shirts jogged past, and two women pushing a stroller laughed at a joke of their own. Music from one of the stages drifted in. I was sitting in a giant living room with all of them. All these people were my friends. My community. They didn't care if I was queeny or not, if my family wanted me or not, or even if I was gay or not. We were all *together*. The feeling rushed over me, powered through me. I wanted to run and sing and laugh and dance and let all the fabulousness come pouring out. No one cared what I was, but everyone cared about me. It was better than the cast party.

My phone buzzed right then with a text from Wayne. Time to meet him. I didn't want to go, but you always have to leave just when the party's most fun.

I gave my card-mates a hug each, and if David's hug was a little longer than the other two, so what? We were family.

A few minutes later I met up with Wayne and Jake, and on impulse, I gave both of them a hug. "Thanks for bringing me," I said.

"You're more chipper," Wayne observed.

"Yeah!" I said. "It's…. I'm not…. I'm all buzzy and shit. It's great!"

"You've been struck by the festival fairy," Jake declared and tapped the top of my head. "Ping! You're one of us now."

"Just in time for us to head out," Wayne said with a glance at his watch.

Something in the crowd caught my eye. "Hold on a sec."

I ran over to where Eutha Nasia was laughing with some guys. On the way I grabbed a Pride flyer from a booth. "Hey, Eutha!"

She turned. "If it isn't that tender young thing I met earlier. What's up, honey?"

"Can I get your autograph?" I held out the flyer to her. "My friend forgot to ask before."

"I'm honored, sweet thing." Eutha signed and drew a big flower under her name. "Enjoying the festival?"

"Absolutely." I took the flyer back. "I'm letting all the fabulousness out."

"I'm thrilled!" She batted her eyelashes at me, and this time I grinned at her. "Kiss, kiss, darling!"

Wayne admired the autograph all the way back to the car.

ACT III: SCENE I

KEVIN

WHEN WAYNE and Jake dropped me off, I thanked them lots, and Wayne reminded me rehearsal started in less than an hour. Jake kissed me on the cheek, and the Jeep sped off.

Dad's truck was gone, but Peter's car was still parked in the driveway, and my heart did a backflip at the sight of it.

Someone had cut the grass. That was usually my job.

Inside, the trailer had been totally cleaned—floor mopped, carpet vacuumed, bookshelves dusted, even the windows washed. Dad and I kept stuff pretty clean, but this was level-one OCD. Peter was in the kitchen unpacking bags of groceries. I kissed him hello, feeling like a husband getting in from the office. It was a real "Honey, I'm home" moment.

"I got your texts," Peter said. "How was it?"

"Weird at first, awesome at the end." I looked through the bags. Full stock of food, more than we ever had in the place at once. "You didn't have to do all this."

"Gotta do something," he said. "Your dad left just after you did, and I had to keep busy, you know?"

I nodded. You're not supposed to let people buy you food when it's your own house, but hell if I was going to turn down a full fridge, clean windows, and a mown lawn.

"Well... thanks," I said awkwardly.

"Keeping my man fed." He put a jar of peanut butter in the cupboard. "Show me more pictures."

We sat on the couch and thumbed through the photos I'd taken of my Euchre friends.

"He's cute," Peter said about David.

"Hey!" I said, even though I'd been thinking the same thing. And then I wondered if Les had thought the same thing about me, and then I started to feel creepy, and my good mood faded away like fabulousness on a hot sidewalk.

Peter had no idea what I was thinking, and he snorted. "Just because we're seeing each other doesn't mean we don't notice other guys. But you're the only one I want to kiss." He did, and out of the blue, I flashed on Les again. "Infinity!"

It was a total reversal. Suddenly I didn't want Peter there. A whole hive of bees was buzzing inside me. I was going to fly in a thousand directions, blasting pain wherever I went. I wanted to be left alone. I wanted to yell and scream and punch and kick. When Peter was there, I couldn't do any of those things.

"What's wrong?" Peter asked. "Is it that remark about David? Look, I'm not—"

"No." I shook my head. "Long day, long drive. Going to my room."

With the door shut, I flopped down on my bed and stared at the picture of Robbie on my nightstand. Did he feel the same way about me that I felt about Les? That made it worse. I was filled with blackness, worthless and broken. I shoved my face into my pillow and yelled and yelled and yelled. I didn't stop until my voice was scratchy and my eyes were sandpaper.

And then Peter was there. He wrapped his arms around me, but I pushed him away. "Don't." I sat up. "I'm not worth it. I'm not worth anything."

"You're worth everything to me," Peter said quietly.

I just sat there, feeling heavy and stupid, but Peter stayed with me until it was time to leave for rehearsal.

That evening at rehearsal, I couldn't get anything right. I flubbed lines. I blew entrances. I wrecked my accent. The beehive was still buzzing angrily inside me, and I couldn't concentrate. Iris looked unhappy, which only made things worse. I was a shitty actor, and I should never have been cast in the first place.

Finally when I screwed up the same left-right move three times in a row, I exploded. "I'm leaving!" I snarled and stormed off the stage. I stomped into the green room. The pop machine glowered at me, reminding me I didn't even have a dollar for a fucking soda. I kicked it and hurt my foot.

"Gonna break something, buddy." Wayne was leaning against the doorframe.

"My whole fucking life," I said with my back to him. Why couldn't he just go away? Why couldn't everyone just go away?

"When I was a kid—and by kid, I mean a little younger than you—I got into some bad shit," Wayne said. "I was mad all the time, and I hurt people. My parents. Iris. My best friend. I wasn't angry at them, even though I acted like it. I was angry because I didn't like who I was."

"You think that's what this is about?" I snapped. "You think you can tell me some nice story about when you were my age, and I'll break down and reveal what's wrong with me?"

Wayne shrugged. "You'll tell me or you won't. But you'll feel better if—"

"I was raped, okay?" I yelled at him. "Les Madigan didn't just attack me in the park. He raped me. He made me into a little pervert, and then he died."

Wayne closed the door and sat on the aging red couch with his hands folded.

"I'm so sorry," he said quietly. "That was a horrible thing he did to you. No one should have to go through that. I'm very sorry."

I'd been expecting shock. I'd been expecting horror. I'd been expecting disgust. I didn't know how to respond to an apology.

"It wasn't your fault," I said after a second.

"I don't think it was my fault," he said. "I don't think it was yours either. I'm sorry this happened to you because it was a crime against you, and I wish it hadn't happened."

I sat on the other end of the couch. My nose was running, and I sniffed hard. Wayne just sat. Finally he said, "Have you told anyone else?"

"Peter," I said.

"Is that why the police think he killed Les?"

"No." I wiped my nose with the back of my hand. "They don't know about me. And you can't tell them."

"I won't." Wayne slid a dollar into the pop machine, pulled a can out, and handed it to me. "Have *you* thought about telling the police?"

"I can't tell the cops," I shot back. The can was cold in my hands. "They'll figure out about me and Peter, and then they'll think Peter killed Les even more, and he didn't. Besides, what would it matter? Les is dead. He can't go to jail or anything. And…."

Wayne waited a second. "And?"

"And I'd have to tell people," I whispered. "Everyone would know what happened to me."

"You didn't do anything bad or shameful," Wayne said. "Les did. It wasn't your fault. It was Les's. But it's your decision what to do."

"I don't *know* what to do," I said helplessly. "It's stupid. I'm stupid."

"Les wanted you to feel stupid and powerless," Wayne said. "Guys like him get off on that shit. But he's dead, and the only power he has is what you give him. If you live in fear and anger, he wins." He paused. "Do you know the Parks Community Center a block over? By the police station?"

"Yeah," I said suspiciously.

"They have counselors who work on a sliding scale. You can see someone for free. And it's totally confidential. No one has to know."

"Counselor won't help me."

"You'd be surprised," Wayne said. "Beats being pissed off all the time and wrecking your acting. I can tell you love theater, but what goes on the behind the scenes affects you onstage. You can't escape it."

"I just want to be alone for a while," I said. "Thanks for the pop. Don't tell anyone."

He got up. "If you do want to talk to someone, you've got my number. I'll go make excuses for you and play Algy for an evening."

After he left, I drank the pop and stared at nothing until Peter came in and said rehearsal was over. He seemed uneasy. I didn't care right then. We rode home without talking.

In the morning Dad was working again, which was great, but the trailer seemed empty. Peter said he was going to find an apartment somewhere. "I can't sleep on your couch forever," he said. I didn't disagree. He asked if I wanted to come with him, but I didn't. Instead I watched videos on my phone most of the day in kind of a dull haze.

Then I remembered Les's phone. A little shock went through me. Peter had cleaned the whole house. Had he seen it? Had Dad? Scared, I searched for it. Peter must not have vacuumed under the couch, because the phone was still there. The broken screen made a dark mirror that cracked my face into a hundred pieces. It was pieces of Les, and I was one of the last guys who had seen him alive.

Another thought—Peter said he'd deleted the video of him and me, but did Les have anything else about me on there? Pictures? Other videos? Had he talked about what he'd done? Taken selfies while he....

I couldn't throw the phone away without knowing. The cops probably weren't watching the phone's GPS every second, right? Besides, Peter said that he put the phone in airplane mode, so no one could see it anyway. I pressed the power switch.

The phone came to life. A little jet plane in the upper corner told me it was still in airplane mode, so I felt safer. I called up the photos and scrolled through them. He didn't have a lot. A bunch of photos of a random cat for some reason. Some more of a really messy apartment—Les's, I supposed. No photos of me. No videos at all.

I let out a long, shaky sigh. I don't know what I'd been expecting or hoping for, but I hadn't found it. Yay?

Then I checked the text messages. A cold spear went through me.

son of a bitch

I hate u

u should die, fuckwad

They all came from different numbers. No names attached to them—just phone numbers.

I shut the phone off. Now what? I had planned to throw the phone away, but now... what if the messages were clues? Or evidence? My mouth was dry. If I wanted to give the phone to the cops, how would I explain that I had it? I could get in trouble—and I was still on probation. I'd land in juvie. I had no idea what to do.

I paced a circle in the tiny living room. The messages might not be clues either. They could just be hate stuff. Or prank texts. Didn't everybody get those? I might turn over the phone and go to juvie for nothing.

Peter still had lawyers too. His family wouldn't let him get convicted of murder, even if they were pissed at him. Come to that, though, his lawyer wasn't following him around anymore. Damn it, why was all this shit getting dumped on me? I didn't know how to decide. Suddenly I wanted my mom, even though I hadn't seen her in years.

I shoved the phone under my mattress. I'd figure out what to do later, when I'd had more time to think.

Three days passed. Things got strained in our little trailer. Dad's under-the-table job ended way sooner than he expected. Other work all dried up, which was weird in the middle of construction season, but what can you do, right? So he was home all the time.

Peter was having trouble finding an apartment—there isn't a lot of stuff to rent in Ringdale because Morse Plastic sucks up almost everything for their temp employees. Ironic. And sometimes the landlords didn't want to rent to him—no murder suspects allowed. Peter tried to keep quiet about it, but I could see it hurt him. So the three of us were in the trailer a lot. I asked Dad if Peter could move into my room instead of sleeping on the couch, but he just stared at me.

"If Peter was your girlfriend, what do you think my answer would be?" he said.

And I had nothing to say to that.

Rehearsals stank. I still couldn't concentrate, though I didn't freak out again. Wayne didn't say anything about what I told him, but I could tell he was thinking about it, so I avoided him. The rest of the cast was screwing up too. Melissa lost her accent completely. Meg giggled whenever she had to kiss me. Thad missed two rehearsals—something about his mom—and Wayne had to fill in for him. Iris wasn't happy. Only Peter didn't seem concerned.

"We're supposed to open in two weeks," I raged on the way home after one really bad night. "We'll never make it, Peter Finn."

"We will," he said.

"How do you know?" I asked. "What makes you so wise?"

"It happens in every single play," Peter said as we turned down my street. His headlights pierced the night, and bugs splattered against the windshield. "There's always a point halfway through where everything becomes a disaster. And then, about a week before opening night, suddenly everything snaps together, and *boom*."

"*Boom?*"

He snapped his fingers. "*Boom*. We have a play. Do you think Jack and Algy have a thing for each other?"

"*Pffff*. Completely." I checked my phone for messages. It was becoming a habit now. "I mean, the only thing the women care about is whether Jack and Algy have money and if their names are really Earnest. Jack and Algy talk about all kinds of shit together. They have fun together, and they argue and make up, just like… like…."

"Like we do?" Peter finished with a smile that was so cute I wanted to put it in amber and keep it forever.

The next day, Peter and me didn't have rehearsal, so he went apartment hunting. He came back a few hours later—no luck. Dad still hadn't found work, so we hung around the trailer playing cards and shit the rest of the day. Peter offered to go out and buy us a TV, but Dad wouldn't let him.

"I can handle a cell phone for Kevin," he said, "but a TV's too much. And you need to save your money, young man."

Just before suppertime, a strange car pulled into the driveway. I got all tense. I didn't feel any better when Mr. Dean, the lawyer, got out. Peter and I exchanged looks, and I could see he was a little panicky too.

"What now?" Dad muttered. He flung the door open and called, "This isn't going to be a good-news visit, so let's get it done."

Mr. Dean said, "First I need to talk to Mr. Morse."

"Yeah?" Peter moved next to Dad in the door, so I had to stand on tiptoe to see over them.

"Your preliminary hearing is scheduled for July eighth at nine at the courthouse," Mr. Dean said from the porch. "The prosecuting attorney will present his evidence so far to the judge. We'll try to refute it and move for the charges to be dismissed. The judge will turn us down. The prosecution will move for your bail to be revoked on the grounds that you're a danger to society and a flight risk. The judge will turn that down too. Then everyone will go home."

"You're still my lawyer, then," Peter said slowly.

"Your parents haven't told me I'm not."

"Is there going to be a trial?" Peter asked.

"We hope not," Mr. Dean said. "It wouldn't go well. The prosecution will paint you as a rich, spoiled brat who committed murder and got away with it. Juries hate spoiled brats."

"Peter isn't spoiled," I said hotly.

"The jury won't see it that way," Mr. Dean said. "Our best hope is that sometime between now and the actual trial, we can find evidence that proves you innocent. Just stay away from the press between now and then, especially about your relationships. This is a deeply conservative town, and if the prosecution can add *gay* to *spoiled brat*, it's over for you."

"I didn't do it," Peter said through tight teeth.

"That doesn't matter in court," Mr. Dean said. "All that matters is what the jury will think of you." Then he handed Dad a thick envelope. "Mr. Devereaux, I'm mainly here representing Scott and Helen Morse. It's come to their attention that you don't own this trailer or the land it occupies. Nor do you pay rent."

Dad hesitated. "That's right. We're housesitting for a buddy of mine."

"I didn't know that," Peter said in my ear. I took his hand.

"This... buddy of yours is one Daniel Treckman, who is currently serving time in Jackson State Prison for assault and armed robbery."

A chill went over me. How much did the Morses know?

"What about it?" Dad said.

"Mr. and Mrs. Morse made Mr. Treckman a generous offer for the land, the trailer, and its contents. He accepted this morning."

The chill turned to ice. I couldn't breathe. Peter's hand became a ghost in mine. Mr. Dean's other words swirled around me in a polar whirlpool.

"You and your son can either vacate the premises within forty-eight hours or sign the lease enclosed in that envelope and agree to pay rent in the amount of one thousand dollars per month."

"A grand a month?" Dad spluttered. "For this hellhole? You're shitting me!"

"Or...," Mr. Dean said.

Peter stepped forward. "Or I can go home and be the good little straight boy, is that it?"

"There's a clause in the lease stating that if Peter Finn Morse vacates the premises and agrees to remain at least one hundred yards away from young Mr. Devereaux at all times, the rent will be forgiven," Mr. Dean said.

Dad said, "You can shove your *forgiven* up your—"

"May I remind you, Mr. Devereaux, that if you do not provide your son with adequate shelter, you violate a number of Health and Human Services regulations. If HHS learns of the problem—and the Morses have instructed me to tell you that HHS will definitely learn of the problem—your son will be removed from your care and placed in a foster home."

Wet cement filled my chest. Air wouldn't move. I staggered backward into the hot living room. Blood thudded in my ears. They wanted to take me away from Dad. They wanted to throw us out. Dad was going to be homeless, and I would have to live with strangers.

"Is this why I can't find work?" Dad's voice was sandpaper. "Did those two kill my name around town?"

"I'm not able to comment on that," said Mr. Dean.

Peter's face was white. "Leave, Mr. Dean."

"Mrs. Morse also wanted me to repeat that her earlier offer of a foreman position in Toledo is still open," Mr. Dean said. "You have forty-eight hours to decide."

He got into his car and drove away.

"Jesus." Dad dropped the envelope on the table and sank to the couch. "Jesus."

Peter was already on his phone. "Dad? What the *hell*? You think screwing up Kevin's life will make me come home?" Silence. "Don't lie, Dad. If you really cared about Kevin and his dad, you'd offer him a job here, not down in Toledo." Silence. "No. I'm leaving their house right now. I'll stay in a hotel until I can find a—what?" Silence. "Then I'll commute from Vine City. Even you can't rent every apartment in Michigan. And if you ever say anything to Mr. Devereaux about rent, I'll go straight to the networks and tell them all about myself. I'll tell them you threw me out of the house, and I'll tell them you stole my money." Silence. "You can do that, Dad, but it's like you always told me, 'If you're explaining, you're losing.'" Silence, longer this time. "Then take the company public, Dad. Look, I'm not talking about this now. Leave Kevin and his dad alone." He hung up.

"Jesus," Dad said again from the couch.

"I think I fixed it so they won't throw you out," Peter said slowly. "But I need to leave. I'll get a room somewhere until I can get an apartment."

"Peter Finn," I said, "you don't have to—"

"Yeah," Dad interrupted. "He kinda does."

I turned, surprised. "What?"

"I can't lose you, Kevin." Dad wouldn't look at me. "You know how many times I've waited for HHS to knock on that door? Every time I can't put enough food on the table, I worry they'll take you away from me. Every time I sign that damned free lunch form for school, I worry. Every time you go outside with knots in your shoelaces, I worry. I'm a felon out on parole. You have any idea how easy it would be for them to decide I can't be a dad? Especially if the all-powerful Morses tell them I can't?"

His words punched me in the gut with cold fists. I dropped into the chair, my throat thick and heavy, suddenly too tired to fight. "What about *Earnest*? I have to stay in the play because of probation. And you have the lead, Peter Finn. You can't drop out now."

He knelt next to the chair and put his arm around me. "I'm not dropping out."

"Mr. Dean said you had to stay a hundred yards away from me—"

"One thing I learned from being around lawyers all the time is that everything is negotiable," Peter said, "including the name at the bottom of the contract. Don't sign that lease, Mr. Devereaux. You've got legal rights as a squatter, actually."

"Until I leave the trailer," Dad said. "Then your parents can swoop in and change the locks."

"I'll go home and talk to them," Peter said. "I have to check on my sister anyway. Don't sign the lease and don't move out. If worse comes to worst, I'll pay the rent."

"Peter, I can't accept—" Dad began.

"Yes, you can," Peter said. "This is my fault, and you can let me help. Unless you've got some gold buried in the backyard."

"Don't I wish."

"They're going to pull more rug out from under you if you don't do what they want, Peter Finn," I said. "They'll take the car away—"

"I'll buy another one."

"And your phone."

"Phones are cheap."

"And your lawyer," I finished dully. "What if they cut loose your legal people?"

That stopped him. He thought a long minute. "They wouldn't do that," he said at last. "I think. It would tarnish the Morse name and hurt the company if I went to jail. Look, I have to go. I'll see you at rehearsal tomorrow. Text me."

He packed up his stuff and left, leaving a swallowing darkness behind.

"Hate to say it," Dad said after his car was gone, "but he is kind of spoiled."

I rounded on him, angry now. "What do you mean?"

"His parents throw him out, but he still figures on having money and a lawyer," Dad said. "It's a little setback. So inconvenient, looking for a hotel and buying a new phone. You and me? We're on the street. Our family broken up."

Hot anger made my eyes scratchy. "Being accused of murder isn't just a setback."

"When his parents get angry at him, they take it out on *us*, Kevin," he said, "not on him. The Morses don't care who they hurt, and Peter's a Morse. He'll hurt us too. He might not mean to, but he will."

"He *left*, Dad. He left to protect me. Us."

"I know. But he didn't say he'd stop seeing you. If he really wanted to protect you, he'd—"

"Shut up!" I bolted to my room, slammed the door, and hurled myself onto my bed. I wasn't going to cry.

Robbie stared at me from his picture frame. I drew back a fist to smash the stupid thing but then made myself stop. Carefully I rolled over to face the wall and lay there. Peter was gone. I might not see him again.

If I didn't have Peter, why had I told anyone I was gay? All that pain for nothing.

Jesus, this was messed-up. Peter was still in trouble with the cops, and his parents were coming after me and Dad. I was still on probation after, and Les had… had….

Shit. I'd said the word to Wayne, but I didn't want to think it. My eyes were still dry and scratchy. I was such a loser. Nothing. Nobody would want me. That was why Peter had really left—he couldn't stand being with someone who'd been wrecked and ruined.

Dad left me alone, and when I dragged out of bed in the morning, the living room smelled like stale whiskey. I looked in the kitchen wastebasket. The empty bottle lay at the bottom. It had been more than half-full when he'd given me some a few days before. Jesus.

Feeling worse, I tiptoed into Dad's room. It was dog hot in there, but he was snoring hard on his bed. The whiskey smell was strong in here, too, but mixed with a nasty kind of sweat. I stood under a rock of guilt, and last night's anger faded beneath it. It was me. I'd pushed him into drinking like that. Did Dad still have the nightmares about that guy he had punched going over the edge? I hadn't thought about that. He was scared of losing me, and I—

I couldn't think how I'd handle it if I lost him. Last night I'd been so freaked at Peter leaving and what Dad had said that I hadn't thought too much about being taken away from him. The idea stole my breath and tightened my skin. I'd already lost Mom, and Dad… Dad had helped me, even when I was shitty to him. And he hugged me when I said I was gay while Peter's mom had chased him out of the house. He let me go to Pride Fest while Peter's parents made him hide from it. And he let Peter stay here with us and stood up to Detective Malloy for me. Peter had his lawyers, but I had Dad. Which one of us had it better?

I watched him sleep. God, when was the last time I'd told Dad I loved him? I couldn't remember. What a shit. I'd been mad at Dad for leaving me, but that was before I knew about his nightmares and how scared he was about losing me.

Les had hurt me, and I had tried to keep that to myself, but how could I keep it now? Les was hurting Dad. He was hurting Peter. He was hurting everyone.

Maybe I could stop it. If I was brave enough.

Les laughed at me in my head. *Little pervert. You like it. You love it. You won't ever tell.*

Dad shifted in his sleep. I slipped out and went back to my own room, where I paced up and down. *You won't ever tell.* I'd already told Peter. And Wayne. What was one more person?

I got Les's phone from under my mattress and called up the text messages again.

son of a bitch

I hate u

u should die, fuckwad

These could point the police toward other people, toward the real killer, and I was holding on to them because I was afraid of telling what Les had done to me.

Well, yeah. Telling Peter about it had set off everything bad. If I had kept my mouth shut, Peter would never have gone to Les's house and beaten him up. No one would have seen him or his car, and the cops wouldn't have found bruises on his hands. Telling was a disaster, a coward's way out.

You told Wayne, said another little voice.

But he was like me. He wouldn't tell anyone else. And I hadn't meant to tell him. It had just happened. Now I would have to tell someone who didn't like me.

I started to sweat, and my stomach twisted into a knot. Oh god, I was going to throw up. I ran to the bathroom and stood over the toilet, breathing deep and trying to hold my stomach down.

Little pervert.

At last my stomach stayed put. I splashed some cold water on my face and stared into the mirror. My reflection was pale.

You won't ever tell.

No. No, I wouldn't. I couldn't handle facing everyone after they knew how filthy I was.

But again I thought about Dad. How much this was hurting him. What would happen to us if this went on? Dad had been brave for me, and now I needed to be brave for him. I *would* be brave for him.

I marched into the kitchen and scribbled a note to Dad. *Out for a bike ride.* Then I hopped on my bike with Les's phone heavy in my pocket and pedaled away.

ACT III: SCENE II

KEVIN

THE LOBBY at the Ringdale Police Station had cranked up the AC, and the marble floor sucked the heat out of my bones as the automatic door whooshed shut behind me. My teeth chattered a little, but it wasn't from the chill. The sergeant on the other side of the bulletproof glass gave me an eye. I didn't recognize him, and I had no idea if that was good or bad.

"Help you?" the sergeant asked.

"Uh… maybe." I had to work to make the words come out. "Is Detective Malloy here? I need to talk to her. About a case."

"Your name?"

I gave it. He picked up the phone and told me to have a seat like I was at the dentist's office. I sat on a plastic bench and stared down at the knots in my shoelaces. Would Detective Malloy notice them and use them to take me away from Dad? I'd run away first. I'd—

"Kevin?"

Detective Malloy was standing in an open door. I swallowed, nodded, and stood up. My heart was beating hard, but it was heavy too. I needed to go to the bathroom.

"Come on back," she said.

I followed her into an area with a bunch of desks and computers. It was the same place I'd been taken in the spring when I was arrested for beating up Robbie, and both times I'd wanted to climb on my bike and bolt for the Rocky Mountains. Last time the handcuffs on my wrists had kept me from doing that. This time I stayed because of something stronger than steel.

The big room hadn't changed. Most of the desks were taken up by men and women typing, some in uniform, some not. A few had nonpolice people sitting near them. Most of those people wore handcuffs.

I tried not to look at them, but the cuffs made me feel sick. Phones rang, keys clicked, and voices chattered. Smells of stale coffee and burned microwave popcorn hung in the air, and harsh overhead lights glared down at us.

"Have a seat," Malloy said beside what I figured was her own desk. "Can I get you something? Water? Can of pop?"

I shook my head and sat down while she took up a squeaky chair at the computer. She wore a sharp blue suit jacket with a crisp red T-shirt under it, and her hair was pulled into a french braid like it had been before. My heart beat faster. This was the detective who had arrested Peter and interrogated me. She didn't like me. She thought I was trash. I *was* trash.

"The sergeant said you wanted to talk to me about a case," she said expectantly. "Is it the Les Madigan case?"

I nodded. My words had gone away. I was a mouse in a roomful of slit-eyed cats.

"Shoot, then," she said. "What do you have for me?"

I started to speak, then stopped. Fear clutched me in a fist of ice and squeezed all the words out of me. I couldn't think of Peter or Dad or anything except getting out of there.

Little pervert.

Detective Malloy must have noticed. She said, "If someone is scaring you, Kevin, we can go somewhere more private. We can protect you. It's what we do."

"You can't protect me from this," I said in a small voice. "It already happened."

"What happened, Kevin? Did someone hurt you?" Her voice was full of sympathy now, and it almost broke me. Stupidass tears gathered behind my eyes. I didn't want to do that there... or anywhere. Instead I pulled the phone from my pocket and set it on the desk in front of her.

"Here," I said.

She didn't touch it. "What is it?"

"It's Les Madigan's cell phone."

Detective Malloy reached into her desk, pulled on a pair of latex gloves, and picked up the phone. "Where did you get this? It's okay, Kevin. I'm not going to arrest you. You can say."

I stared down at my knotted laces again, fighting for words.

Little pervert.

But I had to help Dad.

"A couple nights before Les was killed," I hunched over, and my words were slow as quicksand, "I was on my way home after rehearsal, and I stopped in the park by the golf course. But Les was there too. He followed me. He grabbed me and he… he…." Hot tears dripped from my eyes, straight down onto those stupid laces. I gasped for air. "He…."

"Kevin," Malloy said. "Did Les Madigan sexually assault you?"

I stared at my damp laces a moment longer.

You won't tell.

For Dad.

"Yes," I whispered.

A small pause. Then just like Wayne, Detective Malloy said, "I'm so sorry."

I wiped at my eyes with the back of my hand, and a pink Kleenex appeared in my line of vision. I looked up. Malloy was handing it to me. I took it and blew my nose.

"It was brave of you to come down here and tell me that," Malloy said. "Really brave. You should be proud of your courage."

I just shook my head. I felt a little better. I had told a stranger and hadn't died. But I still didn't know what was going to happen.

"Have you told anyone else, honey?" Malloy continued.

"No," I said. "Well, yes. Sort of."

"Who have you told?" Her voice was always quiet and gentle, like she was talking to a rabbit that might bolt away any second.

"Yesterday I told Wayne. He's the new stage manager at the play. And I told Peter Finn."

"Peter Morse," Malloy said.

I took a shaky breath. "Yeah."

"Was that before or after Les died?"

"Just before. He got really mad and went over to Les's apartment. That's why that lady saw him over there."

Malloy nodded. "Did Peter beat Les up?"

I was freaking out and scared, but I wasn't going to answer that one. "I wasn't there, so I can't say."

"Why did Peter get so mad when you told him?" Malloy pressed. "I thought you two barely knew each other."

"We didn't," I stammered. "I mean, we didn't then, but now we... we're...."

"Is Peter your boyfriend, then?" Malloy said.

Jesus. "You can't tell anyone," I blurted. "His family—"

"They don't know."

"They know. It's just... they don't like it, and they're being shitty about it."

"I see." She was scribbling in a notebook. "Where did you get the phone, Kevin?"

Here I lied. I didn't want Peter to get into any more trouble than he already was. "Les dropped it when he attacked me, and I found it. I kept it."

"Why?"

I shrugged, but my heart was pounding now. "I don't know. I was mad at him, I guess."

"Understandable." She dropped the phone into a plastic evidence bag, sealed it, and scrawled something across the top.

"Am I in trouble?" I couldn't help asking.

"No, honey," she said. "No trouble. You absolutely did the right thing."

A chunk of relief hit me then, and some of the tension faded. I felt limp.

Malloy added, "But why did you decide to bring this in now?"

"I had it for a long time, but couldn't make myself touch it," I said. "Then I read the text messages on it, and I thought they might help."

"Text messages?"

"I guess some people were mad at him and they sent him hate texts. I thought they might help you investigate more suspects."

"Did the texts have names on them?"

I shook my head. She still thought Peter was the killer. It wasn't the way this was supposed to work. "It just shows phone numbers. But you can trace that, right?" I got more desperate. "Look, Peter F—Peter didn't kill Les. He didn't."

"How do you know that, Kevin?" she asked quietly.

"Peter wouldn't do that." Suddenly I couldn't seem to stop talking. "The day after Les died, I was at Peter's house, and I touched his hands. They were so big—way bigger than mine, I remember that—and they had bruises on them like you noticed, but that doesn't mean Peter killed him. It's not proof."

"Kevin, we can't—" Malloy stiffened, and for a second I thought I was in trouble after all. "Oh my god." She snatched up her notebook and flipped pages. "Oh my god. Say that again."

"That doesn't mean Peter killed him?" I said, mystified.

"No, before that. About his hands."

"Uh… I touched his hands, and they were way bigger than mine." What was she talking about?

"Oh my god," she said a third time, and she could barely sit still. "Kevin, where is Peter now? Do you know?"

"No. He said he was going to have to get a hotel room, but he was going to check on his sister, so he might be home or he might not," I said.

"I'll find him. Kevin. This helps a lot."

I was confused. "What? How? You know Peter didn't do it?"

"I have to do more checking," she said, getting herself under control. "Listen to me, now. Have you told your father about what Les did to you?"

The chill came back. "No. Are you going to tell him?"

"Not if you don't want me to. I'll tell him if you like. If you don't, I won't say anything."

More relief. But I shook my head. "I don't know."

She rummaged around in her desk and handed me a card. "Normally I'd ask if you wanted to press charges against Les. That's not a question anymore. But this is the contact information for a counselor at the community center up the block. She works with sexual assault survivors just like you. They don't charge if you can't afford it. We can call her now, together, if you want. Would you like that?"

I shrugged. "I'm okay."

"It's up to you, honey." Malloy paused. "I know how hard this is. I've been through it too."

"You have?" I wasn't sure what she meant.

"When I was at the academy," she said matter-of-factly. "No need for a lot of detail, but a guy I knew got me in a bad situation, and he raped me. I was too scared and upset to say anything, and he got away with it."

Whoa. I eyed her carefully. She was a tough detective, and she had let this happen to her?

Yeah. And I had "let" Les happen to me. Shit.

"What happened?" I asked.

"It took me a long time to say anything about it to anyone," she said. "I was sad and mad a lot. My performance at the academy suffered. I almost had to drop out. Finally I talked to a counselor, and she helped me. I learned that I felt ashamed of it, like it was my fault, and it took me a while to understand that it wasn't my fault and I'm not a bad person because of what some asshole did to me."

That cracked a smile from me. I looked at the card in my hand. It was for the same place Wayne had told me about.

"I have to go." Malloy stood up. "Are you going to be okay for now?"

"Yeah." I stuffed the card into my pocket.

Malloy told me to call her anytime if I had something else to tell her. Then she escorted me outside into sunlight, touched my arm, and left. A few seconds later, I saw her drive away in a regular car.

I DIDN'T call the counselor. Instead I called Peter. He didn't answer, and I was kind of worried and got more worried while I rode home. What if I hadn't done the right thing? I played my conversation with Detective Malloy over in my head, and with a chill, I realized I had basically told her Peter had beat up Les, even though I said I hadn't seen it. Did that give more evidence against him? She hadn't said Peter was going to be okay. My breath came in short gasps, and I had to stop my bike to get myself under control. What if I had just sent Peter to jail?

When I got home, Dad was gone. He'd left a note at the bottom of mine saying he was going to look for work in Vine City. Unspoken message—maybe the Morses hadn't killed him off over there. The fat envelope Mr. Dean had delivered lay open on the kitchen table, and papers were spread all over. I leafed through them. The lease. The job offer. They sat on the table like leaves of poison ivy. I couldn't think about them.

I tried Peter again. Nothing. I texted him. Nothing.

An hour went by, then two. I made some lunch. Peter had bought lots of ramen, mostly as a joke, I think, but it made me think of him. Maybe I should call his house. Yeah, like his parents would talk to me. Maybe one of the help guys would, though.

The ramen bowl grew cold, and I pushed it away, not as hungry as I thought.

I got out my script to go over my lines, but they kept falling out of my head. Eventually I slammed the script shut and went out for a bike ride, just for something to do.

Some big puffy clouds had rolled in to give us shade, and the heat had let up a little. The air smelled like dry grass and warm asphalt. I passed shambling houses and overgrown fields. Only a few cars coasted past me on these back roads. My legs were a little sore from the ride to the police station, and I grimaced. I'd gotten used to Peter driving me to rehearsal, and I was out of shape. How did Peter look so good if he drove everywhere? He never talked about working out. Maybe he was one of those lucky bastards who got a cut body without doing a thing. Me, I rode hundreds of miles a week and still looked like a stick. But I liked riding my bike. Even if I got car someday, I'd keep riding my bike, especially in summer.

A green SUV came toward me. It wobbled a little in its lane and slid over the dividing line. I gave it a wary eye. Lots of people don't watch for bikes when they drive, and they don't give a shit about anything without at least four wheels. This bozo might be on his phone or yelling at his kids in the back seat or even jacking off, for all I knew. I moved over into the grass, which dragged on my tires. The SUV came closer, then moved back into its own lane just as it reached me. It passed without a problem.

Should I call the lady on the card? I still didn't know. The thought of sitting on a couch and talking about Les for an hour made my stomach churn with salt and ice. Talking about it with Detective Malloy had wiped me out, and I'd only talked to her for a few minutes. What would talking to a counselor do to me? No. Just no.

By the time I was almost home, a line of warm sweat was creeping down my forehead. The air was growing more oppressive, the clouds getting thicker. We were probably in for a thunderstorm.

Why hadn't I heard from Peter? And why had Malloy gotten so excited when I mentioned Peter's hands? I wondered if Peter had found an apartment, and I was starting to get pissed off. What was the point of him giving me a cell phone if he didn't use it?

Maybe I should text him again. I touched my pocket, but it was empty. I'd left my cell phone on the kitchen table. *Shit!* What if he'd called me while I was out? I gunned it toward home.

An engine noise was growing behind me, and I threw a glance over my shoulder. That green SUV was coming up behind me again. What the hell? It wasn't weaving, but it still made me nervous. My driveway was only a handful of yards away, so I went for it.

The SUV sped up. Its headlights stared at me like hard silver stones, and the tires whooshed ahead and ate up the pavement. I couldn't see who was driving. My heart pounded. I tried to tell myself it was nothing—just someone running to the store and back or something like that. But it looked a lot like that SUV was coming straight for me. A little voice inside shouted at me to dive into the ditch. But how would it look to that driver if some random kid on a bike leaped away when he passed? I pumped it and pushed for all I was worth.

The SUV was really close—maybe ten yards. I could hear the gear changes in the engine. The driveway was only a few feet ahead of me. I tore around the turn into my own yard, and my bike nearly went out from under me. The SUV cruised past the driveway, serene as a nursing-home parade float. It disappeared past the pine trees that cupped our yard. I stood there for a moment to let my heart slow down. Jesus, was I going to be scared of every damn thing for the rest of my life?

I leaned my bike against the trailer and was heading inside to check my phone when gravel crunched in the driveway. I turned around, nervous and relieved at the same time. Dad was home, and maybe he knew something.

The big green SUV was pulling in. A tight chill ran down my spine. I backed up to the trailer steps and flicked a glance to the trees. I could run for it. The SUV couldn't make it between the trunks. I could—

The driver door opened. It hung there like a loose tooth, and the space behind it gaped dark and angry. Something moved inside, and for a cold moment I was sure Les Madigan would lurch out, leering at me with a sick, wide smile. *Ha, ha! I'm not dead. Come here, you little shit, and show me how glad you are to see me.*

Thad Creeker hopped down. All the tension burst out of me in a rush, leaving me light-headed. It was had-a-thing-for-Meg Thad. Not some weirdo. And not Les. I breathed out a sigh of feathers and lead.

"Hey, Thad," I said.

Thad saluted me from the nose but didn't say anything right away. That was weird. We had a couple-three scenes together, but we weren't close friends, though we'd talked at the pool party a little. He'd asked about the murder case and told me Les used to deal drugs.

Maybe I should have told that to Detective Malloy. I totally forgot.

Thad walked toward the porch. His face was tight and pale beneath messy sandy hair. Was something wrong at rehearsal? With Peter? A little stab went through me.

"Is something going on?" I asked him.

"Oh good," Thad said. "I got the right place."

"If you're looking for me, yeah." I rubbed my face. "Was that you driving past before when I was riding my bike? You kinda freaked me out."

"Sorry. I was looking for your place, but it's hard to follow the GPS, and I saw you riding your bike, but I couldn't turn around and shit."

"Okay." Still weird. A thought struck me. "I didn't know you were old enough to drive."

Thad glanced at the SUV. "I have my permit. Mom lets me drive. Sometimes I have to when she…. Well, sometimes I have to. You got a minute?"

"Uh, sure. What's up?" I was dying to check my phone, but he looked unhappy.

"You probably heard about what just happened to Peter."

Another cold stab. My knees wobbled and I had to grab the stair railing. "No. I've been trying to call him, but he—"

Thad reached the steps. "The cops dropped all the charges against him."

The words breezed past me so fast I didn't understand them at first. I stared at Thad for a second, and my fingers went white around the rail. "What?" I managed.

"Yeah. They dropped the charges. He's cleared."

"Oh my god." I threw both fists to the sky as a wave of pure joy swirled through me. I could have leaped to the clouds and pulled stars from the sky. "Yes! Yes! Jesus, yes!" Then I remembered I wasn't supposed to be that close to Peter, so I made myself calm down. Still, the huge grin wouldn't leave my face.

"That's fucking awesome," I said. "How?"

Thad's face remained stoic. "I guess it was his hands. That detective lady realized that the bruises around Les's neck where he was choked were smaller than Peter's hands, so he couldn't have done it."

I touched his hands, and they were way bigger than mine.

Oh wow. That was why Malloy had gotten so excited. It wasn't the phone—it was what I said. I'd given her what she needed to realize it couldn't be Peter. Yes! I wanted to hug someone, but I didn't think Thad was a great choice. Where the hell was Peter? Why hadn't he called me?

"Yeah, so, the detective investigated some other stuff," Thad said. "They found texts on Les's phone and they looked at the drugs he was selling."

And suddenly I remembered the conversation we'd had at the pool. A splash of cold water went over me. The interest Thad had shown in the murder case. The way he kept asking who the killer might be if it wasn't Peter. I looked down at Thad's hands. They were smaller than mine. An electric shock drilled through me.

"You killed him," I said. "It was you."

"Les was selling drugs to my mom," Thad said in an awful, flat voice. "If it wasn't for him, she'd be clean. But she passes out in her own vomit and I clean it up because I can't stand to watch her, and I can see she's forgetting shit. She's forgetting *me*. They were going to take our house because she's missed so much work, and it's all because of the son of a bitch who sold to her."

"Jesus, Thad," I said. "I'm sorry."

"She's been clean lately because she can't find a new dealer," Thad said. "But she's looking. Always looking."

"How did you do it?" I asked. The words just slid out.

"I only finished what Peter started." Thad was staring at the bottom step of the porch like he might set it on fire. "I was going over there to… I don't know what. And I found him lying on the floor in that shithole apartment. Two of his teeth were knocked out, and he had blood all over his face, and he was only half-conscious. Shit. He looked up at me when I came in, and he whispered, 'Help me.' Can you fucking believe that? *Help me.* All the mad just pounded at me right then. The fucking bastard was killing my mother, and he says, 'Help me.' So I put my hands on his neck and choked him to death. He couldn't even fight back."

"Jesus," I whispered.

"Afterward I was scared to death the cops were coming for me. I about dropped dead when that detective came to rehearsal, but then she arrested Peter. I was saved."

"At Peter's expense," I blurted.

"I figured he was rich. He could buy his way out of prison. Fuck— Peter the golden boy. Shit doesn't stick to him. He was even allowed to stay in the play."

"Thad—" I began.

"But then it all went fucking south when Malloy realized Peter's hands were too big for the choke marks. And she got ahold of Les's phone and found out I sent him texts. And one of the neighbors they had missed last time said just today that she saw me going into Les's apartment. She thought I was buying. Can you fucking believe that? And it's all because of you."

I froze. "Me?"

"You gave her Les's phone, didn't you?"

"Yeah."

"That's what I figured. I couldn't find it in Les's apartment, which means Peter must have taken it. But Peter wouldn't leave it at his house, so I guessed he gave it to you, and you gave it to the cops."

He was right but for the wrong reasons. I didn't enlighten him. "What do you want, Thad? You took your mom's car, and you don't even have a license. The police have to be looking for you."

A hard look came over his face. "Fuck them. And fuck you, Kevin."

I backed up a step. "What did I do?"

"You wrecked my life, you bastard!" He balled up his fists, and I remembered Hank when he got angry. "If you had kept your fucking mouth shut, none of this would have happened! It was all good until you ruined it!"

I automatically felt in my pocket, but my phone was still on the kitchen table. *Crap.* My nerves hummed like tight wires. "Look, Thad, I'm not trying to—"

"Shut up!" he screamed. Tears were streaming down his face. "I'll make you shut up!"

He bolted back to the huge SUV and jumped inside. The engine roared to life. I ran back inside the trailer, locked the door, and leaned against it. My heart slammed against my ribs. *Jesus fuck.* What the hell was going on? My phone was in sight on the kitchen table, a few steps away. I was lunging for it when the SUV's engine suddenly boomed louder than the devil's thunderbolt. I saw movement through the tiny windows in the front door and dove into the living room.

A thunderous crash smashed through the trailer. The front of the SUV burst through the trailer wall, obliterating the front door. The trailer screamed and shuddered. Carpet burned my elbows, and I wrapped my arms around my head. Glass shattered. Books and wood and plastic flew everywhere. The SUV snarled like a demon. Thad gunned it again, and the SUV shoved farther inside. The ceiling creaked and cracked. Dad's bookshelves collapsed. Blood and fear pounded in my ears, and sharp exhaust filled my nose. I scrambled to my feet. The trailer had a back door, but we never used it because it was stuck shut.

Gears ground. Thad shoved the SUV in reverse, and it pulled out of the trailer. Siding screamed along its sides. The trailer shifted and came off the cinder blocks that held it up. Everything dropped a foot. Water burst out of the kitchen sink as the pipes broke, and I caught the sick scent of stove gas. Groceries jolted out of the cupboards, along with the dishes. The hole partly collapsed, and the roof sagged toward it. Across the debris I saw my phone on the kitchen floor. Thad was still backing up.

I lunged across the debris. Cold water sprayed over me. Thad slammed the SUV into drive. I dove again and made it past the hole half a second before the SUV smashed into the trailer again only a yard away

193

from me. The floor shook and the walls groaned. It knocked me to the floor again. Oh god, oh god, oh god, oh god. Where was Dad? Where was Peter?

Thad blasted the horn. The sound bellowed through the wreck that was my only home, and radiator fluid, sweet and poisonous, leaked across the floor. Through the car window I saw his face, a mask of twisted rage. My phone was only inches away. I rolled over, and pain sliced white-hot across my arm. Broken glass. Blood gushed toward my elbow—so much of it. The sight made me dizzy.

The engine roared again, and the SUV's tires spun and chewed up the flimsy floor. I grabbed the phone. Blood made my fingers slippery, but I managed to poke 9-1-1.

Thad backed the SUV up a third time. It took a chunk of the trailer with it, and I lost my balance again. More pain shot down my arm, and I dropped the phone.

"Nine-one-one. What is your emergency?" said a tinny voice from the floor.

"Help me!" I shouted. "My name is Kevin Devereaux! He's trying to kill me."

"Can you tell me where you are, sir?"

The hole was open. Thad had backed away. I made a choice. Ignoring the 9-1-1 operator, I scrambled out of the hole, trailing hot blood. Thad saw me and floored it. The SUV lunged at me, snarling like a tiger. At the last second, I dodged out of the way. Air brushed past me, and something smacked my back—the side-view mirror?—and I was on the ground. Jesus Jesus Jesus. Pine needles stuck to the warm waterfall of blood that poured down my arm, and stupidly I thought about Cheez Whiz. The SUV crashed into the trailer a third time. I scrambled backward, trying to regain my feet. The driver's-side door opened, and Thad half fell out. A cut on his forehead dripped blood down his face. The ground under me swayed a little. Loss of blood? Freaking out? Both?

"Thad," I said. "You don't need to hurt me."

"You hurt *me*, Kevin." He picked up a chunk of wood like a club. "I had everything fixed, and you wrecked it. I'm gonna wreck *you*."

He stood over me with that club, ready to bash my brains out. I reached out, clawed the ground around me, and closed my hand over something cold and hard—a piece of metal. Red anger thundered over me. The tiger roared in my head and clawed at my ears. Everything that had happened to me in the last days, months, years bellowed inside me, filling me with hot lava and molten lead. Strength raged in me, and all the pain and fear burned away. I gripped the metal tightly. With two swipes, maybe three, his bit of wood would be nothing. The fucker who had broken my home, wiped out my life, would be *dead*. The metal was power in my hand. I aimed for Les's kneecaps.

I froze. *Les? Wait.* Who was I fighting?

The tiger boomed inside me and demanded to be used, to attack. Thad had destroyed my home, blamed Peter for murder, fucked up my whole life. He deserved to—

What? Die? Yes. Oh yes. I was going to kill him. Like he had killed Les. Like Dad had killed Mark Brown. Like I had almost killed Robbie Hunter. Like Thad meant to kill me. How many people did anger need to kill?

Something shifted inside me. It had to stop. It had to stop with someone, somewhere. I swallowed. It could stop with me.

The tiger tried to roar again, but I turned my back on it. I turned my back on anger. The tiger tried to roar one more time, but I wouldn't listen, and the roar died. Deliberately I dropped the piece of steel. The tiger faded into a pair of slitted eyes that closed and vanished.

"I won't fight you, Thad," I said. "We have to stop. Just stop. Once you start stopping, we can all quit forever."

I was half-babbling, not quite sure what I meant, only sure I didn't want to be angry anymore. The rage was draining away, the lava cooling to hard rock. As it retreated the slicing-hot pain came back to my arm, and dizziness rocked the ground under me.

"You're a cowardly shit!" Thad snarled. Spittle from his lip landed warm on my cheek, but I was too unsteady to wipe it away. He raised the club higher. "You took everything. You're a fucking corpse, Devereaux."

He swung, and I made myself roll. My arm screamed in agony and left a puddle of blood behind me. Thad's club smacked into it, spraying scarlet. I shoved myself backward, dirt and pine needles grinding into my skin.

"Thad," I said. "This isn't right. It won't make anything better."

"Hell it won't!" He kicked me, and the blow landed on my wounded arm. Fiery pain lashed all the way down to my bones. I screamed. Thad kicked me again, this time in the side. I was going to die.

I lay on the ground at Thad's feet like Robbie had lain at mine last year, looking up at Thad the way Robbie had looked up at me. And in Thad's eyes I saw the same fear and hate in him I'd felt in myself the night I beat Robbie, the same fear and anger I felt when I yelled at Peter's mom, the same fear and anger I felt about Les. Thad and I were alike. We were both so scared we were alone.

We're alone.

And that was it, wasn't it? All along I hadn't been angry at Robbie or Peter's mom. I'd been afraid I was alone. But Peter had shown me that there were other guys like me. Dad had shown me that my family loved me. Wayne had shown me there was a whole world of people who would accept me. Detective Malloy had shown me that other people got hurt the same way I did, and they could get through it. I wasn't alone. And if *I* wasn't—

"Thad," I said, "you aren't alone. I know what it's like. My dad went to jail and my mom left, and I'm scared about that all the time. I know how it feels. The whole world is against you, and you think everyone hates you because of what your mom does, but it's okay. There are lots of people out there who are going through the same thing. I'm one of them. You're like me. You don't have to deal by yourself."

Thad raised the club again. I tried to back up some more, but I was tired and too dizzy. My side hurt. White coals of pain burned my arm, and my vision was getting blurry. Faint sirens screamed far away. I looked up at Thad and said the only thing I could think of.

"I'm sorry, Thad," I said softly. "I know it's awful. I'm sorry. But you aren't alone. I'm here, even if you do want to kill me."

Thad clenched his jaw and started to bring his arm down. I braced myself for more pain, said a silent goodbye to Dad and to Peter, and hoped they knew how much I loved them. The club came down—

—and smashed the ground next to my head. I stared in shock. Thad smashed the club against the ground again and again and again, screaming more and more with every blow. Then he dropped the club and went to his knees, sobbing. The sirens grew louder. Water trickled from the wreck behind us and made a stream under the pine trees. I crawled through it to Thad and managed to get my good arm around him. The bones in his shoulders felt light and hollow.

"It isn't fair," he said between sobs. "It isn't fair."

"It's okay," I told him. "I'm here. You aren't by yourself."

The first police car pulled into the driveway.

ACT III: SCENE III

KEVIN

TURNS OUT the cops figured out where I was from my name, just like the Morses had. I ended up in the hospital with a bunch of stitches and a blood transfusion. It was kind of creepy watching that red bag empty into my arm, knowing it was someone else's blood.

Detective Malloy was with me, taking notes, when Dad arrived. He burst into the room with a wild look on his face and all but crushed me in a hug. I yipped about my stitches, and he let go. He was crying. Did everyone in my life have to do that? But I was secretly glad he was being a drama dad over me.

He made me tell him everything from the start, even though I'd just told it to Detective Malloy, and when I was finished, he hugged me again, but more carefully. I asked him what the damage to the trailer was.

"The gas company got the gas shut off, and we turned off the water, but the trailer itself is totaled," Dad said quietly. "I don't know what we're going to do, Kev."

"There might be some social programs to help," Detective Malloy said.

Dad shook his head. "I'm a felon on parole. There aren't any programs for me."

Malloy said, "Maybe we can—"

Right then Peter burst in. He didn't speak, just hugged me like Dad did, and I had to warn him about my stitches too. I inhaled his scent and touched his hair and felt light and clean as sunshine now that he was here. Then he kissed me, and I kissed him back.

"Infinity," he said. "Are you okay? Do you need anything? Something to drink? A snack? More blood? I have lots."

I laughed at that. "I'm filled with O-positive goodness for now."

"You're my hero."

"I am?" I was a little red from him kissing me in front of Dad and Detective Malloy.

"You got the charges dropped." Peter's eyes filled with ecstasy, and he hugged me again, carefully. "You're…. I can't say how fantastic, Kevin. The nightmare is over. Thank you. Just… thank you." Then he started to cry, which made *me* want to cry.

Then I saw Mr. and Mrs. Morse. They were hanging back in the doorway. Had they seen Peter kiss me? I braced myself for shouting, but I was too tired, and suddenly I didn't care what they thought.

Dad spoke for me. "What do you two want?" he demanded. "I don't have a job, and our home was destroyed. We're sleeping in the back of my truck when Kevin gets out of here. There's nothing else for you to take."

"It's not like that, Mr. Devereaux," Peter said quickly.

"He's right, Jerry," said Mr. Morse. "May we call you Jerry? I feel like after all we've been through—"

"We're here to thank Kevin," Mrs. Morse blurted.

"You are?" I said stupidly.

"You saved Peter," she said, and her eyes were bright. "That's…. It's everything to me. To us."

"What about all that other stuff you said?" I couldn't help asking.

Mrs. Morse came into the room and carefully, slowly approached my bed. I was wearing a hospital gown, which was basically a pillowcase tied around my neck, and her nearness made me uneasy. But she only touched the back of my hand.

"I was startled and angry and surprised, and I suppose I still am," she said, and her voice grew unsteady. "But I was wrong, and so were the things I said and did. I'm sorry. You are the light of my son's life… and you saved him. Thank you."

"See, Kev?" Peter said with that heart-wrenching smile. "Save me from false arrest and you're in."

Everyone laughed a little at that, but before I could respond, the doctor came in. She was a short Indian woman with a long black braid and a stethoscope around her neck. The room was getting crowded. "Everything looks fine," she told me, "but we'd like you to stay overnight for observation."

Dad looked concerned. "Um… how much will this set me back, Doctor? I mean, if Kevin needs it, we'll find a way to handle it, but—"

Mr. Morse stepped forward. "Doctor, could my wife and I talk to you for a moment? In the hall?" The three of them left.

"What do they want?" I asked.

"Heroes," Peter said, still grinning, "don't pay hospital bills."

APPARENTLY THEY don't pay for anything else either.

First, though—Thad. I don't know exactly what happened to him. Yeah, he was arrested and stuff. He did kill Les, and he tried to kill me, but I still felt bad for him. I mean, he didn't *really* try to kill me. After I got done freaking, I figured that out. If he had really wanted to kill me, he would have done something more direct with a knife or a gun. He wouldn't have smashed into the trailer with an SUV.

Anyway, Thad was arrested and charged with Les's murder and a bunch of other stuff related to wrecking the trailer and attacking me. He was going to juvie, but that's all I really knew. That and the Morses were paying for Mr. Dean to handle his defense.

His mom's drug problem was dragged into the open during the investigation, and she was charged with child neglect and endangerment and ordered into rehab. Joe, Thad's older brother, was put into foster care.

All this created a lot of ruckus behind the scenes at *The Importance of Being Earnest.* We had to open in two weeks, and Iris said we couldn't delay anything—another Teen Scenes show was scheduled to take the theater the day after we closed. So we had to figure out what to do.

Thad had been playing my butler, Lane. Ray Nestorovich was playing Jack's butler, Merriman, a very small role, so Iris offered him Lane's role and asked Wayne to step in as Merriman. It would be a little weird having an adult onstage with us teens, but Merriman only showed up a couple times. Ray had to work his butt off to memorize the new lines and blocking, but he was ready by dress rehearsal, and everyone was impressed. Iris said the challenge made him really grow as an actor.

Joe insisted he wanted to stay in the play. He had lost his family, and he didn't want to lose the play too. We were all extra nice to him until he told us to stop doing that, but he did have a couple of freak-out tantrums like mine. Wayne ended up talking him down, and he was able to hold on as Dr. Chasuble in the play.

Our trailer was a total loss. Dad and I weren't even supposed to go back in to salvage stuff because it was dangerous, but we did anyway. There wasn't much. Just about everything was broken or flooded or buried. I was moving carefully because of my stitches, and all I managed to get out were some clothes, a couple of stuffed animals from when I was little, and the photo of Robbie Hunter. The glass in the frame was cracked. I looked at it for a long time, started to knock on it, then set it back down in the rubble. My nightmares about Robbie were gone. I could leave him there.

I rescued my bike too. It had been parked in the yard, and Thad hadn't even come close to hitting it. I was glad about that. If we had been in the Old West, my bike would have been my horse, and losing it would have been even more crushing.

We stood in the yard and stared at the ruined trailer, side by side. Dad and I had lived there ever since he got out of jail and Mom left. A lot of stuff had happened in that little trailer.

Finally Dad and I tossed our stuff into the back of his truck, and we drove off. I watched the trailer disappear into the pine trees in the rearview mirror.

"We'll never see the place again," Dad said.

"I don't care," I said, lying. "I don't."

"Yeah." Dad touched my shoulder. "Me neither."

No matter how crappy it is, home is home, right?

We drove around the edge of Ringdale and finally arrived at our apartment. It's a nice one, with two bedrooms and two bathrooms—I have my own—and a laundry and a swimming pool. It turns out when you buy property with a house on it, even if the house is a trailer, you have to buy insurance for it. If the trailer is destroyed, the insurance company pays for a place for you to live until everything is fixed. That was awesome news. The funny part came when the insurance company tried to say Dad was just a tenant, not the owner, so the company didn't actually have to give us anything, but Mr. Morse asked the insurance guy to repeat the name of the insurance company. The guy ended up saying

"Morse Insurance" three times to Mr. Morse before he got it. There was probably a pile of shit bricks under his chair when he figured that one out. And we got a cool apartment.

The Morses also offered Dad a foreman job—a for-real one—here in Ringdale. His first project? Building a house on a piece of pine-tree property the Morses had just bought on the east side.

"Once it's done, we'll turn the deed over to you," Mr. Morse promised. "Call it your signing bonus."

I could see Dad wanting to turn it down, but he didn't. Instead he shook hands with the Morses and made plans to meet with the architect. I've never lived in a house that had blueprints before. I'm excited. Still an east-sider, but now I'll be in an actual house. With his first paycheck, Dad bought me my own cell phone and new shoes. Peter's sister Emily went shopping with us. Since that was a Thursday, Emily clapped her hands with glee and picked out a pair of purple ones. I like them.

A few days ago, I also went to the community center and asked to see the lady on the card. Her name was Natalie Hernandez, and just like Detective Malloy and Wayne said, she didn't charge me anything. Natalie—she told me to call her by her first name—was a plump woman who had the word *Mom* practically written all over her. Even though I'd told more than one person what Les did to me, I still couldn't bring myself to tell Natalie right off. At the first appointment, I could only tell her that I was sad and angry a lot. At the second appointment, I told her someone had attacked me. At the third one, I told her Les had raped me. She didn't look shocked or judgy or even surprised. She only nodded and, just like Malloy, said I was brave for telling her and asked if I wanted to say more. And I did. I think it's helping. Les doesn't tell me I'm a little pervert anymore.

Natalie asked if I'd told Dad about Les, and I said I still couldn't, even though he knew I was gay.

"You being gay has nothing to do with why Les assaulted you," she said in her office. I liked Natalie's office. It was clean and tidy. The simple furniture was soft and beige, and the window looked out over Morse Memorial Park. "People like Les want power and control. He doesn't—didn't—care whether you were a boy or a girl, L or G, B or T.

Don't fall into thinking it had to do with who *you* are. It was about him and his selfishness. The question is, do you *want* to tell your dad?"

I nodded. "But I've already told him so much."

"How about we tell him here?"

That's how it happened. Dad knew I'd been seeing Natalie because he'd had to sign forms, and he was glad about it—he'd already said he wished I could see a counselor, even before Les—but he was a little surprised to hear he needed to come in. On the day I asked, he sat down in Natalie's sparse, uncluttered office with me.

And I told him. He hugged me and said it was okay, and I cried yet again. I hated that, but I was glad he knew. I feel a little lighter every day.

SCENE IV: FINALE

KEVIN

THEN THERE'S Peter and me.

Everyone keeps reminding me that Peter is my first boyfriend and that I should be careful. "Doesn't matter if you're straight, gay, bi, or trans, buddy," Wayne said. "Everyone falls in and out of love, especially when you're young."

I don't care. Neither does Peter. Every time I see him, my heart speeds up. Every time he touches my face, I'm touching the entire universe and all the stars. I'm careful not to spend every second with him—even *I* know that's a recipe for a big cookie filled with chocolate-chip disaster. I found a job at a pizza place, completely on my own, and Jess was right—don't ever order the sausage special. I get lots of hours, which makes my time with Peter a little rare and all the more powerful.

Peter has compromised with his parents. He's taking both business and architecture classes this fall. Rumors are floating around that the Morse family will take Morse Plastic public, but I'm supposed to say that those are just rumors. Really. They're also working harder on getting Emily to be less dependent on Peter so that one day he can leave Ringdale without worrying about her.

OPENING NIGHT arrived fast. I hovered backstage with makeup and powder caking my face and everyone else in the cast pacing about muttering lines and gesticulating to themselves. The set was painted, the lights were hung, the furniture was in place. We even had little trees at the edges of the stage. A big bouquet of red roses arrived for me with a card signed *Infinity*. I melted over the makeup table. Peter also sent flowers to everyone else in the cast and to Iris and Wayne, but theirs were carnations. That was an hour earlier. Now my stomach was in knots, and I was sure I was going to throw up.

"You aren't going to throw up," Peter said in my ear. He looked stunning in his Jack costume—a dark Victorian jacket with a high collar and a tie, iron-straight trousers, and patent-leather shoes. I was wearing a similar outfit. Peter had already said I looked good enough to eat with a spoon, and I was glad my makeup hid my blushing.

"How did you know I was going to throw up?" I whispered.

"Everyone thinks they're going to throw up," he said. "You're going to kill."

I threw Joe a glance. "Probably not the best choice of words."

Iris had warned us it was unprofessional—and bad luck—to peek at the audience before the play started, so I made myself not. But I could hear a whole lot of people talking beyond the heavy red curtain across the stage. Dad was out there. So were Peter's parents and Detective Malloy. Even Natalie was there, though she said that, for privacy reasons, she couldn't tell people she knew me. Iris was watching from the audience too. Once a play goes into performance, the stage manager runs everything. My mouth was dry and my heart was pounding.

"One minute," Wayne said quietly. He was in his Merriman costume. "Places. Places."

We all scurried away. Ray, as Lane the butler, went to the sideboard to pretend to arrange a tea tray, and I hid just beyond an open doorway. Recorded piano music filtered through the house, as it had during technical and dress rehearsals. The audience quieted, and Wayne hauled on the rope that brought the curtain up. The lights burst on, and the audience went dead silent. Lane arranged silverware onstage while the piano recording played. I waited, heart still pounding, until the music stopped. My cue.

I was stepping forward when I realized I had forgotten to spin the Algy shell around me. I was still Kevin Devereaux, still a teenager from Ringdale, still me. I stumbled and wondered if I should wait a second. But Ray-as-Lane was alone on the stage with no lines and nothing real to do. The audience was waiting. Ray glanced sideways toward my doorway.

Wayne stood with his prompt book open a few steps away. He made a shooing motion and mouthed, *Go!*

I went. No Algy shell. The lights blinded me, but I was ready for that from tech rehearsal. The house was all in shadow to me except the first two rows, and Dad was right there, front and center. Peter's parents sat behind him. My mouth dried up. Everything was silent. I was screwing up. I was messing it—

Then say your line, dummy.

I opened my mouth, and my first line, the one I'd rehearsed so often I could say it asleep, came to me. *"Did you hear what I was playing, Lane?"*

I blew my accent. I wrecked the timing. But I said it. And then a weird thing happened. As I said the words, the Algy shell came to me. It spun around me, sheltered me, protected me. There was no audience staring at me. I was in my flat in London, wearing clothes I wore every day, talking to the butler who'd worked in my house for years. My posture straightened. My eyebrows quirked. My head tilted. My hands went arrogantly behind my back. I was Algernon Moncrieff.

"I didn't think it polite to listen, sir," Lane said, and the audience chuckled. I—Algy—didn't notice.

"I'm sorry for that, for your sake," I said. *"I don't play accurately— anyone can play accurately"*—a bigger laugh—*"but I play with wonderful expression."* More laughter, easy laughter, like soft butter on warm bread. Algy still didn't notice it, but I did, and the audience pulled me through the play. They weren't the enemy or something to be feared. They were friends, and they liked the play. They liked *me.*

I was home.

The play ticked along. Yeah, we made some mistakes—a few dropped lines, a missed entrance—but no one really noticed. The audience laughed and gasped and even applauded. In the green room after our first scene together, I did a little ecstasy dance with Peter.

"You're brilliant," I said, grinning.

"You make me that way, Kev," Peter said with a grin of his own. "Come on. We're up again."

And then, all too soon, it was the final scene. All the deceptions about being named Earnest were uncovered, all the problems were solved, all the couples were together. Jack and Gwen shared a kiss, and Lady Bracknell interrupted.

"*My nephew,*" she harumphed, "*you seem to be displaying signs of triviality.*"

"*On the contrary, Aunt Augusta,*" Jack said, and he turned to speak to the audience, "*I've now realized for the first time in my life the vital importance of being Earnest.*"

The curtain came down.

Applause pounded through the house—I mean, *big* applause. It crashed through the curtain and washed over us in thrilling waves. Triumph swept me. I'd done it. *We'd* done it. They loved it. I couldn't stand still. I was closest to Meg, whom I'd recently smooched onstage, and I hugged her hard. She laughed. All of us were laughing. Peter threw both fists into the air.

The applause was dimming a little. "Curtain call!" Wayne shouted.

All of us, including Wayne, hustled into a line, and one of the stage hands pulled up the main drape. The applause rose again. The house lights came up a little so we could see the audience. We all bowed once together. Then butlers Wayne and Ray took bows. Charlene as Miss Prism and Joe as Dr. Chasuble took bows. Meg and Krista took bows as Gwen and Cecily. Melissa did an elaborate curtsey as Lady Bracknell, earning grander applause and some cheers. Last, Peter and I came forward for Jack and Algy.

The applause boomed into thunder. People whistled and cheered. I stared, caught completely off guard by the noise. Then Peter bowed, and I quickly bowed with him. Dad was clapping with both hands above his head. The Morses were smiling, and it was the first time I'd seen them do that. I couldn't quite believe it, but it was happening. Peter bowed again, so I bowed with him.

Then they were standing up. First my dad, and then Mr. and Mrs. Morse and Detective Malloy, and then the people around them, and finally the entire audience. They were on their feet and still applauding. I stared, shocked all the way through. They were standing for Peter, and they were standing for *me*. The applause ran and ran and ran. It was a sunlight river overflowing its banks. It was liquid diamonds and drinkable laughter.

The fabulousness came pouring out. I caught Peter in my arms and kissed him there, in front of the cast, in front of the crew, in front of the world. He stiffened, and I wondered if he'd pull away, but he was only surprised. He kissed me back, warm and hard and full.

The applause faltered for a tiny moment and then burst back into full power—full support. I thought I might float away right then. Peter and I kissed for a long moment, then separated and bowed one last time. Dad hid a smile behind his hands, and Mr. and Mrs. Morse continued their own applause with the house. Maybe the town was changing.

Meg ran into the audience, pulled Iris onto the stage, and made her take a bow too. I still had my arm around Peter's shoulders, and I mouthed *Thank you* at her and at Wayne. Iris wiped at her eyes, and Wayne's lower lip trembled. Then we all took one last bow together, and the curtain came down.

The second the drape touched the stage floor, we all burst into wild cheers that morphed into an orgy of hugging. And shouting.

"We kicked ass!"

"You and Peter? When the hell did that start?"

"I knew it. I knew it from the start."

"Standing O! We got a standing O!"

"Cast party at my place!"

Wayne caught me in a hug of his own. "Congrats, kiddo," he said. "For everything."

Peter, of course, kissed me again, and everyone laughed.

"How long?" Meg demanded.

"We met just after Iris posted the cast list," Peter said. "Kevin literally ran into me, and from then on, I was wrecked."

I laughed, but I couldn't let go of Peter. I didn't want to, even with everyone looking. Best of all, I didn't need to.

"No wonder you were so freaked when Peter was arrested," Ray said.

"Yeah," I said, not looking at Joe. "It was rough for everyone."

"You never know what's happening behind the scenes," Melissa observed.

And then a little coldness went through me. I'd been so focused on myself and Peter that something else had fallen totally out of my head. I pulled away from Peter and turned to Wayne, upset now. "Wayne—I forgot something at curtain call."

"What did you forget?" Peter asked, mystified.

"They're still applauding out there," Wayne said, and I realized he was right. The noise hadn't stopped. "Let's give 'em a second curtain call, everyone."

Oh! I hadn't heard of this. We rushed back into line and took hands. Iris took a place with us as the curtain came up again. The applause increased. I held hands with Peter and Meg for a moment, and then I dropped Meg's hand, stepped forward, and saluted my dad, the most important guy in that audience. His smile widened, and he blinked hard.

We all took one more bow, and the curtain came down.

STEVEN HARPER PIZIKS was born with a last name no one can reliably spell or pronounce, so he usually writes under the name Steven Harper. He grew up on a farm in Michigan but has also lived in Wisconsin and Germany, and spent extensive time in Ukraine. So far, he's written more than two dozen novels and over fifty short stories and essays. When not writing, he plays the folk harp, lifts weights, and spends more time on-line than is probably good for him. He teaches high school English in southeast Michigan, where he lives with his husband and youngest son. His students think he's hysterical, which isn't the same as thinking he's funny.

Visit his webpage at www.stevenpiziks.com or www.stevenharperwriter.com

CPSIA information can be obtained
at www.ICGtesting.com
Printed in the USA
LVHW080157011220
673106LV00041B/918